IN THE LAND OF TWO-LEGGED WOMEN

We gratefully acknowledge the support of the Canada Council for the Arts and the Ontario Arts Council for our publishing program. We also acknowledge the financial support of the Government of Canada through the Canada Book Fund.

Cover design: Val Fullard

Library and Archives Canada Cataloguing in Publication

Alcaro, Huey Helene, 1938–, author
        In the land of two-legged women : a novel / by Huey Helene Alcaro.

(Inanna poetry & fiction series)
Issued in print and electronic formats.
ISBN 978-1-77133-241-5 (paperback).-- ISBN 978-1-77133-242-2 (epub).--
ISBN 978-1-77133-244-6 (pdf)

        I. Title. II. Series: Inanna poetry and fiction series

PS3601.L27I52 2016   813'.6   C2015-904997-0
                                                                        C2015-904998-9

Printed and bound in Canada

Inanna Publications and Education Inc.
210 Founders College, York University
4700 Keele Street, Toronto, Ontario, Canada M3J 1P3
Telephone: (416) 736-5356 Fax: (416) 736-5765
Email: inanna.publications@inanna.ca Website: www.inanna.ca

MIX
Paper from
responsible sources
FSC® C004071

IN THE LAND OF TWO-LEGGED WOMEN

A NOVEL BY

HUEY HELENE ALCARO

inanna poetry & fiction series

INANNA PUBLICATIONS AND EDUCATION INC.
TORONTO, CANADA

For women who refuse to be treated with contempt.

TABLE OF CONTENTS

…People who may have long been patronized and casually discounted, can pick themselves up out of comfortable humiliation and, by so doing, find unsuspected resources, a whole other personality even, within themselves.
—Rolf Fjelde, on Henrik Ibsen's *A Doll House*

1. NO

THEY WERE GOING TO CUT OFF HER LEG. They were going to cut off her leg. They were going to cut off her leg. She ran screaming through the house. NO.

She woke screaming. Glom was running his hands on her. NO. She propelled herself from the bed and crashed to the floor, hitting her forehead on the wall. The next day she'd have a lump that would darken to an ugly purple and fade through green into yellow as it receded.

Glom was reaching for her. She moved back using her hands and one leg. Scrambled toward the corner, like a scurrying insect.

2. BEAUTIFICATION

SOMETIMES SHE'D LET HERSELF FALL into remembering. Sometimes she couldn't stop it, remembering the days before her leg was sawed off and the 'l was added to her name, denoting woman, one in possession of one leg. She remembered running, running across her grandfather's field, the grass soft under and around her feet; Spirry running with her, his body wiggling even as he ran, little legs pumping. She'd stop and pick him up, hold his silky almost black fur to her face. He'd keep wiggling. A joyous companion in running, running, running across fields, down streets, around and around the patios surrounding the house. Her running, jumping, tearing along friend. Oh, how she loved him.

What would he do, feel, when she could no longer run with him? She sometimes wished her father had not given him to her. Then there wouldn't be the loss of him. And she would lose him in some measure because she would not be able to run with him. She couldn't think about it, not on a day of perfect blue, green, white beauty. No, not on such a day. So many days to think about not running any more. So many days when there would be no running. Nor walking.

"Come on, Spirry, let's run!" Solanj and her best little playmate would take off once again across the field, racing, racing, racing in pure delight of being alive. Joy.

* * *

Itching. Cramping. Itching. Hurting. In the thigh, the calf—and the desire to run her hand down her legs, just for the knowing of herself. There was one leg to touch, but she wanted to feel both. She needed to scratch the itch, rub the cramp, but there was nothing to rub, or to scratch. Nothing except the stump. Her friend Toka lost her leg to the saw several months before Solanj and had gone mad with the pain in the leg that was no longer hers. When she was eight she'd fallen out of a tree, piercing her right leg on a broken limb as she dropped. It had bothered her in cold weather. She felt the old and new pain as it lay in the disposal pits. She twisted and turned and screamed that one of the cats from the mountains was eating her leg. Its teeth were ripping into her calf, her foot.

Some women lived with pain all their lives. A grimace would cross the face for no apparent reason. The lost leg had appeared once again. A ghost that cried out in itching and cramps and shooting pains.

Solanj had loathed the Beautification Ritual as far back as she could remember. All girls feared it and cried before and after the leg was sawed off but they went on, doing what was expected. Few tried to prevent it. Solanj did. She asked, begged her mother, Luranj'l, and father, Hect, to not have it done to her. At first they smiled and thought she was being a nervous little girl, then realized she was serious. They kept a servant with her at all times, even when she slept, knowing she might try to run away. Her woman's blood came and the day was set for removal. She only pretended to take the drug that was to make her senseless for the three days prior to The Beautification. On the sawing off day, she'd thrown the drug across her room and run screaming out of the house and down the street. It was a blue and golden day, so beautiful it hurt and they were going to saw off her leg. It took three servants to catch and carry her back to her waiting parents, the parents deeply embarrassed by her unseemly behaviour. The drug was forced down her throat.

She said nothing after her leg was sawed off, flung into the bloodstained wooden bucket and carried to the wagon that would transport it to the pits. She continued to say nothing as the weeks went by. She held Spirry and stared at people, her mouth a straight, tight line, her eyes hard. Her mother tried to cajole her into appropriate young lady behaviour then threatened with various restrictions. Solanj'l looked at her in a way that said there was nothing anyone could do that was worse than what had been done.

Her father prided himself on his reserve and dignity but finally yelled, "What is wrong with you? All females do this. It is natural. It is what the God wants. It is what we all want. Why must you act as if something bad has been done to you? Without Beautification you would never have a man. I do not know what is wrong with you."

Casanj'l, her older sister with flirty eyes and giggly little girl ways, told Solanj'l she was being dumb. Every girl knew this was needed to get a husband. Casanj'l lowered her lushly-lashed eyes, turned pink, and moved her shoulders this way and that, signalling sweet, docile, malleable to every man who came into the house.

Solanj'l did not wiggle and twinkle for the men. She merely flicked glances at them with her rage-filled eyes. When no one would see, she cried. She put her head against Spirry's soft little body, rocked back and forth and cried. Spirry licked her tears and whimpered.

3. A PARTY — AND SEX

A DINNER, A FEAST FOR MEN WHO WOULD, if they wished, ease Glom on his way to being a man of increasing significance, a man to be heard, a man to whom others would defer because it could be to their advantage. The men brought their wives, using one of the possible methods—carried by a household servant, rolled in a chair by servant, rolled by husband, carried by husband. When not moved by others, a woman used props, poles with hand grips held under the arms. She'd move the poles forward then drag her leg after. If that became tiring she could stand for a bit, leaning against the curved crosspiece connecting the poles even though it did not provide much support. Solanj'l believed the way in which a woman moved or was moved conveyed her relationship to her husband—highly prized property tended by husband, property to be handled by staff or property fending for itself.

Glom had wanted her in a wheeled wood chair with intricate carved flowers and a plush red seat and back, to be rolled by him, but she said as hostess she needed to be able to move herself when he was occupied with entertaining the men. He accepted the logic of this. Solanj'l always chose to move herself unless Glom insisted she be propelled by him as he sought to impress a particular individual or group.

As they sat at the women's side of the fireplace in the Master's Receiving Room, sipping the before-meal wine, Solanj'l asked

Janka'l, wife of a Minister of Commerce on the rise, "What is your preferred method of moving about?"

Janka'l looked startled by the question and Solanj'l saw her eyes had golden flecks in them, like the great cats that lived in the mountains and were sometimes trapped when they came too close to the city, then caged in the park. Solanj'l had gold flecks, too, in her light brown eyes, making them yellow in some lights.

Solanj'l smiled and said, "I've been thinking about this. How do I like to get around? How do other women like to move? I'm sure there are differences. It's an interesting idea, don't you think?" She addressed this to all the wives.

Janka'l nodded in the way one does to keep a hostess happy. Petra'l, wife of a major furniture producer, said, "I've thought of that too. I like to have Metak, my husband, carry me. I find it so … intimate." She presented a we're-talking-about-sex smile and casually lifted her skirt to show her foot and a bit of ankle for anyone to see. She threw a quick glance to where the men sat. She was wearing a sheer blue stocking and a deep blue shoe with a silver heel. Her husband did not object to her behaviour or she would not have done it. A wife covered or revealed as directed. Glom did not want Solanj'l "exposing herself." He, on occasion, would use a cane to slowly raise the hem of her skirt so men could see what he possessed. Solanj'l always knew when this would be; the only time he carried one of the canes was when he planned to put his property on display. Her skin, top of head to sole of foot, tightened as the hem of her skirt rose slowly, as she felt the air against her leg, the cloth touching, dropping away, touching as it moved higher, stopping at the knee. Glom would push the skirt back with the side of his hand so more of her could be viewed. He had great pride in her narrow foot, slim ankle and shapely calf. Even her thigh had just the right amount of flesh, not too much. And not too little as can happen when there is no fullness on the inside as it rises to the channel of love. Not that the men would see her thigh; they could only imagine the titillation that hid beneath the fabric covering the thigh next to the stump—the real titillater. Their looks of appreciation and Glom's smug smile sickened her. How many women were sickened by display? How many were stimulated? How many felt nothing, having gone dead inside?

Glom carried no cane tonight. She would not be on display. The muscles in her neck and back weren't rigid, her skin ready to tighten. She could appear to be the gracious hostess, playing the role of loving her life.

The wives spoke of advantages of being carried, rolled or moving with props. Morgani'l, wife of Bantant, and Solanj'l's best friend, wondered why a chair couldn't be made to be moved by the woman in it. Janka'l looked at her as if deeply puzzled.

"I wouldn't want that at all," declared Petra'l. "I want to be cared for."

Deba'l, wife of Hunak, the Minister Second Only to The First said, "It does become bothersome not to be able to move freely, having one's hands available at all times when one must arrange a night like this, which Solanj'l has so beautifully provided."

Her use of "bothersome" indicated the high regard in which her husband held her. Wives did not presume to suggest their condition was anything less than perfect. Solanj'l would get to know this Deba'l better. She'd invite her for an Afternoon Break, a term she'd always found amusing. A break from what? Other than boredom.

They moved into the dinner, which Solanj'l had not arranged. Wives did not make arrangements for guest meals; the stewards did. Women could not be trusted to create anything so important, but the lie lived because possession of the illusion of a good wife-manager indicated a man had chosen very well; he had gotten something more than a source of erotic satisfaction.

Kracak, the steward who came to Glom when he'd taken Solanj'l as wife, had deigned to tell her what he planned because he wanted to be told how very clever he was. They would begin with airy puffs made from the best goat cheese, served with a light wine, pale green from the herbs that flavoured it. The main course would feature a roasted bullock. "Oh, not the entire bullock," he said and laughed in his deprecating way when Solanj'l raised her eyebrows. The bullock would be accompanied by a puree of yellow tubers, a nut and berry dish, crunchy greens fresh from the countryside and crusty rolls—a specialty of Glom's kitchen—served with fresh butter. One of Glom's best rich red wines would enhance the course. Next would come individual ginger custard tarts with dollops of clotted cream. The meal would end with teas and the traditional fruits and sweets. Solanj'l had praised him, as she always did. A steward could create great misery for a wife.

Glom sat at the prime end of the dining table, Solanj'l at the lower. The family escutcheon was carved in the middle of the table. It featured a coin, an ancient one with a pillar that looked like a stylized penis, surrounded by wagons, buildings, food animals, and men. A forefather had wanted to illustrate his family engaged in a multitude of enterprises, one not being enough. The guests exclaimed about the table, as guests always did. The rest of the room had little else to distinguish it, wood-panelled walls, one containing a window draped with heavy tapestry fabric. Paintings of mountain and lake scenes decorated the other walls. Because the city-state of Ramprend was built on flat, dry ground—except where greenery was forced—scenery had to be provided by paintings of what was known of the world beyond it.

The male guests were seated to Glom's right, the wives to his left. The men did not sit across from their own wives, whom they could see at any time. They wanted to see a different face even though they could do nothing with the body under it.

Guest dinners usually gave Solanj'l a raging headache, as if an axe had split her head open right down the middle. Tonight was only mildly painful, due in part to the antics of Petra'l who was thrusting her breasts at Doam, Janka'l's husband.

They strained against the tight bodice she was wearing, the kind worn by all women at these events, covering from the top of the breasts to waist, squeezing the ribs, pushing the breasts up and forward. Solanj'l was certain these bodices contributed to her headaches. Petra'l's breasts reached out and her eyelashes fluttered as she simpered her way through conversation with Doam, who seemed dazed. Petra'l's husband, Metak, occasionally looked at his wife, a smirk on his face. He'd beat her for the performance, or he savoured watching his wife act the termer, a woman-of-short-term use. Perhaps he savoured, then beat.

As they were enjoying the fruits and sweets, Kracak came in and whispered in Glom's ear. Glom nodded and Kracak went to Hunak and whispered. The Minister Second Only to the First scowled, rose and left the room after quietly speaking to Glom. A group of hooded men had broken into a mill on the northern edge of the city. It was not known if they had come out of the mountains or were from the Land Across the Lake. Such an occurrence had not happened in memory. It was so surprising the usual conversation pattern was broken, guests speaking not just to the one across the table, but to any who would listen. Solanj'l said nothing. She had no information; there was no point in speaking. She leaned back cradling a glass of icy flower-scented wine and listened. When the guests were gone Glom would want to talk and talk, speculating on his fortunes and how this raid might affect them. She needed to know who said what and be ready to knowledgeably agree with each of his assessments. He was in his glory, an unusual event had occurred and Hunak and other important men learned of it in his home. He sat very straight, glancing around smiling. He looked as if a light had gone on inside him. His glow-look, Solanj'l thought with a sinking in her stomach. She'd have to perform tonight.

"How fortunate the Minister was readily available," he said to no one in particular, hoping all would hear.

Solanj'l imagined him saying in the future, "Hunak, The Minister Second Only to the First was in my home when we learned of the invaders." He had reason to be pleased about Hunak's presence. Most citizens forgot there was a First Minister. It was assumed he did nothing, if in fact he existed. Hunak was considered the primary government leader.

When it was time for their guests to leave, Glom said he would accompany Deba'l home.

"It is gracious of you to offer," she said, "but not necessary. Hunak's servant is especially capable."

"I insist. How could I have one of my women guests leave my home alone?" He put his hand on his chest and gave her his thoughtful smile.

Deba'l nodded in what looked like acquiescence. She held one of Solanj'l's hands with both of hers as they said their good evenings. A tall, large-boned woman, she held herself erect in her wheeled chair, not rigidly erect, as Solanj'l usually did, but with an ease that conveyed she had attained a sense of worth in a world of humiliation. Her dark brown eyes gave the impression of knowing things not readily seen by others. She spoke her mind more than most women, due to having been chosen by a man willing to acknowledge her intelligence. His regard for her was well known and a frequent source of puzzlement. She was a woman to cultivate. Solanj'l's smile was one of gratitude and anticipation when Deba'l accepted the invitation to an Afternoon Break three days hence.

Glom returned aglow. Attending to Deba'l was a step forward, small perhaps but significant in his movement toward gaining the position of great importance he so craved. He talked of what he'd said, how Deba'l had attended, how she would speak approvingly of him to Hunak, how he would speak with Hunak the next day, ask him about the new information on the raiders. He would show he was willing to do anything he could to be of assistance to the Minister Second Only to the First. Solanj'l smiled, nodded, said oh, yes, in an admiring voice, asked easy questions, all the while hoping he would talk himself into sleep.

In his state of elation and anticipation, Glom was not about to sleep. He patted the bed on which he sat and graced Solanj'l with his it-is-time-for-you-to-perform-your-primary-function smile. He had no idea Solanj'l considered their erotic activities an unwelcome demand rather than a joy dispensed by him onto her. As far as she had been able to discern, all men thought women were delighted with the sexual arrangements of Ramprend. Women were used to produce pleasure and the men did not possess, or chose not to use, sufficient imagination to conceive of how it felt to be treated as a thing. Solanj'l occasionally wished men would experience what women did, but undoubtedly the only result would be men offering prayers of thankfulness to the Great God Ploch that they had not been born women.

With sinking stomach and throbbing head, Solanj'l opened her arms. Glom lifted her out of the wood and plush chair and propped her up against one end of the bed. All four posters were carved with that portion of the family escutcheon that was the stylized Member of Joy and Pleasure. She did as expected, slipped out of her private pants, dropped them on the floor and started to undo the buttons holding her outer bodice together. Glom bent next to the bed, watching eagerly, running his hands up and down his thighs, encased in the tight-fitting pants men wore for formal events, pants constructed to draw eyes to penis and testicles, which some men enhanced with pleasurepads. Glom said he had no need for enhancement. Solanj'l's bodice was made of thickly textured red, blue, and purple fabric with gold threads, a fabric only men of wealth could purchase for their wives. She pulled the bodice open and leaned forward so Glom could ease it off her shoulders and down her arms. The first few times she felt the fabric slipping away from her had brought such anger she learned to shut her mind to what was happening. Do not think. Do not feel.

If she did, she would become a thrashing, screaming mass of raging energy. She would be a danger to Glom and she would join those in the House of the Demented.

The smirk of anticipated satisfaction came to Glom's face. It always did when she sat in her under-bodice, deep blue tonight to complement the one worn for public view. She could never predict when he would remove the under-bodice or leave it on. The skirt would usually remain, titillation enhanced by partial covering. She watched as he moved his hands under her skirt and lifted it to see the Sacred Site of Love, a description to make her gag if she allowed it to fully enter her thinking. He gave a little sigh and dropped his mouth to kiss and lick the end of her stump, her Pretty Little Spot, where the skin had drawn together. Solanj'l closed her eyes and went to the field behind her grandfather's home. She ran and ran with her beloved Spirry, down the field and back and around and around.

Glom was murmuring something. She returned to hear him say, "You don't mind do you. You don't miss your leg when you know this gives me so much pleasure." He smiled at her, then dropped his eyes to admire what the Beatification Ritual had wrought. She produced her agreeable wife smile and returned to the field as he pulled her flat on the bed and entered her. She and Spirry raced and raced. And raced.

4. DEBA'L VISITS

SOLANJ'L FOUND HERSELF ROCKING back and forth as if trying to hurry up time as she impatiently waited for the afternoon when Deba'l would come for teas and tasties. And talk. Could she even hint at the unthinkable? The bizarre idea that grew into desire had come suddenly and seemed stupid. How could she do that, and more to the point, who would let her? Yet it seemed right. If she could do something to help herself, all women, she wouldn't feel.... What was it she felt? Could one be angry and dead at the same time?

Women standing and moving on their own. Without props. Wouldn't that be fine?

She'd been sitting on the side patio and the man who lived in the nearest house walked by, the father of beautiful Nalani who would one day have her right leg sawed off. He was striding in the way men do when they feel particularly good about themselves. She supposed he had gained a large sum of money or bested another man. Glom walked like that when life was going well with him. A strut. Strutting up a hall, down a street, looking as if he owned the world. Well, men did own their world, at least men of privilege. Privilege they hadn't earned but acquired from fathers who acquired it from theirs and so on back through the generations. Women, of course, could not strut. Strutting on one leg would be quite a feat. Walking on two, even if one was not real, would also be a feat. Could she make that happen?

How did one walk? She didn't have a clear memory of it. How did this neighbour move?

One leg swung forward, down, back leg forward, down, first leg and so it went. She'd have to watch Glom more closely. She could also watch girls—before their legs were sawed off.

Why this idea now? It didn't matter; there it was—growing. Rather than sitting in a chair to be wheeled around or foot-dragging with props, a woman could be up and moving with arms free to work as well. When you lost a leg, you also lost at least partial use of your arms.

She could imagine Casanj'l going on and on about no God-loving woman would want wooden legs. How utterly awful. How could anyone think of such a thing? Solanj'l's question had always been who could love a God that wanted girls humiliated and disabled? A question not spoken. Each week she went to the Temple reeking with sickish sweet smoke that made it difficult not to retch. She mouthed adoration, knelt (with difficulty), stood, sang the praises, knelt, implored, "Oh, Great God Ploch, I am unworthy. You and you alone know my heart yet love me. Oh, Great God Ploch, continue to look with favour on me." Chanted even when life was anything but favourable, over and over, years after years. To a God that demanded mutilation as an act of adoration.

Deba'l did not appear to be a Ploch-lover but Solanj'l could not rush her. She arrived with a bouquet of huge red poppies. "I think of you as a woman best seen with red," she said, handing them to the servant attending Solanj'l. "With your colouring, red is prime."

She was on props, not relying on a servant to move her. She and Solanj'l swung along side by side to the Sitting Room usually used only by family. Solanj'l said it was more comfortable than the much larger Receiving Room when there were only two people.

Privileged Ramprendians lived in usually square homes, providing little of exterior interest, with the possible exception of patios. Clay blocks were stacked to form walls, leaving space for windows of glass. Beams held up wood planks to form roofs. Only the wealthiest of families had homes made of wood brought from the mountains. Glom's was one of them. People admired its alternating light and dark hues formed by the grain. The guest entry door was a version of what was carved in the dining table and on bed posters. It opened to a hallway with the Master's Receiving Room, Dining Room, and Sitting Room to the left. Kitchen, Storage, and Bathing and Elimination Rooms were to the right; a hallway connected the two sides. Beyond the public rooms was another hall with the Pleasure/Sleeping Room and two Child Rooms. If necessary more rooms could be added along that side of the house. It was surrounded on three sides by patios with tables, benches, small trees, and pots of herbs and flowers, all costly due to the necessity of paying to have water hauled in from streams flowing out of the mountains. Glom could build a comfortable neighbourhood for all his workers with the money spent on his patios and the field at the back of the house.

Deba'l nodded about the Sitting Room. "It is comfortable. Filled with light." She smiled at Solanj'l as if they were about to share secrets.

They sat at a table near the floor to ceiling window. A house-maid brought the hot water pitcher with a tray of teas. Other trays held biscuits and cream cakes. Solanj'l said she would ring if anything more was needed. The young woman left as she had come, nudging the rolling table with her leg as she swung along on her props.

Deba'l watched her, then turned to Solanj'l and said, "So inefficient. Think how much easier her work would be with two legs."

Solanj'l's felt her eyes widen, then looked down and motioned for Deba'l to choose which tea she would prefer. "Do you suggest we stop the ritual on servant women?"

"It would make sense."

Solanj'l prepared the pot of tea and passed it to Deba'l, who chose a biscuit not much bigger than a mouthful and nibbled on it as she waited for the tea to steep.

"Is there more information on the raiders?" Solanj'l asked.

Deba'l shook her head and shrugged. "No. They came and went quickly. Apparently they took nothing. The few men who saw them said they wore dark cloaks and perhaps had beards. No words were spoken. We know so little about other people. We keep ourselves isolated. I think that contributes to our lack of imagination." She poured her tea, leaned forward and peered at the biscuit tray before choosing one with tiny berries in it. "Or do you think we are a people of imagination?"

"No," Solanj'l said after a beat. "I don't."

"Do you think we could do something about that?"

Solanj'l consciously kept her eyes neutral, not wanting to give away what she was feeling. "What do you have in mind?"

"I've been considering the possibility of a women's group at the Temple."

Solanj'l's heart sank. The last thing she wanted to be involved in was a Temple supported group.

"I see my suggestion is not met with enthusiasm," Deba'l said.

Solanj'l scowled.

Deba'l laughed. "Your eyes were unguarded for a moment." She waved her hand as if brushing something away. "Temple business is not the point. But ... meeting there would give a group legitimacy. The idea came after your question about women moving around. I so enjoyed discussing something other than the cost of fabrics and all the other nonsense we jabber. Thank you for raising that question."

"What purpose would the group serve?"

"We could talk about our lives, as we did before your dinner."

Solanj'l looked out the window, feeling alternately hesitant and excited. She knew Deba'l was watching her. She turned from the view across the stone patio to the field. "I'm not known as a particularly fervent believer in the Great God Ploch. My participation could be suspect."

"You and your husband go to the weekly service, as do I and mine. Two women of our station asking to make the Temple more important in our lives should please the priests very much."

Solanj'l took a sip of tea and stared at the biscuits and cakes. The flower-flavoured cream cakes were a special favourite of hers, but she didn't feeling like eating one. She reached out and took a plain biscuit to give herself something to do. "I'm sure the priests would have something to say about what would be discussed."

"There are ways to keep them happy."

Solanj'l's eyes betrayed her again.

Deba'l leaned back and laughed, a low rumbling laugh. "Oh, don't think I'm suggesting that. I have no interest in being locked away for the rest of my life. And, I have no interest in humiliating my husband. He is a good man."

Solanj'l felt a twinge of what she thought must be envy. A woman who respected her husband, perhaps even loved him. How was it possible to respect and love a man who desired you because part of your body had been removed?

Deba'l said they could present their idea in a way that would make it acceptable to priests. If the group started discussing questionable topics, doubts could be removed. Money could be passed. Hunak was willing to share his money with her. Pay the priests enough and you could do much that was not in keeping with religion.

"You know this from experience?" Solanj'l asked.

"We are not to engage in pleasurable activities on specified days. We are to go to the Temple and do penance. Is that not so?"

Solanj'l nodded.

"You know the High Priest has a house on the lake shore."

Solanj'l knew of its existence. She'd heard people mumble about it not being right for a High Priest to have such a home.

He had one next to the Temple; that should be enough. Deba'l explained it was a "little gift" from Hunak. He'd become tired of penance days. Now they went to their own lake shore home during those times Ramprendians were to be confirming their insufficiency in the eyes of Ploch. She'd not seen the High Priest at his house on one of those days, but it would not surprise her if she did.

This revelation was stunning. Deviation from established practice was punished by ostracism. Perhaps that was not true for the Minister Second Only to the First. Deba'l went on as if nothing unusual had been said, talking about how being of greater value to their husbands could be the starting point. Who knew where their discussions might take them?

Deba'l was proposing something so out of the ordinary so soon after their initial meeting that it was somewhat frightening. Could she be trusted? Had she, Solanj'l, made a mistake that made her suspect? Was she being tested?

Deba'l chose a cream cake. "I should not eat so many of these tasties but I find yours particularly difficult to resist."

"Eat as many as you want. There are more."

"I do not need temptation thrown in my path."

"Is temptation always bad?"

"It depends on who's doing it … and who's judging." Once again she presented a sharing secrets smile.

Solanj'l took a cream cake and bit into it. The flavour filled her mouth and she closed her eyes.

"You know how to enjoy a tasty morsel," Deba'l said.

Solanj'l told her about Glom's baker who claimed others used only a floral essence in their cakes. "I make the flowers into flour," he'd say with pride in his voice. "That is the way to make flower cream cakes." He'd bring his hand down on the worktable to emphasize the importance of this.

"If you're going to do something, do it the whole way," Deba'l said. She bit into a cake and closed her eyes.

5. THE MEETINGS BEGIN

PRIEST GUNG RAN THE TIP OF HIS TONGUE around and around his red, puffy lips. Women meeting to talk of ways to please their husbands. How delightful. How loving. He rubbed his hands together. The Great God Ploch would be so pleased, as would the High Priest. Another tongue revolution. That she didn't have Gung's mouth hanging over and slobbering on her as she performed sex duties was one thank you Solanj'l could offer to Ploch.

Priests allegedly were chaste but few believers trusted Ploch's servants were sufficiently uplifted by the God to abstain from copulation and related activities. They snuck into homes to be with servant girls, who had no choice but to lie down, spread their legs and stumps, hoping worse wasn't coming. Solanj learned about what priests could get up to when she was ten. Two or three times when she'd gone into the kitchen for a late night drink she'd found a favourite servant, Rana'l, crying. She asked what was wrong. Rana'l would shake her head and say, "Nothing." She sounded so sad. One night Solanj found a priest in the kitchen sitting next to Rana'l with his hand resting on her stump, which was covered by her skirt. He jerked his hand away and left without a word. Solanj said it was good of him to come and see her. Rana'l gave her a look filled with anger and said, "You don't know what you're talking about." She'd never before spoken sharply to Solanj.

When Solanj told her mother she thought the priest should not to come to the kitchen at night because it made Rana'l unhappy, Luranj'l became angry. What was she talking about? How could she say a priest should not come to their home? Priests were good men. She was mistaken. Rana'l was fine. Solanj was not to speak of this again.

Solanj resolved to find out more. For several nights she forced herself to stay awake and watch for the priest. On one of his regular nights she hid in a kitchen closet. The priest made Rana'l lie down on a bench near one wall and pulled her skirt up. Solanj was so surprised to see that Rana'l wore no undergarment that she didn't immediately question why the priest was looking at a part of Rana'l he should not be seeing. The priest put his mouth on the stump that had once been a leg, like he was kissing it. He put two or three fingers—Solanj couldn't be certain of how many—into Rana'l's private place and started moving them back and forth. Rana'l's face was turned toward the closet. Solanj had never seen a face like that before. She didn't know how to describe it; there was no word. It was like sadness and anger were all tangled together. She felt a clutching in her stomach. Was that what the future would be for her? Did all women have to let men do things to them that made them sad and angry? Did her father do what the priest was doing? Did her mother look like that sometimes?

The priest kept kissing Rana'l's stump, saying how beautiful it was, how tempting. Solanj had thought sawing off girls' legs was just a vicious thing Ploch wanted done. A new understanding was coming. An icy chill climbed up her back and moved onto her neck when she saw the priest pull up his robe and there was a huge finger-like thing between his thighs. He put it into Rana'l's private place and she made a whimpering sound. He kept poking it in and out, in and out, then gave a great groan and fell on Rana'l, crushing her against the bench. Solanj held her teeth together to keep from crying out. After what seemed a very long time, the priest pulled away from Rana'l and left.

No words. Rana'l sat up and pulled her skirt down. After a minute or two she heaved herself up onto her props, and like a very tired old woman barely hanging on, dragged herself to the door that lead to the servant quarters. Solanj wanted to run to her, to say she was sorry she couldn't make the priest stop coming, but knew this would upset Rana'l even more. Even a little girl knew servants feared being sent away. She could not tell her mother or father what she'd seen.

* * *

Gung would arrange for the meeting room and refreshments himself. Such wonderful, wonderful women. His tongue slid over his lips, leaving saliva in the corners. He was so happy to help them, to know them. Such lucky, lucky husbands. How he envied them.

Six women attended the first meeting, which took place midweek during an Afternoon Break. Petra'l was thrilled with the idea. She must belong to any group that included Deba'l and Solanj'l. Solanj'l considered her a scatterwit but Deba'l thought she had promise. Of what, was not identified.

Janka'l also accepted an invitation. Solanj'l had the impression her husband had urged it. She was small with a triangular face that made Solanj'l think of a human Spirry. Her eyes were bright, suggesting little went unnoticed.

Morgani'l came out of curiosity. A woman of ironic high spirits, and about the only person who could make Solanj'l laugh wholeheartedly, she considered the purpose of the group inane. She threw her head back so far her dark blonde hair came to her waist as she laughed at the invitation.

"You are going to think up ways to better please Glom? I don't believe it. What are you really planning to do in this group?"

Solanj'l shook her head and shrugged. "It can do no harm. It might have uses."

"It's the uses I want to know about."

Solanj'l smiled and said nothing.

Casanj'l was there, the sister Solanj'l never liked or respected.

A simpering seeker of male approval. As a little girl she would climb onto their father's lap, eyelashes aflutter, whispering who knew what into his ear. Then pulling away to smile sweetly at him, bringing forth a not-quite fatherly smile. Their dignified, no nonsense father liked Casanj's game. First lesson in the relations between the sexes: Female, play the fool. The girls were equally beautiful, tall, but not too tall so as to threaten boys and men. Just the right amount of enticing roundedness of the body. Creamy, finely textured skin, a contrast to lush chestnut hair that fell to the middle of their backs when they let it go free. And there were the clear light brown eyes with gold flecks, Solanj's larger and elongated at the outer corners.

Solanj'l had shaken her head when Deba'l suggested including Casanj'l in the group but she was present, informed of the meeting by Gung with whom she had a reciprocal fawning over arrangement. Unfortunately Solanj'l could find no convincing reason for excluding the once flirtatious girl who'd become a tight-lipped, judgmental woman whose presence was like a negative force sucking air out of a room.

Gung had wished to be present at the meeting. Licking his lips the whole time Solanj'l assumed. Deba'l smiled sweetly at him. How does she do that? Solanj'l had wondered.

"Now how can women speak freely of their husbands before a priest?" Deba'l had asked.

"Ah," Gung intoned as he nodded his head. "Of course that must be considered. Yes, you are correct. After a Temple greeting, I will depart to let you wives do your talking." He gave a bow and muculent smile.

The Temple was a depressing place—huge, grey, and clammy. It thrust itself up in the city centre, constructed of porous stone boxes squat and broad or tall and thin. It was a visual representation of lack of imagination. There was little to relieve the stony dreariness that continued inside, except for the nondescript fabrics that hung down in the altar area and the wood covering the seats of wealthy worshipers. Poor people sat on stone. It was always uncomfortable, enervatingly humid in summer and frigid in winter—except at the altar where priests were warmed by wood burning braziers.

Around the sanctuary were rooms for various purposes, all equally unappealing. Some of them contained mould, a rare occurrence in a dry country. The Temple sat over a spring. Water seeped into the basement and oozed up the porous stone walls. The Great God Ploch had instructed the priest-builders to cover up a source of water in an arid land.

Solanj'l conducted the meeting. Deba'l said with a smile that since she'd arranged to meet with the priest, it was Solanj'l's turn to work. Gung was introduced and thanked for his assistance. He went on and on about a renewed adoration of the Great God Ploch, how pleasing to the Great God and the High Priest. The only statement that stayed with Solanj'l was, "We look forward to the expansion of the group."

As soon as he exited Casanj'l asked why Solanj'l was leading the group. Shouldn't the group decide who would be the leader? She wasn't saying she thought she should take that position, but she was older than Solanj'l and... Deba'l cut in and pointed out she and Solanj'l had done the work to bring about the meeting. That qualified them as leaders. They'd agreed Solanj'l would conduct the meeting. Casanj'l's face snapped into harsh lines as she tapped her thumb on her stump, but she kept her mouth shut. How could she argue with the wife of the Minister Second Only to the First? Petra'l said it was fine with her, she didn't want to be a leader of anything. She thought it amazing Deba'l and Solanj'l had taken on a man's job.

"But we women are the ones who are to provide pleasure," Deba'l said. "We are the ones who must consider how to do it. It is to our advantage to share ideas."

"Husbands tell us what they want," Janka'l said. "There is no choice."

"Then why are you here?" Casanj'l asked. Her face was still angry.

Janka'l cocked her head to one side. "I thought it would be good to be with my own kind. And to talk about something other than clothing."

Morgani'l had been sitting with arms crossed, looking as if she were merely an observer, the role Solanj'l had thought she would play, but then she spoke. "Think of all the things we could say to each other."

"We know what we are to do. What do we have to talk about?" Casanj'l snapped.

"Whatever we want."

Casanj'l opened her mouth but Solanj'l, with a warning glance at Morgani'l, pointed out they were present to talk about ways to please husbands so they should do so.

"I know my favourite way to do it," Petra'l said with a flirty smile.

"It would be so strange to talk about … that," Janka'l said.

"I would find talk of *that* an abomination," Casanj'l said pursing her lips into a tight line.

They were in a peculiar situation. Their purpose in life was to please husbands, primarily with sex, and yet women rarely spoke of it. There was no specific proscription, it simply wasn't done. They sat and looked at each other warily, none ready to enter into revealing what was usually kept to themselves, not even Petra'l apparently.

"There are many ways to please husbands," Deba'l said. "I, not the steward, am always ready to serve Hunak food and drink no matter what time he comes home."

Solanj'l said it pleased Glom when she asked him questions that helped him with business dealings. Morgani'l said Bantant liked for her to do that as well. Janka'l said she thought she pleased Doam by laying out his clothing each day because he didn't like to choose and said she was better at doing it than his steward.

"Aren't we going to talk about … intimacy at all?" Petra'l finally asked.

Morgani'l laughed her throaty chuckle and said they would call her their Leader of Intimacy.

"Petra'l, you have the courage to suggest we should," Deba'l said. "Start us on the discussion."

Petra'l gave a great sigh. "If I must."

What on earth will she come out with? Solanj'l wondered.

Petra'l gave a little wiggle in her chair. "One thing I do is, when we're having dinner, I raise my skirt so Metak can caress my stump while he eats. He likes that greatly."

Solanj'l felt the familiar tightness in her head.

Casanj'l looked at Petra'l as if she'd been slapped. "Do you do this in front of his steward?"

"No," Petra'l scowled. "Of course not."

Casanj'l moved around in her chair as if she felt something poking her, then said such talk was not right; she hadn't thought they would talk about ... personal matters.

"I don't see how we can avoid it if we are to talk of new ways of pleasing husbands," Deba'l said.

"Are you ashamed of what you and Carn do?" Solanj'l asked.

"How dare you ask such a thing? How could I be ashamed of what my husband wants? It is the duty of the wife to like what a husband does."

"Always?" Morgani'l asked. She'd married late because she was as averse to marriage as Solanj'l. She had finally agreed to the offer of a widower fifteen years older than she. Many people thought he was too lenient with her because she was free to do and say surprising things. It was even reported she had once put her hand on her skirt to hold it down when Bantant started to display her leg to impress a business associate. Solanj'l knew this to be true.

Casanj'l declared *The Book of Ploch* instructed a wife to obey her husband in all ways and to *like* it. Solanj'l asked when she'd read that. She hadn't. There was no need. Carn had told her.

Deba'l asked Casanj'l if she had a way of pleasing Carn, one they could suggest to their husbands. Casanj'l again shifted around in her chair, looking uncomfortable. She said nothing.

No other ways of pleasing husbands were offered until Petra'l broke the silence. "I feed Metak bits of food. Especially fruit at the end of the evening meal. You know ... before our time ... together." A wiggle and little girl smile.

With varying degrees of enthusiasm the others said they could try feeding their husbands bits of food. Solanj'l found it difficult to envision herself, as well as Deba'l and Morgani'l doing it, but it could be tried. If she was going to provide women with legs she'd undoubtedly do many things she found ridiculous and unpleasant.

It was the first of the Pleasure Ways.

6. THE WOODWORKER

"BUT, WHEN THE CHILDREN COME..." Glom said
"When the children come my work will be finished," Solanj'l replied.

"But what is my pretty little wife going to do in a workroom?"
Solanj'l presented her agreeable-wife smile, "Work."

"Ah," Glom smoothed his hair back from his face with his right hand, making the thick bangs stand up, producing a untidy look, but one of his I-am-pleased gestures. "I know. You are going to work on a surprise for me."

And so Solanj'l went to work on a surprise—but not one Glom would imagine. Legs. Legs that could give women a degree of mobility, a glimmer of freedom, maybe a reduction in the sense of just hanging on in a world of woundedness.

When the idea came to her she didn't know how she would convince people to accept such an incredibly outlandish, non-Ramprendian idea. Then it hit her. It was obvious. To expand on the pleasuring of husbands. Girls had their legs sawed off because useless stumps were exciting to men. How exciting for men to repeat the Beautification. Remove the wood leg and ... ah ... The Stump dangling from the woman maimed for his pleasure. Over and over and over. Private Beautification.

There would be resistance, of this she was certain, and more resistance from women than men would not surprise her. Casanj'l, a true believer in the ways of Ramprend, would be outraged, but that would be of no consequence if Carn wanted her to have a leg. Solanj'l thought Petra'l and Janka'l would respond hesitantly, with Petra'l being the first to accept it because "intimacy" might be enhanced. Morgani'l and Deba'l would be interested immediately. Deba'l would put the index finger of her right hand against her jaw, middle finger under her lower lip and thumb under chin—her thinking pose. Possibly she'd smile as well. Morgani'l would look like a cat speculating on a tasty meal, if she had a tail it would be switching. They'd be the first to learn of it. She smiled, imagining their surprise; she must remember that anticipated response when she became discouraged, which she knew would happen.

First there had to be a leg. Glom ordered Kracak to set up the future children's playhouse as Solanj'l directed. Kracak said nothing but his eyebrows did their I-don't-believe-this lift. She needed two tables, one for sitting, another at which she could stand. She also wanted a rolling chair left in the workroom. She'd move from workshop to house on her props. Kracak produced one of his little sniffs of displeasure, disapproval, disbelief when Solanj'l told him she would be working with wood.

Standing without props was the first problem to solve. Her hands had to be free so she could manipulate objects and reach farther than was possible from a chair. She also needed to experience being upright, remember what it was to stand on her own. Creating a pedestal would be her first step to not only standing but also walking. Running undoubtedly never a possibility. She told Kracak to bring her a round piece of wood twenty-seven inches long and twenty-four inches around, hollowed out ten inches in and with a two-inch rim on one end. It was to be painted red, her prime colour according to Deba'l. She'd use it as a symbol of encouragement. Kracak did as asked, not without grumbling about being taken from his "real" work.

She assembled cloth for padding to put inside and around the rim. She'd insert the stump in the hole and have a pedestal on which to stand. How was she going to do this? She would have to touch *it*. It revolted her. She used mitts for bathing; her hands against the stump was more than she could bear. To insert the stump into the wood leg would probably require touching. *Don't think of that now, not yet. Work up to it.*

The pedestal was not right. She didn't have to try getting into it to know it was too tall, the stumphole not deep enough, and the top too thick. It needed to angle up so it wouldn't stick out too far and it had to be much thinner on one side or she'd have to stand with spread legs. She should have thought of that. Kracak carried it off to be adjusted. It came back too short, hole still too shallow and the top shaved all the way around, so thin in places she knew it would break through. She suspected Kracak deliberately mis-remembered her instructions. A new piece of wood would have to be shaped from written instructions. How was she ever going to make legs for women when she couldn't get a simple pedestal made?

Luranj'l had told the young Solanj she could not hurry or organize life. Patience was a trait women must develop if they did not possess it naturally. Solanj's existence would be an unhappy one if she didn't learn to let life happen *to* her. Solanj'l's frustration at the slowness of creating a simple usable pedestal brought this back. As she tried to change the Ramprendian way of life, she'd have to accept reversals. After all, she was trying to do something never done before. There were no examples. Men who lost legs through accident were in the same circumstance as women. If a poor man lost one it was generally assumed he caused the accident and deserved what he got. Men of privilege rarely lost a leg. When it happened they were treated with deference and provided with servants at all times. Berating herself for failing at first attempts was useless.

After a basically acceptable wood replacement arrived, she worked for three days to get the padding to what she hoped would be the right thickness and softness. She covered it with purple plush, purple being her favourite colour, and hung gold tassels around the top, except for the side next to her flesh leg. It stood by the table looking like a stool for a wealthy child. It stood there and she sat and looked at it. How was she going to get into it without help? How was she going to deal with the stump?

She stared at it for two days, trying to imagine herself in it. It was rather gaudy, all red and purple and gold. Not usually liking ornate objects, she wondered why she'd decorated it like that. Perhaps to amuse herself as a distraction from being terrified by her own intent.

Without the embellishment it should be the beginning of a leg. Make it leg size, give it shape. There would have to be a way to keep it on. Women were to move, not just stand. Oh no. Women who didn't use props undoubtedly wouldn't have enough strength to get into the leg and move with it. Before any woman could use the wood leg, she would need to build strength in the flesh one. Even she, who used props regularly, needed to build more strength in her flesh leg and her arms.

She told Kracak to remove the footrest from the chair she used in the workshop.

7. SMALL TRIUMPHS

TRIUMPH, SMALL BUT A TRIUMPH nonetheless. At first she had to push or pull on the wheels with her hands to help move herself in the chair, her leg not strong enough to move her and the chair without the assistance of hands. With practice though she could, hands used only for guidance.

She pulled her way across the workroom to the window and moved the curtain aside. It was a bright blue and gold day with a few white clouds idling across the sky, what she'd thought of as a happy day when she was a little girl. She tried pushing up the window but couldn't from a sitting position.

Wait, she'd forgotten something. The leg needed to bend at the knee so women could get into and out of their chairs more easily. How could she have not foreseen that? The leg needed a joint, a knee bend so women could sit, but if that were the case it wouldn't be stable when a woman stood. All right, don't despair, just another problem to solve.

A man was standing at the edge of the Glom's field. How long had he been there? He wasn't familiar. He appeared to be staring toward her but the angle and intensity of light might not let him see her. He moved north, stopping frequently as if examining the property. He was taller than the men of Ramprend generally were and was wearing a cape, something not done during the day. She put her arm on the window ledge and leaned her chin on it. She'd have to tell Glom about him; he might be up to no good.

The Raiders, who'd moved to initial capital status, had paid another visit, breaking into a mill, dismantling a machine and taking away gears. Glom wore his glow-look when he proudly reported Hunak, Minister Second Only to the First, had asked him, an important man of business, to be a member of the committee to discuss and stop these invasions and thefts. He'd been missing evening meals due to running here and there to talk with this and that person about what to do. It was decided guards would be posted, men recruited from the unemployed because the Sheriff did not have sufficient staff for the extra work. When Solanj'l questioned their qualifications for dealing with outsiders, Glom's mouth formed the straight line that meant he did not like to be thought wrong.

She rolled to the tall table. The time was at hand: time to put the stump in the hole and stand. One morning she'd gritted her teeth, closed her mind as much as she could, and washed the stump by hand. It felt dead, even if there was some warmth in it. She could feel the skin on her palms trying to withdraw from contact. She hung on and rubbed up, down, around. When the time came to wash The Pretty Little Spot her nerve left her. It took seven days for her to get to the point she could touch that sad, puckered skin. Do it, curse Ploch. There'd be a lot more she didn't want to do. DO IT. She had, then put her head against the tub wall and gulped her revulsion. Fortunately she would not have to touch that spot to insert the stump in the pedestal, or leg.

She rolled to where the pedestal stood in a corner made by the high table and a wall, pulled herself up onto the props, then leaned her left hip against the table and pushed the props aside. Her efforts at making her own leg stronger were working, but she didn't know if she could stand on it for any length of time, leaning against the table or not. She took a deep breath, grasped the stump and held it up with her right hand, and leaned forward to tip the pedestal toward her with her left. She crashed to the floor. When she'd fallen in the past, her father or Glom had been there to pick her up and put her in a chair. She wasn't going to call Kracak to handle her like a sack of meal. She crawled to the pedestal, pulled it out of the corner, and nudged it along against the wall. The falling, crawling, pulling and nudging were exhausting. She needed more physical strength. She lay on the floor for several minutes, then hitched herself to the chair and pushed it into the corner where the pedestal had been. Because it was wedged in the corner she thought she'd be able to rise up enough on her knee and push-twist herself into it. It didn't work. Her skirt got in the way so she twisted and turned herself out of it. Tried for the chair again. Her shoe slid and she hit her chin on the front of the seat. She dropped onto the floor and panted. She took off her shoe and stocking and after two more failed attempts finally got into the chair.

She'd thought she understood how debilitated women were. She had no idea. Because she used the props as much as she did, she had some arm strength. Someone like Petra'l who sat in a chair all the time wouldn't be able to do this and she had to assume there would be a lot of falling as women tried using the legs. It might prove more of a challenge to get women into a condition to use them than to make them. There was so much to anticipate, to figure out.

In her eleventh year, Solanj had decided she would build her own little house on the edge of the patio at the rear of her father's property, a place of her own to read and make things—whatever came to mind. Her father was amused by this intention and told his steward, Chanuk, to give her what she wanted. Chanuk thought it quite funny. He chuckled and she knew he would have ruffled her hair if such familiarity were allowed. Casanj was right: amusing men had its purposes.

She decided to start her little house by laying down planks to form a base. She assumed it was a way to start but had no idea how she would erect walls and get a roof put on. Something would come to her. Chanuk had the planks brought and laid down. A neighbour boy appeared. His name was Nanic and he was three years older than she. What did she think she was doing? Girls didn't build things. When he learned her father approved and the steward was to help, he said he would guide her.

"I don't need your guidance," she'd said.

After considering several useless ideas about erecting walls, it had come to her that she would peg her little house together, like the leaves in the dining table, only upright. First there had to be a channel in the floor planks to slide a wall board along and onto the pegs in the one next to it. Chanuk looked skeptical when she presented the idea but he shrugged, ordered a channel cut, and provided her with wall boards and drills that make holes. He provided pegs to insert into holes where needed. She was grateful.

Nanic came each day to "help," complaining the entire time that he should be in charge. She'd tell him to go build his own house, but was glad for the help. The wall boards were too heavy to stand and slide onto the pegs by herself. The work was slowed because he did more strutting and issuing of pseudo-orders than drilling, pounding, lifting, and sliding whenever Chanuk was within sight. Solanj knew by looking at him that Chanuk thought Nanic was funny.

She left out three wall boards for a doorway. She connected the boards and had Chunk help her put hinges where needed to make a door. Workmen were brought in to "help" secure the corners of the house and put on the roof because Solanj realized this to was beyond her alone. The men thought it funny for a girl to be out there with them but saw she was a quick learner and a good worker. Chanuk told Hect the men were impressed he had such a child. She also was the talk of her neighbours and her parents' friends.

"Imagine thinking of such a thing and actually working to bring it about."

"So clever."

"Unfortunate she's a girl."

What they did not say out loud was, "How strange."

In her current workroom, Solanj'l put her left forearm against the back of the chair seat, grasped the right arm, pushed with her foot, twisted her body, and was able to get her left hip on the seat. With some pushes and wiggles she was in the chair, panting but seated. She'd had frustrations with building her little house but she had done it, just as she'd gotten herself into this chair. Glom's pretty little wife needed to hold onto the tenacity of the girl with two legs—two strong legs—and arms. She'd do it; she'd get into that pedestal.

Someone was pounding on the door.

"Solanj'l, I have something to tell you," Glom called out.

He'd agreed to not enter the workroom until his surprise was finished. After her initial work, she'd realized Kracak also had to be kept out. The surprise could be ruined if Kracak knew she'd asked Glom with her hands thrown up in little girl despair to tell Kracak to stay out of the workroom. She explained she was afraid Kracak might tell another steward who would tell his master who would unwittingly tell Glom and spoil her surprise for him. Glom had said Kracak wouldn't tell others if ordered not to. She cocked an eyebrow at him. Stewards had a fine reputation for talking amongst themselves about what occurred in their households. Glom allowed she had a point when she reminded him the neighbours knew about a new carriage before it'd been purchased and of the time Glom's father knew what gift he would be receiving on his Arrival Day. Kracak was told he should not enter the workroom. He'd lifted his chin and given a grunt. This was an affront but nothing could be done if that was what his master wanted.

Glom had had a surprise of his own. "For my pretty little wife and her little secrets," he'd said as he handed her the key for the playhouse. She'd never understood why a playhouse needed a key but was now grateful he'd thought so.

She said she'd be out in just a bit. After she got her skirt back on. She didn't tell him that.

Hunak and Deba'l were coming for dinner, just the two of them. Glom had spontaneously issued an invitation after a meeting and Hunak said they could come the next night. Solanj'l listened, thinking of a little boy. It meant so very much to him to be connected to men with power. Providing women with legs meant she too needed the powerful. She was certain Deba'l would want a leg. Could Hunak, *the* man of power be convinced of their desirability? A private dinner could be useful.

8. THE PEDESTAL AND PRIVACY

EVEN STRENGTHENED, HER LEG GREW TIRED quickly. It trembled from the exertion of standing and she'd start to wobble, the pedestal moving with her. If there were music she could sway and pretend she was dancing. Would women be able to dance with wood legs? Only strangely. She had to lean against the table or put the props under her arms to give her leg assistance, but she was standing and could reach around on the table in a way she could not from a chair. She did have to be careful not to reach too far or she'd capsize.

She'd learned how to get into the pedestal without falling to the floor, but only after several more crashes. Glom had asked about her bruises. She laughed them off with statements about the recalcitrance of the surprise for him. He'd shake his head and say no surprise was worth her damaging her body. She'd pat his arm and tell him not to worry. A few bruises were worth the result. She hoped that would be true.

She decided to let Glom see the pedestal. He came to the workshop after a day of reviewing the men allegedly guarding against the Raiders. She proudly stood at her table, skirt drawn up to reveal the pedestal, waiting for compliments. This surprised her. Girls of her station could create delicate, generally useless items with fibers and threads but to do serious work was not part of the world of privileged females. She'd stepped out of that world and created something unique. Without her being conscious of it, her view had shifted. She wanted acknowledgment.

"What is that? Is that my surprise?"

She laughed in an appropriate wifely way. "Oh, dear no. The pedestal will help me create the surprise."

"You will do more work?"

She nodded.

"What an extraordinary little wife I have. It's pretty."

Disappointment filled her, pushing against her skin. She became heavy with it. All he saw was pretty. He didn't understand how difficult and frustrating it had been to create this object holding her in a standing position. He couldn't imagine how alive it made her feel. And how sad—remembering when she could stand. And walk—and even run.

Glom put his arms around her and kissed her, reached down and put his hand on her hip under the skirt, the one above the absent leg. He moved it around and attempted to slip it between the stump and pedestal.

"Ah," he said, "We will have to lift you out of this pretty thing, my pretty little wife."

She would so like to tell him what she felt when her called her his pretty little wife but one did not speak of striking one's husband.

"Such a wonderful man," her mother had said from the beginning of the courtship. Solanj'l did not want to marry any man including this one, even if he was attractive enough with his dark hair, long straight nose, and almost black eyes. Not much taller than she. Slim, which was good. She had an aversion to men who let the fat build up on their bodies. One suitor disgusted her with his shaking belly. Glom did not look like he'd go to jiggling flesh; but she still didn't want to be his wife. He was full of his worthiness and she could see no reason for it. He was successful because he had been born into a privileged family. He was smart enough not to ruin what had been handed to him but had no interesting ideas, merely uttering what was current with the men of his station. She could not take him seriously. Her parents, however, thought him a great prospect. Casanj'l told her she should be very happy a man of such stature was interested in her, particularly when she didn't do anything, anything at all, to encourage him.

"I don't want to encourage him."

"You are a fool. What do you think will happen if you do not accept him? You have rejected more men than anyone I know. Mother and Father are very upset with you. They won't turn you out of the house, but the embarrassment of having a daughter who did not marry would kill them. How could you live with that?"

Solanj'l told her engaging in hyperbole was counterproductive, but she hadn't known what she would do if she didn't get a remotely acceptable husband. Unmarried women existed in shadow. People would acknowledge her existence only when she was with her parents, out of respect for them. She'd be even more of a nothing than she already was. She capitulated after her father brought the son of a colleague to dinner one night, a bulky and loud man who had opinions on all subjects. Her father later said he had too many opinions with too little knowledge. Solanj'l knew she was being threatened when a man her father did not respect was brought in to look her over. She told Hect she would marry Glom.

He did possess one asset. She'd sensed she'd be free of disgusting sexual practices. She hadn't wanted to even consider what the loud, muscle-waiting-to-go-to-fat man would do to her. She knew no particulars about repellent practices, but she did know she'd have no recourse but to go along with whatever a husband wanted. Nothing said by her mother or Casanj'l, who'd been married a year when Solanj'l agreed to accept Glom, led her to think sex would bring pleasure. If Luranj'l or her sister enjoyed it, they didn't tell her. A man had urges; it was the woman's task to satisfy them. Her desires did not signify.

Some women apparently found sex pleasurable, Petra'l spoke fondly of it. She occasionally had feelings she thought must have to do with sex, but her rejection of the world in which she lived was so great it was hard to believe a woman would willingly be that way with a man. How could you desire someone who regarded you as a thing maimed for his purposes? Nothing in her experience with Glom had brought her a desire for more of what was done—but she had been right in thinking he would not do things she found unbearable.

At this moment he was having urges he wanted satisfied before they had the evening meal. He rolled her to his bed. Not the acknowledgment she'd hoped for.

9. REVELATIONS

SOLANJ'L FOUND EVERY MEETING a two-headed experience, one head thinking of how the women would react to the legs, the other attending to what was being said and what might be behind it. What were these women capable of feeling and doing?

Janka'l, who was becoming more talkative, had wanted to marry her husband's brother but he was not interested. She smiled shyly as she said, "He was interested in you, Solanj'l. Doam and he called on you a few times. I guess you didn't welcome them with eagerness." Solanj'l had no memory of the brother or of Doam before she met him through Glom. She merely smiled, not wanting Janka'l to think she had a forgettable husband.

"I'm certain Doam is quite pleased with his choice," Deba'l said.

"I hope so."

"You don't know?" Petra'l asked. She looked stunned and said nothing more, unusual in that she would chatter on and on if the others let her.

"He doesn't complain," Janka'l said rather hesitantly.

Petra'l found her voice, "What about gifts? Does he give you gifts?"

Janka'l opened her mouth but Casanj'l broke in, "Gifts aren't a mark of appreciating a wife."

Petra'l gave her an angry look. "I think they are."

"How does Carn express his appreciation for you, Casanj'l?" Morgani'l asked. Whenever she addressed Casanj'l her voice had an edge of contempt.

"He ... he says I'm a good wife."

"Oh," from Morgani'l.

"That is enough."

"I'm with Petra'l. Gifts have their place."

Earlier they'd all admired the necklace Morgani'l was wearing, spheres of pale green anzonian hanging from a heavy gold chain. A fifth year anniversary present. Petra'l had been particularly impressed. She'd undoubtedly tabulated the cost of chain and stones, then estimated how long it would be before Metak could appreciate her the way Bantant did Morgani'l.

"I know Doam is pleased with his choice," Solanj'l said. "He told Glom they both were fortunate in their wives. Glom told me."

"Really?"

"It's the truth."

"Thank you for telling me."

Deba'l said they should discuss how husbands expressed appreciation; it would help them in finding ways to please their men. "Casanj'l, tell us how Carn expresses his."

"I told you. He tells people I'm a good wife. He does it all the time."

"Does he say it privately?" Morgani'l asked.

"That isn't necessary."

"Does he say it about anything in particular?" Solanj'l asked. Casanj'l shook her head.

"For flower arranging?" Petra'l asked, motioning toward the flowers sitting on the table against the wall.

The once bleak room in the Temple was less so, largely because of the complaints of Petra'l and Morgani'l. Petra'l said meeting in such a place was worse than being in a dirt cellar for vegetables. Deba'l had secured Gung's permission to make the room more hospitable. Morgani'l and Solanj'l brought in brightly coloured wall hangings. "How exquisite," Gung had said, rubbing his hands together, then pawing Solanj'l's arm while profusely thanking her, with complete lip-moistening action. Each of the members was responsible for bringing flowers on a rotating basis. Deba'l and Solanj'l had been providing teas and tasties. At this meeting, Petra'l and Janka'l offered to take their turns with refreshments. Casanj'l was of the opinion food distracted from discussion, an opinion that did not prevent her from eating as much as, or more than, the others.

In response to Petra'l's flower-arranging question, Casanj'l shook her head. Morgani'l asked Petra'l if she arranged flowers for Metak. She said no, the steward or one of the servants did. Her mother had told her she should learn the art because men liked it. She shrugged as if a woman of her allure didn't need to bother. They'd all gotten this advice from mothers but Deba'l was the only one who actually did it. Morgani'l surprised them when she said Bantant liked to arrange flowers; he found it relaxing. She would sit and talk with him while he did it and even make suggestions about placement of flowers. Now that she thought about it, she realized she enjoyed these times with him.

Her friends wanted to know what Solanj'l did for Glom. She waited a beat or two, then told them she was working on a surprise for him. She held up her hand, "Don't ask me what it is. I'm afraid if I say anything, he'll hear about it in advance."

Morgani'l asked if he knew she was doing it. When Solanj'l reported she used the playroom as a workroom and Glom had ordered Kracak to provide her with what was needed, Casanj'l said he was being very indulgent if he gave such orders to a steward.

"For Ploch's sake," Morgani'l said, "she's working on a surprise for *him*."

"That doesn't matter. And do not use the great God's name in that way."

"I'll use it any way I want."

Petra'l put in, "I think it's wonderful. What fun. I want to make a surprise for Metak."

"It is clever of you, Solanj'l," Janka'l said.

They all agreed and asked for just a little hint. She refused but said they could talk about other surprises they could create. Deba'l said the best she could do for Hunak would be give him more time from work but that wasn't possible, she'd already taken over the giving of orders to the steward so Hunak wouldn't have to think about it.

"You run his household?" Casanj'l asked, looking as if Deba'l had just announced she'd been named a Minister.

"It was the kind thing to do."

"It's a man's job."

"Hunak was glad to be relieved of it."

Janka'l said Doam seemed to like the embroidered pillows she made. Perhaps she could make him a scarf to wear on festive occasions. What a radical idea. Men of privilege were outfitted by a few tailors. Women actually made the clothing, but men had to decide how to clothe men. Would a husband wear an object made by a wife? The only way to find out was to make something and see if it pleased him.

"I make a mess of embroidery," Petra'l more or less wailed. "I can't do anything well with my hands." She held them up. "No knack at all." She shrugged. "I guess I shouldn't worry. Metak always tells me I'm a good wife after… "

"We know," Morgani'l said, throwing her hands in the air. "After intimacy."

Petra'l didn't know why they made light of her interest in intimacy. Didn't they all want to be good at that? Janka'l said they were told what to do and they had to assume they were doing what they should.

"But you have to make up things on your own," Petra'l said. "Suggest little … actions you'd like to try."

"Oh," Janka'l said.

Morgani'l asked for an example of … actions. Petra'l wasn't

certain if she wanted to give any. Why did she have to talk of such things when they didn't? Intimacy discussions hadn't gone beyond her telling of revealing her stump at the table and feeding fruit to Metak.

"Come, Petra'l," Deba'l said. "Can't you tell us one action you created?"

"If I must."

Morgani'l snorted. "You know you want to. Stop playing put upon little girl."

"Well…"

Solanj'l was amused to see them, herself included, lean forward ready to hear something never heard before. Even Deba'l, the oldest and most assured, looked intent. Petra'l sat up straighter, ready to be the centre of attention. What she said made Casanj'l gasp and turn pale.

Petra'l had told Metak to lick … her private place. "He was licking my stump so I told him he might consider moving his mouth up and over a bit." She smiled in a self-satisfied way.

Casanj'l tried to move her chair backward. "I'm not listening. This is … oh … how can you speak of such a thing."

Morgani'l asked, "What does it matter where they lick?"

Casanj'l looked as if she might vomit. "You're disgusting. I've always thought you low in your tastes."

"Deba'l held up her hands. "No fighting among friends."

"I will not listen to filth."

"We're here to speak of ways to please husbands," Solanj'l said. "Petra'l, does this please Metak?"

"Petra'l vigorously nodded her head. "It does." She giggled. "I like it too."

Solanj'l said, "It pleases Metak, Casanj'l. Are you saying it's wrong to please husbands, or is there some reason it's wrong to please Metak?"

"No good husband…"

"Have none of you heard of this practice?" Deba'l asked. "It's something some men like to do. I must assume some women like having it done to them."

How did she know this? Had she discussed it with other women? Did she talk about it with Hunak? They learned that not only did Deba'l talk with Hunak of such things, but that he had come to ask her what she liked, what gave her pleasure.

Solanj'l looked around the room. Janka'l's head was cocked in her questioning way. Morgani'l looked amused. Casanj'l's face was closed, lips tight. Petra'l was beaming. What did her own face show? The sadness she felt? That one emotion appeared every time the nature of Deba'l's and Hunak's union came to her attention.

She rode home thinking about the end of the meeting. She found the idea of talking about sex unnerving. Doing it gave no pleasure. Who wanted to be reminded of that? The courage it must have taken for Petra'l to share that, particularly with critical, sniping Casanj'l present. It appeared Petra'l was a woman of independent thought. How many of those lived in Ramprend? How many adventurous women had been making up new ways to be pleasing? Deba'l said it was a known practice but Petra'l appeared to be unaware of it. She, Solanj'l, should have been paying closer attention to the world around her. How had she presumed to think she could bring about change with so little knowledge?

10. A LEG AND GATHERINGS

MONTHS PASSED WITH SOLANJ'L SLOGGING along with the leg. She started with hope, but came to wonder if she might have expected too much of herself. Kracak had brought her another piece of wood longer than her own leg, scooped out at the top for a stump, like the pedestal. She'd carved and sanded and came up with what looked like an upside down tree stump, lopsided. She told Glom she needed to study with a wood craftsman. He threw his hands up in mock frustration, "What kind of surprise can this be?" but ordered Worak, one of his skilled workers to admit Solanj'l into a company workshop and teach her all he could. She assumed Worak was deeply insulted, being ordered to work with a woman, but had no choice but to do his best. He was a fairly good teacher and she a quick student—she had, after all, worked with wood before.

Knowing how to better use tools didn't ensure proficiency at creating an acceptable result. She realized it would have been wise to start smaller than an adult-sized leg. A vase of flowers sat on her work table. Kracak handed her a fresh bouquet every third morning. Glom said it was Kracak's idea. "Women need a spot of beauty with them," he'd said. She was amused and impressed with his craftiness. Keep the Master happy. Use the wife.

She decided to try to reproduce the vase, a cylinder with a pinched in waist. If she could do that, maybe she could produce a leg. Legs didn't have to be exact replicas of living ones, an approximation would do. It might be advisable to make them anything other than human looking. What would amuse men? Legs like vases, tree trunks, table legs? Penises? Long, long penises? She started to laugh, then bit it back. If she got going she might not be able to stop. Petra'l recently had said men were interested in themselves, as if it were a revelation, which threw the others into laughter that stopped just short of hysteria.

She managed to create something like the vase and drilled a hole in it. Her first sculpture, one in which she could put flowers, dried ones. After the vase came a leg—of sorts—a clunky thing that alternately enraged and made her laugh. How could any woman move with that? A wheel? No—what a dumb idea. It would roll when not wanted. Whoosh, Thud. The woman would be flat on her back or doing splits the way she had as a girl—when she had two legs. Either result would be considered an excellent addition to the Silly Simples but there were already too many of those. How those skits sickened her. A wife crawling toward her husband on one knee, begging forgiveness because she had done something terribly stupid, such as speaking too frequently at a guest meal. There was a favourite that included a woman falling over and flailing like a bug on its back, imploring a husband to lift her into her chair. This would occur after she had had the effrontery to attempt moving her chair on her own. The Great Hall would fill with laughter. And women laughed as loudly as men. Why? Because they had to—or did mutilation of body damage the mind?

After they'd been married two years she told Glom she did not find the Silly Simples funny; she saw herself and women she knew in circumstances like that and it made her sad. They continued to go to the "comedic" performances because a man of Glom's status must, but he didn't demand she join him in laughing even though her unsmiling face was occasionally noted by his friends and colleagues.

The Silly Simples had been discussed at The Gathering, as the Temple meetings were now called. Solanj'l first brought them up with the question of why women laughed. No answer. They did what others did, what their mothers and grandmothers had done. She suggested it was because women considered themselves of no value. No, they didn't think that was the reason.

"Do we ever hear our husbands laugh at men like themselves being humiliated?" she asked.

No, but there were no particular women made fun of.

"All of us are being made fun of. Why not them as well?"

"Men are made fun of," Casanj'l said. "You are speaking nonsense."

"Only servants and workmen."

"I've never thought of that," Janka'l said. "You're right. Men who run the city are never shown that way. Stewards either."

"Because they're the surrogates when the men of power aren't in their homes," Morgani'l said.

Solanj'l didn't ask her friends to attempt to do anything about the Silly Simples but she mentioned them from time to time. Her reminders would be like scratching at one place on the body, over and over. Eventually there'd be an opening and the pain would start seeping out. She felt, without being certain why, that pain was essential to creating a desire for the legs.

* * *

Gung demanded a meeting with Deba'l and Solanj'l and almost rubbed the skin off his palms and lips when he told them women were clamouring to join the group. Such success. Who would have thought women would want to honour Ploch by gathering and discussing ways to please husbands? Of course, he didn't mean women didn't want to please their husbands, or Ploch. It was, however, such a surprise to find that women actually wanted to talk about this with others.

"You must let other women attend. It will grow and grow!" He threw his arms wide.

Deba'l said it would be better if new groups were formed.

New members to their group would not have shared knowledge; they would feel not welcome even though they would be. A group starting fresh would build a spirit of connection, such as they had. Solanj'l admired the way in which Deba'l usually was able to get around the desires of Gung, but on this occasion he was resistant. Why couldn't they just keep adding women? The larger the group the better. Perhaps he thought their meetings were like worship services with one or two talking, all others passively listening.

He was right; there was a demand — larger than they could fill. They finally got him to agree to a new group. One Gathering became several Gatherings to Discuss the Bringing of Pleasure to Husbands. Morgani'l agreed to lead groups. Janka'l, who believed she couldn't possibly do so, was finally convinced she should try and found she liked it. Casanj'l demanded she be a leader. Deba'l and Solanj'l spent hours attempting to match her with those likely to be as rigid as she, not wanting women who might have open minds under her influence. Petra'l refused to lead even one group, claiming Metak wouldn't want her to do it, an assertion not quite believed by the others.

Morgani'l said to Solanj'l after one of their own Gatherings, "It will be interesting to see what happens with all these groups."

"Yes."

"You're keeping something to yourself."

Solanj'l shook her head slowly and smiled in a teasing way.

"I hate it when you do that," Morgani'l said as she was put into Bantant's waiting coach.

Solanj'l watched this process, hating the sight of her friend being moved like a piece of furniture. Morgani'l passively sat in her chair while it was lifted by two servants and slid into the coach, which had all seats raised because no one would be riding with her. Slid in, locked in place, door closed. The servants climbed into the driver compartment and clicked to the coach beasts, great shaggy creatures called moonfaces because of their large round heads, flat noses and small, laid against the head ears. Given their bulky heads it was amazing they could move themselves, let alone a heavy wood, leather, and metal coach carrying several people, but they were amazingly swift once they hit stride. Morgani'l waved as they moved off, a smiling, waving table or sideboard.

Glom's servants waited for Solanj'l to give them permission to do to her what had been done to Morgani'l. A sharp pain shot over her eyes. She would so like to tell them she would walk home. She'd done that as a child, servants trailing behind, not free but getting from here to there on her own two feet. No more. She nodded. The servants picked up her chair; she and it became an inanimate one. She had to get an acceptable leg made. How was she going to find the time to do that with more and more Gatherings to supervise?

11. RAIDERS AGAIN

"YOU WON'T GUESS," GLOM SAID. "You won't be able to guess." He'd pounded on the workshop door, demanding she join him in the Sitting Room. Kracak had set out a bottle of wine. Glom took it up and slowly, carefully poured out two glasses.

"That's the wine you've been saving isn't it?" she asked.

"Yes, a very special one. I have only a few bottles and planned to keep them for when my children are born, when my sons do well and, of course, after the girls go through the Beautification Ritual, but... is something wrong?"

"No ... just an uneasy stomach today."

"My news will make it right." He handed her an icy cold glass, took up his, leaned back and smiled.

Time to coax. Draw the information out as if he were a little boy who had a terribly important secret. Find something plausible but not the truth. If she guessed correctly he would be denied the pleasure of telling her, thus deflating his good spirits.

"You made a big sale today."

He smiled, took a sip of wine and shook his head almost imperceptibly.

This had to do with Hunak. Ever since he'd been asked to be on Hunak's committee he'd been filled with his increased prominence among men. Sex was not the only thing to give him the glow-look.

"I know. You are to direct a new division of the family business." His mouth tightened when she said direct but returned to a look of smug waiting when she said business. He sat and waited.

"You're to start a men's group in the Temple?"

He tightened his mouth and shook his head in mock disbelief at her obtuseness. She picked up her glass and stared at it.

He refilled his and said, "You're not drinking.

She took a sip and said, "I'm waiting for your news. Tell me, I don't seem to be able to figure it out on my own." Her voice had that touch of little girl.

He took a drink, smiled, then put his glass on the table next to him. She waited with what she hoped looked like eagerness. He resettled himself in his chair, like a teacher about to pass on vital knowledge previously unavailable to the callow. "Hunak has asked me to be in charge of the guards at the edge of the city."

He doesn't know anything about guarding, she thought but said, "How can you do that? You have your work."

He explained he didn't have to be present; there would be men to direct the guards but he would be the one to make the major decisions. There'd been a raid the previous night and the guards had been powerless. Solanj'l wondered if they'd been sitting with their backs against a wall, idly talking and enjoying some beer rather than paying attention to what was happening around them. Beer or not, they'd been surrounded by men in black cloaks with hoods and large sticks. "Staves as tall as a man," one guard reported. The Raiders motioned for the guards to move into a mill closed for the night. One guard ran at a Raider and got a chop to his arm. He and the others were herded into the mill then locked in. After that nothing was certain. It was thought the Raiders had penetrated into the city but there was no evidence of that and nothing seemed to have been stolen. But they had to be more vigilant. That was why Hunak had asked him to assume leadership over the guards. She asked about his plans.

He gave a dismissive little chuckle. "I learned of the appointment two hours ago. Give me time, my impatient little wife. I do have one or two ideas."

"I have not congratulated you," she said. "Forgive me."

He waved his hand. "My wife doesn't need to ask forgiveness or to congratulate me. But it is fine you do so."

His primary idea of what should be done was that the guards be given swords. They would not have been overpowered if they had been properly armed. Few people in Ramprend knew how to use swords. The country hadn't been at war in three generations; what need was there for swords? The Sheriff's deputies did not carry weapons, their jobs largely consisted of righting the occasional overturned coach, finding lost pets, breaking up fights among drunks, or marching the occasional thief off to jail.

Solanj'l speculated on what the Raiders wanted and where they came from. Glom said they had to be from the mountains

"Why not from the Land Across the Lake?"

"Because they come from the north. And why would the Lake people come to Ramprend?"

"Why would the mountain people?" she asked.

"You think I'm wrong."

She knew Glom was a tolerant husband, more likely to praise than condemn, but she'd learned early in the marriage that leaving the impression she thought him wrong would put him into a sulk that could last for a week. She didn't know if his silence with occasional grunts was worse, or Kracak smirking because she was in disfavour.

"No, I don't think your ideas are wrong. If people are coming here, rounding up citizens and locking them up in mills, then something must be done. But I wonder why they're coming. They may have a reason that isn't at all threatening."

"They've stolen from us."

"Yes, the gears. I wonder why they've taken nothing else."

Glom shook his head, looking annoyed. Don't raise questions

for which he had no ready answers. She asked—in the little girl voice—if the guards were the most responsible men available. Glom said they probably weren't, given their frequent lack of employment. But he'd have them trained. What was needed were strong men, men who took action. Men who could use swords.

12. PETRA'L

PETRA'L ARRIVED IN METAK'S CARRIAGE And was carried into the house like a piece of furniture. Once having that image of women, Solanj'l couldn't get it out of her mind. Petra'l had been quick to accept Solanj'l's invitation for tea during an Afternoon Break. Kracak rolled her into the Sitting Room and placed her near the window that overlooked the north patio. Sunlight reflected off the glazed pots filled with flowering herbs and threw streaks of light into the room. A servant had laid out trays of biscuits and cakes and the makings for tea.

"Oh no," Petra'l cried

"Are you all right?"

"Now, but who knows how I'll be when I leave? Deba'l warned me of the skills of Glom's baker and I'm afraid I'll stuff too many tasties in my mouth and grow fat and Metak will not be happy and have to punish me."

Solanj'l stopped reaching for a teapot and asked, "Punish you?"

Petra'l laughed. "Oh, not badly. You know. A little slap or two on my bottom."

Solanj'l had wondered if Metak beat Petra'l, but considering a possibility is different from knowing.

"You look as if you've been hit by lightning," Petra'l said. "Surely Glom gives you a slap now and then. Most husbands do."

Solanj'l shook her head. What would she do if he did? Nothing. She could do nothing. She became short of breath, the way she had as a girl filled with rage over her mutilation.

"Don't look that way," Petra'l said. "He doesn't *beat* me. He calls them Correcting Caresses."

"Which tea would you like?"

Petra'l threw her an amused glance, made her selection, and watched her prepare it. "You don't like men do you?"

Solanj'l placed the pot in front of her and said, "There are men and there are men."

"But most of them you don't like."

"I don't like them sawing off the legs of girls."

Petra'l merely looked at her.

"Have a biscuit," Solanj'l said. "I recommend you try one of the ginger ones." She held out a plate and pointed to a crusty white morsel with flecks of yellow.

Petra'l bit in, chewed, swallowed and sighed. "As usual Deba'l is right. This is unbelievably delicious. Can we have our meetings here?"

Solanj'l laughed, prepared her own tea and ate a ginger biscuit. Talk turned to the Gatherings. Petra'l was delighted with theirs. She just loved sitting and talking with her friends and she thought of all the women in the group as friends. She hadn't realized how much she missed companionship until she found herself in it. Everyone was so nice and friendly and they had such fun.

It was true they enjoyed being together. Even Casanj'l looked less like a dried-up berry, or perhaps Solanj'l saw her differently when she didn't have to be with her alone. Members of other Gatherings were also enjoying talking of something other than clothing and related beauty efforts. Only four or five women had dropped out after a couple of meetings and perhaps it wasn't their choice to do so.

"I think we're going to have to get more serious," Solanj'l said.

"Why? What do you mean?"

"We're supposed to be talking about pleasing husbands and we've haven't really been doing that the last few meetings."

"Oh, Ploch." Petra'l looked startled and put her hand to her mouth. "I shouldn't have said that."

Solanj'l said nothing.

After a beat or two Petra'l added, 'I would not be surprised if you sometimes use his name that way."

"I maintain the silence of discretion."

Petra'l, who'd been reaching for another biscuit, threw herself against the back of her chair, brought her hands together and laughed. "We do have fun, don't we?"

"Have another biscuit, or try a cake."

"Which cake should I try first?"

"Dewberry." Solanj'l pointed to a pale green one.

Petra'l sunk her teeth in and groaned in pleasure. "If I could feed these to Metak when we are being … intimate (a self-deprecating move) I could get him to do anything. Lucky you to have these to help you work your wiles."

Solanj'l merely smiled.

"Feeding," Petra'l said, "is better than beating."

Solanj'l held out the cake plate and indicated Petra'l should try a rose-flavoured cream-filled one. "Beating?"

"Really, Solanj'l, with all your intelligence, why do you play the innocent? I suspect you even know some women like it."

Solanj'l looked at her for a moment. "Do you?"

Petra'l shook her head. "Metak really hurt me only once. I guess it was deserved. I got carried away (she wiggled back and forth) in my attentions to a man. Metak took me home and gave me great correction. I had to sit on a pillow for days." She came out with a bark of a laugh. "What he usually does stings a bit. That's all. I can't say I like it but it does no real harm."

"What about your dignity?"

"Dignity?" Another bark laugh. "Women can't have dignity. You know that."

Petra'l was undergoing a transformation. She remained the

happy lover of intimacy but stabs of sharpness had been appearing in what she said, like little claws flicking out through velvety fur. She wasn't as indifferent to women's circumstances as she let on. Now she wanted to talk and Solanj'l was willing to let her.

She was grateful for being married to Metak. Her father had wanted to give her to a thin, dried-up like a stick man with a vicious temper and a reputation for hitting his sisters. For months she'd been violently sick to her stomach with no known cause. She became skeletal according to Stickman who'd grown tired of her condition and married one of her friends who was rarely seen without being completely covered. "Bruises and open wounds are so unsightly, you know."

Solanj'l asked how Petra'l's father could have given her to a man like that. Petra'l's eyes became hard. Her father was an accomplished wife beater, proud of his reputation for "firmness" within the family but those outside were not to know that. He wanted the favour of Hunak, who'd spoken against the beating of wives. She'd told Deba'l about him. He would get no favours from Hunak or any who worked for him. She'd not told her mother what she'd done. Her mother just might tell her father, who'd beat her and undoubtedly tell Metak to do the same to Petra'l.

Solanj'l wondered how many fatal accidents were flights of escape. Keeping a man satisfied enough to not turn vicious could be like standing on the edge of a cliff crumbling under your feet. You could become so tired of terror you'd fling yourself into oblivion—and freedom.

"Some men," Petra'l was saying, "need to beat the wife to get ready for pleasure. Did you know that? Without screams and tears the men can't do it. How unfortunate they aren't always matched with women who like to be hurt." She picked up another cake and turned it around, examining it as if trying to find what made it taste so extraordinarily good.

"Let's talk about things as good as this. Would you consider selling them and the biscuits? They could not only be fed to husbands. They could also be placed on ... interesting ... parts of the body."

Solanj'l laughed and shook her head. "Suggest it as a Pleasure Way at the next Gathering. But the tasties will have to come from another baker. As much as he likes making money, Glom wouldn't want a bakery operating out of his home."

"Metak's steward buys from one who is pretty good ... wait." She held up her hand. "He sells even better custards and jellies. We could put those on our bodies. Then there would be licking. I like licking."

This was getting messier and messier, but it might appeal to some.

"You have interesting ideas, Petra'l. It's time for you to lead at least one Gathering." Petra'l opened her mouth but Solanj'l continued. "I know you don't want to be a leader, but Deba'l and I think you would do it well and you have an obligation. The rest of us are doing it. It's time for you to assume the responsibility of being a member of the first Gathering."

"Oh, poo."

"Think of the fun you can have with a new group. More friends."

That was true, but Petra'l had no idea of how to lead. Solanj'l pointed out that she need do little but keep the women talking. Surely Petra'l could do that. Her group would undoubtedly come up with creative *intimacy* ways of pleasing husbands. After much demurring Petra'l guessed she could try. She then launched into funny tales from her childhood, eating biscuits and cakes the entire time, Metak's alleged opposition to plumpness and her being a leader apparently forgotten.

13. THE LEG

SHE SLOWLY RELEASED HER HANDS from the props. She was ... standing. Standing on two legs. She rocked back and forth, just a bit. She grasped the props and slowly moved her real leg then slid the wood one with the help of her right hand and prop pushing on it. She realized the cross bar on the props needed to be removed. It made it difficult to push the wood leg forward. The stump was useless for moving the leg. She slid her leg and pushed the wood one to join it until she was facing the window. A tightening in her chest. She could stand and move, awkwardly to be sure—she must look ridiculous—but she'd moved and could stand for a bit without props. Tears started. Tears of joy. She stood, without using the props, and wept.

The first leg had been too heavy. She knew that without actually trying to use it. It wasn't much of an improvement over the upside down tree trunk. Why hadn't she thought about that before spending time on measuring, carving, sanding? There was a consolation; it looked rather like a leg with a tapered thigh, rounded calf and slim ankle. It didn't look real but one would know what it was supposed to be. A strong but lightweight wood was needed. Kracak and Womak supplied it. She'd produced an even better looking leg and was fairly certain she'd be able to move it with some degree of effectiveness—which she was now proving, more or less. She slid-pushed back to the work table and leaned against it. The stump was annoyed with its confinement in the hole of the wood leg, even if it had been liberally padded. Her flesh leg was not pleased with being rubbed by the wooden one, even if padded. Perhaps she should sit down. No. She was standing on legs. Too much of her life had been spent sitting. She was going to stay upright and move. Walk. Yes, she was. She took a slow trip to the window, using the props but experimenting with lifting them a bit when she moved her own leg. Kracak would say she was doing a silly shuffle but as far as she was concerned she was walking. She did a little hop and almost lost her balance. She pushed the curtain open and looked out at a world that was different. There was the same expanse of patio and the field behind Glom's property. It seemed larger. She leaned the props against the windowsill and threw her arms out to embrace all she could see and almost fell.

Out of the corner of her eye she saw Kracak coming across the patio and pulled the curtain closed. A shadow told her he was standing outside, trying to look in. In a few days it wouldn't matter what he saw because she would have given Glom his surprise. The shadow moved and after a minute or so she pulled the curtain aside to enjoy the view she would someday move across on two legs. Her own leg was tired and shaking badly. Each day she'd spend more time moving to build strength in it—and that dangling abomination that was necessary for the wooden one.

She slid-pushed her way back to the worktable and her chair and sank down gratefully. This new lighter weight leg had been made in two parts, a thigh portion with a peg at the bottom, and a calf with a hole in the top to hold the peg. After a woman sat down, she could pull the calf away from the thigh so the leg would not stick straight out. Straps on the in- and outside of thigh and calf pieces held them together. She'd always hated the long, tapestry-weight skirts women were required to wear, encumbrances when moving on props, but now they would be an asset, keeping the calf from going astray when released from the thigh. She separated the two halves of the leg and would have liked to remove the thigh piece from her stump, but knew she needed to learn to live with the annoyance; she refused to call it pain. Perhaps the discomfort would never go away but familiarity could move it into the background. At least she hoped that would be the case. On this first stepping out she learned the strapping around her waist was not sufficiently secure. The strap on the outside of the thigh and the two on the inside running up the front and back to a waist strap would be sufficient when the leg was worn for sex purposes, but that was not the point of the legs. The point was women being able to stand and move themselves, no matter how awkwardly. Stand and step-glide and have their hands free. Be as whole as they could be.

Would Glom ever realize her real intention, that his surprise, this gift was not for the purpose of sex? Initially he would be so pleased his little wife, who expressed little interest in what they did in privacy, was presenting him with an object of sex. Oh, would he glow; he'd be so bright and shiny it would hurt her eyes. He'd love his own enactment of a Beautification Ritual, symbolically sawing off her leg over and over, producing a stump with its Pretty Little Spot he could fondle and lick. Her stomach gave a lurch. She clamped her teeth together. Don't think of that.

Pants. That would solve the stability problem. A pair of short pants, like those men wore when they played their games. A garment that covered the abdomen and the upper portion of the real leg and was attached to the wood one would better keep the leg secure. And think of all the interesting designs for them. A wife could embroider messages to a husband on them. Another Pleasure Way. She gave a little snort. She was coming up with more of those than she would have thought she could. Earlier in the day she'd thought of Petra'l putting jelly in the hollow of her wood leg so Metak could lick it off the stump. Something would have to be done to protect the padding.

If the pants were decorated, perhaps the leg could be as well. And there was footwear. She would have slippers made, two rather than one. It wouldn't matter if the one on the wood foot didn't fit exactly right. Glom had never had a particular attachment to women's footwear but some men did. Removing the shoe, fondling it. She supposed it was another symbol of removing part of the woman. Janka'l and Morgani'l had revealed their husbands were particularly fond of footwear, Doam being attached to embroidered slippers, Bantant to short soft boots with small curved heels. He regularly told Morgani'l to go buy more boots. She seemed amused by it. The boot, shoe, and slipper makers would prosper when women had two legs.

What if...? No. It would happen. She would make Glom love her leg, become so excited by it that he'd produce ones for all the women of Ramprend.

She pulled the wood thigh from the stump, realizing the straps made that easier than would pants. But stability was more important than ease of removal. She put the leg across her lap and ran her hands over it. She stroked it the way she'd petted Spirry, her racing along friend. He would be happy for her even if she couldn't run. She didn't want to leave it on the table; she wanted to put it back on, open the door and walk out onto the patio for all the neighbours to see. A walking woman. YES! A walking woman.

Not yet, not just yet. She left her workshop on her props and ordered the carriage. She'd go shopping for fabrics that would be sturdy enough for the leg-pants; but not before meeting with Deba'l and Janka'l and a disgruntled Gathering member.

14. TROUBLE AND ANOTHER SHORT WALK

"I WAS LED TO BELIEVE THESE GATHERINGS were for the purpose of speaking about husbands, their interests and concerns, to contribute to facilitation of their lives." Phylli'l had a naturally high voice; the way she was now projecting it threw it into a piercing register, assaulting the listeners.

Janka'l's face was pale. "We do speak of husbands," she said quietly.

"You talk more about yourselves," Phylli'l snapped. "I told Priest Gung that something must be done."

Solanj'l felt a tightening in her head and an urge to squeeze her hands around this woman's throat. Here was her sister magnified.

"What did he say?" Deba'l asked.

"That ... that I should talk to you, although I do not know why. You are women."

She was medium-tall and stringy with a pinched-in face like a piece of fruit starting to fall in on itself. Her hair, of no readily described colour, was so carefully sculpted it had to be secured with sugar water. She sat straight up, her and the chair's back not touching, and glared at them.

"Gung knows what we do and is confident of our work," Deba'l said. "Perhaps you would be happier in another group."

"I will lead a group of my own."

"How long have you been in Janka'l's group?"

"I have attended once and that was all I needed. I saw immediately this woman does not know what she is doing, nor is she interested in keeping the focus on men." She brought her hands down on the chair armrests to emphasize the absolute truth of her words.

Solanj'l assumed all women had a degree of self-hatred, how could they not? But Phylli'l might be the apotheosis of inner loathing—thus a danger to any group. Could she be coaxed into being more agreeable?

Deba'l was not taking that approach. "You don't have the experience to lead a group." Phylli'l opened her mouth but Deba'l cut her off. "How do I know this? Because the Gatherings are the only groups of women meeting and I am certain you are not leading groups of men." Phylli'l drew in a breath and glared. "If a woman proves to be a good member she is asked to become a leader."

"I can..."

"Solanj'l, do you think Phylli'l would like Casanj'l's group?" Before Solanj'l could respond Deba'l went on. "If that is not acceptable, of course one is free to attend none."

"I think it is an excellent idea," Solanj'l said, leaving the others to wonder which of the two possibilities she meant.

Phylli'l said, "I am perfectly capable of leading a group, and doing it correctly." She threw a disgusted look at Janka'l.

"I'm certain Gung would not take kindly to the idea of having an inexperienced person being a leader," Deba'l retorted.

Deba'l had to be admired for daring to speak for a man, a priest, but Phylli'l did not challenge her, indicating Gung had not been all that encouraging.

"I do think you might like Casanj'l's group," Janka'l said. "You share many views I believe."

Phylli'l pointed her finger at Deba'l, then Solanj'l. "You had no experience when you started."

Deba'l said, "Gung's action of sending you to us indicates he wants us to select the leaders."

Phylli'l's face tightened and she motioned to a servant to be removed. The three watched her rolling departure with relief.

"I so wanted to get rid of her," Janka'l said, "but I wonder if it was wise to suggest Casanj'l's group. They'll feed each other's unhappiness."

"Better to contain the poison than spread it around," Deba'l said.

* * *

As Solanj'l looked for leg-pants fabrics she had an uneasy feeling around her heart. An enemy had been made this day. Undoubtedly Phylli'l would have been one in any event, so it probably didn't matter, and after all, she was only a woman. But the uneasiness persisted.

When she returned to Glom's home with several pieces of cloth there was a note from Deba'l. She'd already talked with Gung. "If a Gathering member speaks to Gung regarding dissatisfaction she will be sent to us. 'It is a woman's matter,' he said. All is well." Perhaps.

What did Deba'l intend for these groups? Something more than they were currently doing? She had more responsibility than other women because Hunak trusted her to perform tasks women normally did not. Was she working toward women being viewed as competent, able to do work as well as men, and, daringly perhaps, better than some? Before she'd started on Glom's surprise Solanj'l had sometimes thought she'd go mad. Sit, read, embroider, attend or host Afternoon Breaks, sit, read, embroider, attend or host Afternoon Breaks. How did women endure it all their days? How had she? She now had work to do, lots of work. It felt good. Right now, it was time to visit her leg before Glom came home.

She locked the workshop door and checked to make certain the curtain was closed. She hoisted herself out of the chair, leaned back against the tall table, let her skirt drop and strapped on the leg. She realized it would be easier if the calf were separate from the thigh. Yes, of course, the straps needed to detach, and the whole process would be better done lying down— with straps or pants. She could lie on the lower table. Why hadn't she thought of this before? Well, next time it would be easier. She eased away from the table and smiled. For the second time today she was standing on two legs. She slid-dragged, using her hand as little as possible. Easier than the first time, but she'd start on the pants the next day in the hope of creating greater stability.

Kracak knocked on the door and shouted that Glom was home. It was time for her to come out. She bared her teeth. Oh, for the day she could do that directly to Kracak. That day would probably never come, but it felt good to think about the possibility.

15. THE SURPRISE

GLOM'S FACE WAS ENOUGH to make her laugh—almost. Such puzzlement. He scowled, he shook his head, he opened his mouth, then closed it.

Solanj'l had told him in advance that his surprise would appear on this night. She'd arranged with Kracak for dinner to be eaten on the patio under an awning, something Glom always enjoyed. It was a little chill but she had braziers lit so they were comfortable. They ate all his favourite dishes, ending with cream cake covered with sweet fluffy white icing and blue-red berries. And wine, a very good one with a faint taste of spring melon. Solanj'l drank only one glass. She needed to be completely stable. Glom ate quickly, not savouring his special foods as he usually did.

"Lean back and enjoy the evening. There is plenty of time before the giving," she said with a smile. She was as impatient as he, but didn't want to spoil the presentation with such speed it took the edge off excitement.

After he finished his cake, carefully scraping up every bit, he said, "I have been waiting for this for a long time. It is very bad of you, little wife, to keep me waiting." He was smiling, but she knew she had to take action.

She told him to come to his Pleasure Room when the moon was over her workshop. "That won't be much time at all."

When he entered the room she was standing by the window. She step-slid slowly toward him, which made him step back toward the door. She slowly lifted her skirt. That was when he scowled and looked befuddled.

"Your surprise, husband."

"What is that?"

"I have a new leg, a wooden leg."

She'd thought about how to present it to him. Thought about it a great deal and still wasn't certain she'd found the right words and actions.

She put her hands on his shoulders and said, "It was made just for you."

"What do I do with it?"

"Wait. ... I'll tell you." Playful was not a usual tone for her; she hoped Petra'l would have approved the tone and pause.

"You were ... almost walking. Women don't do that. I have never seen a woman walk. How can you do it? It's wood? How can you move with wood?"

"I'm not graceful."

"But you were moving without props."

"Yes. I'm moving on two legs."

"Why? Why did you make this? I don't understand."

"Shall we sit down?"

"How can you sit with that?"

She motioned him to his chair near the window and moved to hers across from it. Rather than sit she bent and raised her skirt. "Do you like my slippers?" She'd had a pair made in red with embroidered white lilies, a favourite of his.

"Ah ... yes. They're lovely.... Two slippers."

His eyes moved back to the skirt, which she continued to lift. Another scowl crossed his face. She eased down into her chair, the wood leg sticking straight out. The brown straps that joined the two halves of the leg had been replaced by red ribbons. She reached down, untied the ribbons to loosen the calf, pulled it from the thigh piece and let the foot rest on the floor.

She smiled and said, "Here sit a married couple, together with their legs facing each other. Two people and four legs."

His eyes moved from her leg to the wood one, back and forth as if trying to make a decision about where he should look. Under normal circumstances his eyes stayed on her leg as the skirt rose until the stump with the Pretty Little Spot appeared, the puckered scar, the source of men's excitement, the place where there had once been a leg. His hands started moving up and down his thighs.

"Would you remove the hose from my leg, Glom?"

He looked up at her face. "Remove...?"

"The hose from my leg." She smiled. "You've done it before."

"Yes. Ah, you mean your leg, your own leg."

She nodded.

"Uh, you're usually on the bed."

"It can be removed while I'm sitting." She held up her leg.

He leaned forward and removed the slipper. He held it, looking at it, then at the one on the wood foot. He looked as if he had never seen a slipper before. He slowly put it next to his chair and looked up at her.

"It's all different," he said.

His usual self-assurance was missing. She'd not known how he would respond but had not expected the hesitancy of a boy. He leaned forward and untied the ribbon around her leg and started to roll down the stocking, very slowly, pulled it from her foot and dropped it on the floor.

"Do it again," she said. She'd put hose on the lower half of the wood leg that she'd rubbed and rubbed wax into, making it completely smooth.

"Do it ... again?" He looked puzzled.

"My second leg." She lifted the wooden calf and foot and held it for him.

He took even longer with the wood leg than her own. He'd pause as if uncertain about what was happening.

"Now what do I do?"

"You know what to do, Glom. Take me to your bed."

He picked her up, and almost dropped her.

"What's wrong?" she asked.

"The leg. That wood leg. It feels odd."

"Soon I will have only one." She looked directly at him. "I hope that will give you pleasure. Revealing the Pretty Little Spot. That is the real surprise, Glom. The leg exists so you can perform a Beautification Ritual each time you have pleasure from me."

He looked at her, still holding her above the bed. He kissed her, a long kiss. She felt the beginnings of a headache. Oh, please, she thought, let it stay away until the night is over.

"I think my pretty little wife is clever."

He put her on the bed, lifted her skirt and looked at the wood leg, the calf lying away from the thigh. She thought of a broken doll. Solanj'l unhooked the ribbons that held the pieces together and set the calf next to the table by the bed.

"You'll have to slip off the pants to remove the rest of the leg," she said.

He reached down and untied the top ribbon on the pants, a blue one, then a white, a green, and a red over her private place. She lifted her hips and he slipped the pants and the leg off, looking dazed. When her Pretty Little Spot was revealed he sighed.

"It pleases you?" she asked.

"It is strange. But…. Yes, it pleases me." He dropped his mouth to the spot to kiss and lick it.

She narrowed her eyes and held her teeth together. Tonight she could not go to the field to run with Spirry. Tonight she must be alert, pay attention to each movement. Things might be said or done that could be used to advance the idea of legs for all women. He pushed the leg and pants off the bed and entered her. He reached satisfaction quickly and dropped down beside her. She lay in her usual condition of physical and emotional agitation.

"Put it on again," he said after a time.

She asked him to lift the leg from the floor for her. The performance was repeated but this time it was done more slowly with him laughing and murmuring about how clever she was. What fun this would be for them. He could remove her leg anytime he wanted. It wasn't like a living leg, but what a very clever way to hide, then reveal her Pretty Little Spot, to remind him of what she had given up for him. He would be the one to make her beautiful—and he could do it over and over.

"What a lucky, lucky man I am."

She'd decided to let him relish his special status before advancing the idea of other wives having wood legs. She'd tell him of the glory that would come for sharing such a wonderful Pleasure Way. *He* would get the glory; the idea certainly could not have come from a woman. He would also receive blame from those who would be opposed and there would be some of them; but he was an influential man who didn't need to consider the opprobrium of others.

He was murmuring in her ear. "I knew you were the one I must have when I saw you. You have proved once again how right I was."

"I am pleased you like your surprise."

In response he kissed her, then entered her again, without having her reattach the leg. It was extremely rare he felt the urge three times in one night. Success. She had created a Pleasure Way that would excite and satisfy many men.

And give women a mobility they'd never known.

16. HOW ARE YOU DOING THAT?

GLOM LOVED THE LEG but there was no reason to think it would be a triumph throughout Ramprend, certainly some men would not share his joy of it, nor would their wives. What of Solanj'l's friends? She invited them to Glom's house for the presentation. She'd told them she'd found a new Pleasure Way. Nothing like what they'd been discussing. They settled into the Receiving Room and selected teas and biscuits and cakes, complaining the whole time about how it was bad of their hostess to tempt them.

"Don't keep us waiting," Morgani'l said after several appreciative nibbles on a buttery biscuit. "Tell us of the new Pleasure Way. Ramprend certainly needs another Pleasure Way." She twisted her mouth into an ironic grimace.

Solanj'l rolled to a cabinet under the window overlooking the patio. She took out the wood leg.

"What's that?" Petra'l asked. Murmurs from others.

Solanj'l closed the cabinet, turned her chair and made certain it was securely pushed against it. She leaned forward and put her hands under her skirt and inserted the stump in the wood leg. She put her hands on the chair armrests, leaned forward and ... stood up. Getting up with the wood leg sticking straight out was not easy, but she'd built up enough strength to steady herself with the flesh leg and her hand on the cabinet. Jerks of the heads. Intakes of breath. She step-slid to each one, stopping a second before moving on. She was still shaky without her props but completed the circuit.

"Where did you get that?' Petra'l demanded.

"Well, I never," gasped Deba'l.

Janka'l, "Oh, my."

"A leg?" Janka'l said. "A wood leg?"

"Where did you get that?" Morgani'l asked. "Does Glom know you have it?"

"Would you like to try it?" Solanj'l asked.

Silence. Questioning hesitation in the air.

After several seconds, Morgani'l said, "Yes."

Solanj'l sat in her chair, and demonstrated the releasing of the calf then rolled to a cabinet where she'd placed another leg.

"You have more than one?" Deba'l asked.

"You never answered the question about Glom," Morgani'l said.

Solanj'l smiled broadly. "Oh, yes. He knows. I made it as a surprise for him."

"Ahh," Deba'l said.

"You made this?" Petra'l's voice was raised to an almost-squeak. "You made it? How could you do that?"

"She made a little house of her own when we were young," Morgani'l said. "She should have been born a man."

"We all should have been born men," Deba'l said in a voice of resignation.

Solanj'l told them of Glom's initial puzzlement—and how recovery had come quickly. How he'd been very amourous since that time, blushing as she reported that.

Morgani'l snorted. "He gets to remove a leg himself." There was deep contempt in her voice.

"Yes. In fact that is the point I made," Solanj'l said. She looked from one to the other. "His ... own ... personal ... Beautification Ritual."

"Oh, my," Janka'l said again. She put her hand to her mouth, looking as if about to cry.

Deba'l was staring into the middle distance.

"What are you thinking?" Solanj'l asked her.

Deba'l turned toward her. "How very clever you are."

"I will consider myself clever when all women have legs."

"What does Glom have to say about that?" Morgani'l asked sharply.

It hadn't taken long for Glom to see the value of making legs available to all men—well, men of privilege. He would be seen as extremely clever. The legs would be the focus of the Gatherings. Solanj'l would see to that. He rubbed his hands together then reached up and pushed his bangs up into disarray as he thought of the additional money that would come. He found her suggestion of showing the leg to her friends first a good one. Not that women's agreement was needed, but so much the better if they readily accepted the legs and would help her sell them at the Gatherings. Particularly Deba'l. Solanj'l was truly a clever little wife. If she were a man she'd be as good a businessman as himself. She thanked him for such a high compliment.

He'd put his arms around her and said they would go to the Pleasure Room. "You have a leg that needs to be removed."

The women were reluctant to lift their skirts to attach the leg but curiosity overcame it. Morgani'l went first; she lay on a bench and with the help of Solanj'l wiggled into the pants and leg. Solanj'l had anticipated the problem of length and made the leg too short for any of them. She'd made ankle/foot extensions of different lengths and fitted one for Morgani'l.

Though she found it very uncomfortable Morgan'l managed to do a few step-slides with the aid of props. She looked at Solanj'l and shook her head. "I never imagined, never hoped there could be anything new for us. Even if I never have one of these I will at least have experienced the possibility of feeling almost whole." Her face was a mixture of sadness and pleasure.

Solanj'l helped each of them get into the leg, tie up the ribbons of the pants, and made adjustments for the foot and ankle. It was obvious much work needed to be done to make the leg more comfortable, but it was workable. Each face lit up—between the grimaces. Their own legs were weak and the stumps were useless for moving the wood leg. Solanj'l rolled after each like a patient servant, pushing as needed to slide the wood leg forward. In addition to the smiles, there were tears—not a lot but some. She hoped they were tears of joy. They were on two legs. How could there not be joy?

Deba'l came the next day to request a leg. When she'd told Hunak what Glom had to offer and of the pleasure it was giving him, he'd rubbed the side of his thumb against his chin and said. "That man is a busy one isn't he?" He wanted to know how it was to move with it.

Deba'l said, "How do you tell someone how it feels to stand without props and to move on two feet, no matter how awkwardly, when they have never been deprived of the ability? No man could ever understand what I was experiencing."

"Glom has no thought of that," Solanj'l said. "It's all about what the leg does for him.... I think that is to the good."

Deba'l nodded. "It's better they don't know what this means to us."

17. A PLEASURE WAY FOR ALL

GLOM BROUGHT A MAN TO HELP Solanj'l make legs for her friends. Mill building takes time but he wanted to create a demand so they could start a major production immediately after the plant was finished. Doonak was the supervisor in the furniture portion of Glom's enterprises, a highly skilled craftsman and a trusted employee for many years. He appeared to accept the fact that Glom was married to a woman who could work with wood and that his employer was willing to have her do so. He pointed out flaws in leg construction. Solanj'l knew her efforts had not resulted in perfection but wondered how well he would have done.

Deba'l came for her fitting. The Firsts, as the members of the first Gathering were being called, had started exercising to strengthen their legs. They avoided using chairs whenever possible, props became the means of moving, even for Petra'l. The stumps were a major problem. Solanj'l's ability to slide the wood leg was increasing but she wondered if some women might never be able to "walk" without pushing the wood legs with their hand. Maintaining balance that way wasn't easy. She feared the best any of them, herself included, would be able to manage was extremely slow step-dragging and that it would always be painful to have a big wooden thing attached to a stump that usually hung free. She didn't tell her friends how painful it could be after wearing it for a few hours. But, as Morgani'l had said, the possibility of mobility, if not a constant actuality, could give them a sense of freedom not known before.

Doonak had taught Solanj'l how to take accurate measurements because she was the one who had to do it, as well as the fitting. Men didn't touch women to whom they weren't married—other than termers. He waited outside the workshop in the event Solanj'l needed to consult on adjustments for a proper fit of Deba'l. She gave Deba'l instructions but left her to get into the pants and leg on her own, which she did without too much difficulty. Deba'l rocked back and forth on her props, took a step forward, dragged the wood leg up to join her own. Repeat. Repeat. Then she pitched forward, almost falling, as she broke into great choking sobs. Solanj'l step-dragged to her and put an arm around her. Deba'l breaking down gave Solanj'l a strange feeling of anticipation. Something was coming, something rising out of long-held anger and pain.

Deba'l straightened. "I don't know what came over me. I thought I'd be laughing, exalting."

Solanj'l nodded and said nothing.

"Thank you for your kindness."

"How does the leg feel? Walk around a bit."

Deba'l did as suggested. The leg felt awkward at the top with the padding rubbing her flesh leg. She'd like to try it for a few days. Could it be adjusted later? Of course.

* * *

Doonak started work on Janka'l's leg. Solanj'l was almost finished with Morgani'l's. Petra'l's would be next. The husbands had had varying responses. Doam had to see the leg and talk to Glom before he knew what to think. Bantant had been surprised and amused but said Morgani'l could have one if she wanted. Petra'l said Metak was not quick to accept ideas he hadn't thought of himself, but when he heard about the pleasure other men were getting he'd want one so she was going ahead with having it made. How could he argue with what Hunak and Glom were doing?

Solanj'l had demonstrated the leg for Casanj'l at an Afternoon Break a few days after the presentation to her friends.
Amazement, disapproval, hesitancy, and rejection. Why on
earth would a woman want to drag a thing like that around?
What were Solanj'l and Glom thinking. She didn't want to
criticize Glom, it was not her place to criticize a man but....

"I guess you won't want one," Solanj'l said.

Casanj'l pursed her mouth and said Carn would never want
his wife done up with a thing like that.

"Removing it is for the man's sexual pleasure," Solanj'l said.

"I don't want to discuss such things."

The Firsts, without her, discussed how and when the legs
should be formally made public—at the Gatherings, a special
large Gathering, a public event? Solanj'l suggested it be done
with their husbands present, the idea had to appear to originate
with them. The legs were too radical for women to present on
their own. The tradition-bound would feel free to speak out
against them. Deba'l suggested the couples attend one of the
musical performances in the Great Hall, the women on legs.

"Oh, what fun," Petra'l said. The others agreed.

Glom agreed—what fun. What a scene they'd create.

18. STEPPING (DRAGGING) OUT ON TWO LEGS

GLOM WAS A BUSY MAN. His responsibilities in the family businesses, the work on securing the northern edge of Ramprend, and the creation of a mill for leg production were "extremely taxing." His load was reduced to a degree when Hunak's committee stopped meeting, their concern being security and Glom was taking care of that. No Raiders had appeared after the apparently useless previous visit, but that didn't mean the guards could be left to fall into laxity. Regular reminders to supervisors were necessary to be certain all were "wide awake and ready for action."

Solanj'l saw little of him, except late at night. No matter the time, he usually was not so taxed he could not engage in performing "My Private Beautification Ritual." Oh, what joy it was giving him. She would fall into fits of self-accusation for bringing this on herself. How long could she go on? Surely the novelty would fade eventually, but she and her friends would create new Pleasure Ways with the leg and she'd have to perform them. She tried not to think about it. If she did her head would fill with the heat of anger, and all she wanted was to curl into a ball and go to sleep.

She and Doonak completed the legs for The Firsts. The couples could step out as soon as her friends felt more secure on them. Glom was delighted with the idea of appearing with Hunak and Deba'l at a large public event—the others following along was fine. They would have a guest dinner and then go out and astound Ramprend. He did think it unfortunate a Private Beautification Ritual could not be demonstrated to heighten men's awe and desire for a leg.

Solanj'l mouth dropped open. Surely he would not do that to her.

"What's wrong?" he asked. "You've lost all your colour. Close your mouth."

She stared at him.

"Surely you don't think I would expose our private time to others." A little chuckle. "No, I was thinking of having it done on a termer."

Solanj'l felt her stomach rolling. Women-of-short-term-use were considered the lowest of the low, but to do that to one in public would be appalling. She'd always had a degree of sympathy for these women. They were born, or driven by husband rejection, into their contemptible condition and there was no escape. She had never understood why men would be with women they considered garbage in human form. As far as she knew Glom didn't use termers. He could of course; it was his right. Husbands, usually, did not discuss these women with wives; it was pretended good girls and women did not know of their existence. She learned about them from Morgani'l when they were still girls and had seen a couple of women with veils over their heads moving down a street on props. Morgani'l thought it funny Solanj'l knew nothing about them. Solanj'l found it hard to believe. She'd asked her mother about them and Luranj'l had gone into her hysterical voice and told her to never, ever mention such women again. Where had she heard about such filth?

"Glom?" Solanj'l said cautiously. "Surely you aren't going to make private matters public, even with a termer."

"No. No. I was jesting. I wouldn't debase the Private Beautification Ritual with a termer."

She had no response to this and sat silently watching him enjoy his after dinner ice cream. She finally said she was surprised at how readily the legs were being accepted. True, it was a small group doing the accepting, and the legs could be seen as a horror by many simply because they hadn't existed before. She and the other Gathering leaders were getting questions from members. Were the rumours true? Were there wooden legs? Did Glom make Solanj'l wear one? Of course, she told whoever asked that she gladly did whatever gave Glom pleasure.

Glom told her to find the finest skirt and bodice, hose and shoe—no, shoes—possible, money was of no concern. She would be resplendent when they appeared with Hunak. No, that wouldn't be right. He'd have the finest clothing maker come to his home and create an outfit just for her. She should not wear a costume anyone could buy. And, he would have the shoes made as well. The shoes must be particular for the night.

She was resplendent. As each of the guest couples arrived for the dinner they told her how very beautiful she was. Even reticent Doam expressed an appreciation for the fine manner in which Glom had provided for her. Her skirt and bodice were deep green with gold threads worked in to represent flowers of various types. Her hair had been drawn up on the top of her head with curls cascading down the back and sides, accentuating the slant of her eyes. Gold threads had been worked into the curls. Gold hoops holding green and yellow gem stones were on her ears, and around her neck were strings of tiny gold beads. Her feet, flesh and wood, wore slippers of gold-embroidered green leather so soft they felt made of the lightest of fabrics. The slipper maker had been stunned to find he was to shod a wooden foot, but made no objections when he was told cost was not to be considered. Glom had wanted her in ankle boots but yielded when she showed him there was no way a rigid wood foot would accommodate a heel.

They were a merry group at dinner. They broke from the usual practice of a man talking only to the woman across from him. Each talked to all and the women felt free to participate.

Deba'l always had some degree of latitude in speaking because of the obvious respect given her by Hunak, but tonight it was extended to all women. Glom's Glamour Legs were the topic. How very clever of Glom to have thought of such a thing. The women threw quick little smiles to one another when Glom was praised for creativity. How did Solanj'l like hers? She declared it gave her great joy to give pleasure to her husband.

Glom had hired a coach large enough to carry all of them to a performance of the city orchestra. It was to be a concert of new music, which meant it would be old music recycled into something more lacking in creativity than the original. It had been agreed that Hunak and Deba'l would enter the auditorium of the Great Hall with Glom and Solanj'l a few paces behind. When they were about mid-aisle, the others would follow. Two waves of women on legs. Hunak's position as Minister Second Only to the First gave him special seats in the front with an open space around them, making it possible to stand and talk with all in his group. This night the women would stand as well, without props—for the most part. Petra'l and Janka'l were still unsteady on the wood legs.

When the two couples were six or seven rows into the auditorium a murmuring started. Word was passed. The wives of Hunak and Glom were walking, well, it wasn't really a walk, but they were moving without chairs or props. Their hands were touching their husbands' arms but the husbands didn't appear to be holding them up. The rumours were true. Something new had come to Ramprend. Men stood to get a better look. The buzzing and murmuring became open talk as Bantant and Morgani'l, Doam and Janka'l, Metak and Petra'l moved into the aisle. How many women were there who could move that way? Oh, my, what was one to think? It had to be a good thing if Hunak was involved. And Glom was a man to cultivate, everyone knew that.

The group moved slowly into their seating area but did not sit. They stood and talked. The men nodded to ones they knew in the larger audience. The women spoke to each other and to men who weren't their husbands. They continued to be merry and every eye in the Hall was on them. Hunak was a man of quiet dignity but, given his broad smile, he was enjoying the sensation they were creating. It was obvious men wanted to ask questions but the horn sounded to tell the audience it was time to sit and listen to the new music that would send most of them into a doze, from which they'd rouse to provide enthusiastic applause.

"We will be inundated at the interval," Hunak said to Glom, who smiled and nodded. Surely he was thinking of requests to place orders.

They were besieged. Men swarmed around Glom and Hunak. Glom did most of the talking; it had been his idea after all. There was much interest, but ... what use had women for legs?

Glom spoke indulgently, "They are not for the women." He paused." Think of performing your own Private Beautification Ritual."

Well, maybe one could think of that. But would women get strange ideas, being able to stand on their own?

What could be wrong with pleasing husbands? It pleased him to have Solanj'l wear her leg tonight. It pleased Bantant and Doam and Metak—and Hunak. Furthermore, it certainly hadn't given his wife wrong ideas. She was, in fact, a better wife for the leg. He beamed her his glow-look.

Solanj'l saw her father at the edge of the crowd and quietly suggested to Glom that he invite Hect to join them.

"What are you doing with my daughter?" Hect asked Glom.

"I am making her a better wife," Glom said with a smile. "Is that not what we all want?"

"She is being displayed in an inappropriate manner. Her mother is upset."

"What does that matter?" Metak asked.

"Who are you to be questioning me?" Hect said. "I don't know you."

"We can discuss this at another time," Hunak said. "The program is about to resume."

Hect left with his shoulders held rigidly. Hunak said he would speak with him. His degree of acceptance of the legs was greater than Solanj'l or Glom had any right to expect. Solanj'l wondered what words Deba'l had used to create such a response. Or was it just that he saw the possibility of enhanced sexual satisfaction with the legs?

Going out in public had gone about as well as she could have wanted, but Solanj'l knew they wouldn't move the legs into society without problems. The next day proved her correct when Casanj'l arrived without invitation, demanding to know what Glom thought he was doing.

"Ask him," Solanj'l said. "Surely *you* don't think I should speak for my husband."

"I know you had something to do with this. And I want to know why the other members of the Gathering were with you last night when Carn and I were not.

"You said you and Carn didn't want you to have a leg."

Casanj'l shook her head, pursed her lips and said nothing. Solanj'l reiterated the suggestion that she—or better, Carn—speak with Glom. Casanj'l alternated between abhorring the very idea of the legs and of not having been a part of the concert group. They were standing at the entrance. Kracak asked if Casanj'l wouldn't like some refreshment. Solanj'l gave him an annoyed look that brought a smirk in response. Casanj'l said she'd wondered why she was being treated like a tradesperson. Solanj'l sighed and motioned her toward the Receiving Room. Kracak gallantly rolled her in and Solanj'l followed on her props. She thought it inadvisable to wear the leg all the time; it could give rise to the conclusion she liked it. And there was the problem of comfort.

After a servant had brought a cup of tea for Casanj'l, she renewed her attack. Solanj'l let her run on until she'd repeated herself sufficiently to think she'd won an argument.

"Let me answer you as best I can," Solanj'l said. "You said you didn't want a leg. I know of your devotion to the traditional ways. There was no offense intended. If one occurred, I am sorry. If Carn would like for you to have a leg, you will, of course, have one."

"What is the purpose of them? I see no purpose."

Solanj'l took a second or two before giving the response that would always sicken her. "Glom calls the removal of my wood leg his Private Beautification Ritual."

Casanj'l's face snapped into her pinched, dried-up berry mask. "It is for the purpose of...?"

"It is for the pleasure of the husband. I told you that."

Casanj'l looked off to her right as if not certain of what she was going to say. "I don't think it would give pleasure to Carn."

"Why?"

Casanj'l's head swung around. "How dare you question me about my husband!"

"I'm merely interested in why you think he would not find it satisfying. I need to learn all I can because Glom would like to have the legs introduced through the Gatherings."

Casanj'l got her wide-eyed look of blankness that always happened when she heard something that didn't fit in with her view. She left, declaring she would speak to Gung. He would not approve of this danger to their ways. Women having one leg was of the Great God Ploch. This disgusting nonsense would upset the balance of their world. It had to stop.

19. INTRIGUING MEN

SWOOPED IN AND OUT. Men in black-hooded cloaks. They entered a factory and removed almost the entire stock of harnesses from which workwomen hung in mills, hung so their hands were free to work with whatever was desired by the men who employed them. What would people from the mountains want with harnesses? Their women had legs. Or so it was thought.

"You still think it's mountain people?" Solanj'l said to Glom as they ate a morning meal.

"Why do you keep asking that?"

"Perhaps it's some of our own people."

"What would give you such an idea?"

Her shoulders twitched involuntarily. Ramprenders did steal from each other on occasion. A man starting a business could think theft less costly than buying. She kept the thought to herself.

The guards had gone lax again. If those slackers kept drinking and lying around Glom would lose Hunak's respect and friendship. He was going to have to make regular visits to keep the wastrels doing their job and he didn't have time for that.

"Why don't you have a couple of your trusted men do the checking for you?"

Well, yes, perhaps that would work. If they did what *they* were supposed to do. He thought he'd picked good men to lead the guards and yet they'd had another raid.

"Did the Raiders get into the mill without the guards seeing them?"

"No. They ... they were locked in a room at the back of the mill."

"Weren't they armed? I thought they were going to be trained in the use of swords."

They'd been come on suddenly, hadn't had time to get the swords out of the scabbards.

Solanj'l imagined the drowsy or drunken guards frantically tugging at their weapons to no avail and wanted to laugh, but did not.

Glom left for his day's responsibilities. She went to her workshop to get on with hers. She'd decided she would not give up the making of the legs after they went into production. She'd tell Glom she wanted to continue to experiment with refinements. He'd welcome that. She had to keep working. Being able to create, to solve problems, had given her an energy she hadn't known since childhood. She'd had a goal and achieved it. She hadn't anticipated how alive the process, even the setbacks, would make her feel. Life had been a dull ache; she'd merely been getting along, hoping existence would not become increasingly unbearable before she died. She'd had no idea of what it was to want to live. Now she knew.

Doonak was already working. After they'd finished the legs for her friends, he'd started on adaptations for a more readily adjusted one. He also hoped to create a flexible ankle and foot. Solanj'l's changeable foot and ankle had merit but perhaps other alterations would be better. He, and Glom, knew that not all men would want to wait for, or the expense of, a leg made especially for their wives, thus the need for a standard model readily made wearable for any woman. Of course it would be desirable to sell as many specially made ones as possible because of their higher cost.

Kracak kept entering the workshop. A man did not leave his wife with another, other than his steward. The fact that

Glom had let Solanj'l work with the carver and now Doonak had shocked him. How very hungry for surprises his master must be. He no longer had to stay out of the workshop and he didn't. His master's reputation must be guarded.

After his initial visit of the day, Doonak said, "Glom doesn't trust me."

"Glom trusts you. Kracak doesn't."

"He is rather a fusspants isn't he?"

Solanj'l was surprised at this observation. Men did not discuss other men with women unless it involved praise. She smiled and said, "He can make much of little."

"What are his thoughts on the legs?"

"He has not deigned to tell me. Directly. He sniffs and snorts."

"Do you think most women will want them?"

"Women have nothing to do with it. Men decide what women want."

"Yes, that is the way of our world."

She detected something in his voice. A rueful quality?

"Allow me to ask the question another way," he said. "Do you think women will suggest their husbands provide them with legs?"

"That's what Glom hopes. The women's Gatherings will discuss ways to use the legs to give pleasure to husbands." She shouldn't be saying this. Sex was not discussed, even obliquely, except with one's husband and then only if he wished it.

"Do you plan on getting one for your wife?" she asked.

"I don't have a wife."

How strange. Men married by the age Doonak must be. Why would he not have a wife? Surprisingly, he explained. The woman he'd wanted was given to another man. He had not found a replacement. There must be pressure to do so from family and friends. Women who did not marry were pathetic rejects, but a man who did not was inexplicable.

When Kracak arrived for his second snoop, Doonak asked him if he would get a leg for his wife. He said if it was good enough for his master, it was good enough for him. He'd spoken to Glom about it and would have one of the first legs.

Solanj'l had not known this. She hoped Kracak's wife, Nani'l, would like it. Kracak made no movement toward the door and Doonak went into a long description of the making of the legs. Solanj'l assumed he was doing this to move Kracak toward being a supporter rather than an irritant, and silently she thanked him for it. He took no credit for work that was not his when Kracak offered praise. Kracak kept throwing surprised looks at Solanj'l as if he could not believe she'd had anything to do with the legs even though he'd provided the materials for her. He finally said he had to return to his work.

Solanj'l said, "If you would like to bring Nani'l here, I'll measure her for a leg. You don't have to wait until the mill opens."

He looked at her with a scowl.

"You said Glom said she was to have a leg."

"Yes. I did not think *you* would make it."

"I, of course, must do the measuring, but Doonak can make it if you prefer."

"Yes. Yes, that would be right."

When Kracak left, Doonak said, "I'll keep reminding him you created the legs. It's unfortunate all of Ramprend doesn't know the truth. You deserve the admiration Glom is getting."

Why was he saying this? Men did not care about women being admired for anything other than being good wives. This Doonak was an intriguing character. He was taller and more muscular than Glom. Her mother would say he had the look of a worker. Solanj'l thought he looked like a man sure of himself, without being puffed up in the way many privileged men were, even ones who produced no evidence of intelligence or competence. Doonak had both in good measure and knew it, but also knew he would never rise to the level on which Glom lived.

His hair was longer than that of most men; he wore it swept back but it fell forward when he worked. Eyes—his most arresting feature. Palest blue, a surprising contrast to his black hair. Interesting man. She enjoyed his company.

They spent most of the day talking about the future production of legs. Doonak had given Glom the basic layout and equipment requirements for manufacture but it was time for specifics on how assembly would be done. Adjustments would be necessary as refinements were made in the legs, but they needed to define the starting point.

In the late afternoon Solanj'l looked toward the window, then step-dragged to it. A man was on the edge of the property. She thought it might be the one she'd seen before. She called Doonak over and asked if he knew why someone would be out there. No, he didn't. The man moved north. She said she'd seen him, or someone like him, twice before. The second time the man started onto the property but quickly left, probably because a servant appeared.

"Are you certain it's a man?" Doonak asked.

She turned and looked at him, then pointed toward the window. "Look. He's walking. It has to be a man."

He nodded but said nothing.

20. GATHERINGS AND FEARFUL THOUGHTS

EVERY GATHERING WAS THE SAME: a cascade of words, one message. "Tell us about the legs." Solanj'l was so energy-filled she couldn't sit for any length of time. She needed to be up working. Women wanted legs. Something very unexpected had come into their lives and, going against Ramprend tradition, the new was desired by both sexes. Because a man had been the creator and the man of power, Hunak, readily accepted the result, husbands generally were eager to get legs for their wives. Excitement and desire. Glom's workers would find it difficult to keep up with demand. Many women approached Solanj'l hoping to be one of the first to get a leg. She regretfully told each that her husband would have to place an order. And she, in good conscience, couldn't prefer one over another. She did act preferentially with one. With great (she hoped hidden) amusement, she told Casanj'l she would have one of the first legs to leave the mill. It seemed she'd been wrong. Carn very much wanted her to have a leg. He told Glom he was looking forward to private Beautification Rituals. Though not expressed, this caused Casanj'l considerable distress. Her tired-sad face spoke of it. She reported Phylli'l, who had joined her Gathering, had declared the legs an abomination.

"She actually said abomination?" Solanj'l asked.

"Yes. And I…." Casanj'l stopped.

"How very interesting. A woman declaring something created by a man to be an abomination. I'm certain Glom will be interested in her position. And Hunak."

"Her husband agrees."

"Her husband isn't Minister Second Only to the First. He's not a minister of any degree."

Solanj'l had no opportunity to be concerned about having to give up work. She and Doonak continued to consult on the manufacture of the legs. She had her Gatherings to lead. She had meetings with Deba'l, Morgani'l, Petra'l, and Janka'l. And there was a meeting with Gung. Casanj'l had delivered her complaints.

"Now, what is this I hear about wood legs for women?" Gung asked as soon as they were positioned in his slightly damp, drab office, the one break in dreariness a blood red copy of *The Book of Ploch*.

Deba'l decided Solanj'l would explain the incredibly fine idea that had come to her husband, and she did. Deba'l smiled, nodded her head and inserted approving comments from Hunak. Gung nodded his head, rubbed his hands and lubricated his lips.

"I have had one or two complaints," he said, sounding almost gleeful. "From women. One of them your sister, Solanj'l. Such a fine woman." He paused, waiting for Solanj'l's nodded agreement. "In this instance, however, I find we are not in agreement. It is rare that happens, but I could not allow that something created to give pleasure to husbands should be prohibited. I was rather taken aback by her objection."

This was all he had to say to them. The meeting appeared completely useless, but to him it was not. He'd been to see Hunak. He didn't know what to think of this new thing that had come into Ramprendian lives. Hunak told him and the High Priest to ignore complaints, particularly from women. Gung was sending a message of how supportive he was of the work of the wife of the Minister Second Only to the First.

"Casanj'l has to be livid over the lack of religious support," Solanj'l said to Deba'l when they sat over teas and cakes.

"Yes. But Phylli'l is the one who must be watched. I think she's possessed by the need to conquer all who don't heed (she lowered her voice) The True Voice of Ploch."

In a similar voice Solanj'l added, "A woman can't conquer."

"A woman could make a great mess if she gained support from a sufficient number of men."

"It seems she won't have the priests on her side."

They weren't finished with Gung. The excitement over the legs was giving the Gatherings greater cachet. He wanted to address each of them. No, perhaps it would be best if all the Gatherings met at one time. His words would be heard by all women all together. They should have a Gathering of the Gatherings. He gave a little laugh at his clever wording. The High Priest would approve.

Deba'l and Solanj'l agreed because he was adamant and, in fact, it might be a good idea to have a joint meeting of Gatherings. They, too, could talk to all the women at one time. Casanj'l's group was an ongoing concern and there were some troublesome women in others. A Gathering of Gatherings wasn't a bad idea, or description.

Glom was delighted. He would ask Gung for the opportunity to speak as well. Morgani'l, Petra'l, and Janka'l were not delighted. Men inserting themselves into the Gatherings was not a welcome idea. Was there no way to stop it?

"I don't know that we want to," Deba'l said. "Gaining support of men will help more women get legs."

"Why is it we want all women to have legs?" Petra'l asked.

"You think they shouldn't?" Solanj'l asked.

"Wait," Morgani'l said. "That's an interesting question."

Petra'l lifted her head in a self-satisfied way.

Morgani'l continued, "Why is it we're so pleased with these legs and why do we want to share that? They're for the purpose of giving husbands new sex thrills. Not all women are interested in that. Some would be happy to never again provide their husbands with a sex thrill."

Janka'l and Solanj'l laughed.

"Speak for yourself," Petra'l said.

"I'm not talking about anyone in particular," Morgani'l said. "But we have taken to these legs in a way I wouldn't have imagined. My leg isn't comfortable. It's a constant irritant. It hurts but I wouldn't give it up without a fight. Why?"

There was silence.

Finally Janka'l said, "We're attempting to reclaim ourselves."

All eyes turned to her.

"I think you're right," Deba'l said.

Again silence. They sat looking into the middle distance. What was being thought and felt could not be clearly articulated, even to oneself. Janka'l had breached the interior wall that was erected with the sawing off of the leg, the wall that kept the rage, loss, fear, hate hidden away, the wall that allowed them go on living as if all was perfectly fine.

"It has to stop," Solanj'l said.

"What has to stop?" from Petra'l.

Solanj'l stared into no-space, wondering at herself. Where had this come from? She didn't know she thought this. How long had she been doing so? Did she dare express it?

All eyes were on her. Waiting.

"What?" from Morgani'l.

Solanj'l stared at Morgani'l. Did she dare tell her, all of them, what she'd just thought? They'd think her mad. They wouldn't trust her anymore. Morgani'l opened her eyes wider and spread her hands in a gesture that encouraged her to continue.

Solanj'l took a deep breath. "The Beautification Ritual. Sawing off girls' legs. It has to stop."

All eyes opened wider and stared at her. Her friends looked frozen.

"What if we have daughters?" she said. "Could we allow that to be done to them after having known the joy of walking as a woman? No matter how uncomfortable and awkward it is?"

Silence. Then, "Has it occurred to you, all of you," Morgani'l said, "that none of us has children and we don't discuss it? I've been thinking about how it was a childless group that started the Gatherings. I once asked Solanj'l what she thought we were doing, why we were meeting. Perhaps we've been going toward this ... this ... the entire time."

"We'd be put in permanent confinement," Janka'l said. "Or worse."

"I know of no laws against talking about it," Deba'l said.

"There has been no need for laws." Morgani'l said. "No one imagined it would ever be considered."

Solanj'l felt as if a weight were pressing on her; her body was curling forward as if yielding to that weight. The thought uttered would not return to nonexistence and if she did not heed it she would die, by her own hand, because she could not go on living if she abandoned it. The realization filled her, a force within pushing against the weight without. There was no escape. Please. No headache. Not now.

"This is crazy," Petra'l said. "How could we stop it? They wouldn't let us."

"It would seem Petra'l has joined you," Morgani'l said. She smiled at Petra'l. "You spoke of we, us."

"I did?"

"Um hm. So did Janka'l."

"How would ... you ... do it?" Petra'l asked. She sounded angry.

Solanj'l had no idea of how to do it and the magnitude of the responsibility they'd be assuming kept her from being able to think. She needed time. All she could do was shake her head.

"Are you all right?" Janka'l asked.

"I don't know."

"We're looking into the face of something fearful," Deba'l said. "We need time for individual reflection."

"And to keep our mouths closed," Morgani'l said.

Silence again, while they looked, not at each other, but into middle space where there was something fearful.

"Morgani'l's right," Janka'l said. "Nothing unusual happened today."

men. Not true. The mere idea of standing on two legs opened a door to a wanting deep inside, a wanting for at least the illusion of wholeness, a wanting to be someone, and not just the crippled property of men.

Glom wanted Solanj'l to listen to his speech and help him rewrite it. He thought it a fine one but improvements might be possible. Fortunately Gung was not willing to give him unlimited time. The speech was florid and long but there was only so much she could do about it. She did get him to eliminate the sentence that ended with, "the glorious wives of men who are my colleagues and friends, all the glorious wives of all the men of this city who will be blessed with enhanced pleasure brought by the addition of Glom's Glamour Legs into the practice of intimacy which we all know is the highest satisfaction attained by all who love Ploch." She said she thought references to Ploch should be left to Gung. He agreed, but said he would speak of glorious wives. She could imagine Morgani'l's face at that point.

She requested, repeated times, that he not refer to his "little wife," as he did near the end. This was a surprise; he thought she would be pleased. "You are the focus, Glom. Please. Call no attention to me."

"We'll see."

"I don't believe this," Janka'l said as she looked out at the crowd sitting before them. More women were coming into the room, swinging on props or being rolled into position.

"Believe," said Morgani'l. "Women want legs. And these meetings."

The stage held Gung, Glom, and The Firsts, including Casanj'l. Gung and Glom sat side by side at the front with the women behind them. Gung had been reluctant to let any of the women speak but Solanj'l suggested a few words from Deba'l would be in order since her husband had made the space available. Ah, yes, that was true. He had hoped Hunak would speak but that would not be. Two priests accompanied Gung. Glom had

21. A GATHERING OF GATHERINGS

THEY SHOULD HAVE SCHEDULED the Great Hall. All women in existing Gatherings and women who knew them wanted to attend. Women who did not know anyone in a Gathering wanted to attend. Women hanging from harnesses in Glom's and other's mills wanted to attend. Doonak had brought that piece of information to Solanj'l. The women didn't dare approach Glom or her directly. Solanj'l would have to arrange a special meeting for them. Gung had wanted to use a meeting room in the Temple, one with all the damp, gloomy charm of the rest of the edifice, but Deba'l suggested a large room in the Ministry Building, which Hunak had graciously offered. "It would be so much easier to serve refreshments there," was the reason she offered. Gung ran his tongue around his lips, perhaps contemplating cream cakes and juicy tarts, and agreed.

"What are we going to do with all of them?" Solanj'l asked Deba'l.

"Let them come."

"Even if there is enough room we don't have leaders for all the groups that may want to form."

"It's getting beyond our immediate control. We'll have to let women form their own Gatherings. We'll make ourselves available to help them start."

Solanj'l had once thought eons of accepting mutilation had made Ramprendian women even less imaginative than the asked Doonak to be present, in the event he needed to clarify a technical point. The three males sat in the first row. Except for a few chair-rolling servants, five men and more than two hundred women.

A Ministry Aide reported to Glom there were women outside who wanted to enter and were being prevented due to lack of space. He spoke to Gung, who spoke to Deba'l. She suggested they be told there would be another Gathering in one week's time—if the men were willing. What a very clever idea. The aide went to tell the women they had to wait. He later reported they had acted in an unseemly fashion by saying they did not want to wait. But wait they did.

Gung rose and lifted his hands as if offering a blessing from Ploch. Immediate silence. "Women of Ramprend. And honoured male guests. (Doonak's eyebrows rose.) We are gathered here to honour husbands." When that brought no response he said, "Is that not true?"

"That is true," Deba'l intoned.

Solanj'l cut her eyes in Deba'l's direction. Morgani'l gave a snort, then covered it with a little cough.

"Women of Ramprend," Gung said again.

Solanj'l hoped he wasn't going to keep returning to the beginning.

"It is you who honour husbands I wish to praise this day. You fine, fine women who have only one true desire in your hearts, the desire to bring pleasure to your husbands. (Casanj'l's head bobbed in agreement.) You fine women who are willing to live with the discomfort of wood legs because it is the desire of your husbands that you do so."

Where had he gotten the idea of discomfort? Probably Casanj'l. She would emphasize any discomfort associated with the "abomination."

The women sat and stared at him, faces the masks of attention worn during Temple services. It was the only look they knew to be appropriate at a public event that wasn't a concert or

Silly Simple. Solanj'l wished she could know what they were thinking and feeling. Gung shifted from side to side as if uncomfortable. Had he expected smiles and nods, expressions of approval? Glom looked toward him expectantly, his the only face in the room with animation.

"I have arranged for you fine women to be here today so I may express my appreciation to the one who has made Glom's Glamour Legs possible. But before I present that outstanding man, let me tell you how all of this has come about. I realized that women needed an opportunity to gather and discuss ways to give praise to Ploch, and pleasure to their husbands." Janka'l, Morgani'l, and Petra'l turned and looked at Solanj'l and Deba'l, who looked straight ahead. "Yes, I knew there was a need. I consulted with Deba'l, wife of Hunak, Minister Second Only to the First, and Solanj'l, wife of Glom, the man we particularly praise today. They agreed women could profit from gathering to share ways to better satisfy husbands, which we know is the true obligation of women. And, of course it is their true joy because it is the way of the Great God Ploch."

Hearing him say this filled Solanj'l with contempt. It sounded purely stupid. One group accepting mutilation and subjugation to benefit another. Few Ramprendians gave evidence of seriously following—or even knowing much about—the religion of Ploch. Why would people continue in mutilating and subjugating if Ploch worship had become nothing more than mindless habit? Why did *women* in particular continue to go along? Why hadn't women said no to the mutilation of their daughters and granddaughters? Why would so many wonder why *she* wanted change? She could imagine the outcry at the idea of doing away with the ritual.

The women continued to stare at Gung. He undoubtedly didn't realize he was not the attraction. Glom and his legs, and the women who started the Gatherings were the reason they were here. Most of them knew it was Deba'l's and Solanj'l's idea to start the groups.

Gung went on with praise to himself and the success of the Gatherings. He did express his appreciation for Deba'l and Solanj'l, thus connecting himself to Hunak and Glom. He continued, adding nothing new to what he'd said. Solanj'l's attention was quickened when he said, "It is my hope that all the women of Ramprend will be members of a Gathering." It sounded more like an order than a hope. Did it come from him or the High Priest?

He finally went into his praise of Glom. "He is a man of enterprise, a man of honour, a man of accomplishment, a man of large responsibility. As you know, he is the man who makes certain we are not harmed by these vicious Raiders who invade the northern edge of our city. He is a man of vision. He is a man who can act on his vision. Glom, Creator of Glom's Glamour Legs."

There was shifting in the room, then clapping. Perhaps this man would say something worth hearing. After several minutes of fulsome palaver, he did. He told them legs were in production; they were available to all interested husbands. Of course, not every husband could have one at once, therefore, it would be prudent to order one immediately. He told them of standard sizes and of ones made especially for a wife. He said the women with him on the platform would demonstrate them.

"Now," he continued, "I would like to introduce someone who is dear to me, someone who is a help to me, someone, who in her modesty, requested I not speak of her assistance, but someone I cannot ignore. I am speaking of my pretty little wife. Solanj'l, would you stand and come to my side?"

Yes, she would. What choice did she have? She reached under her skirt and inserted the wood calf into the thigh. With her own heel she pushed the footrest under the chair, an adaptation she and Doonak had made, along with a braking device readily used by the one in the chair. She put her hands on the armrests and raised herself into a standing position and step-dragged to Glom's side. It was the first time the majority of women present had actually seen a leg in use. Oh ... ah ... oh my... murmur on murmur ran through the room. She smiled at Glom and he rewarded her with a glow-smile. His pretty little wife was a sensation. He turned and asked her friends to stand and walk to the front.

Solanj'l looked down into the crowd. She felt tears surfacing and wasn't certain why. She could hardly call this a triumph. There was so much to be done. She glanced at Doonak, whose face shifted from neutral to pleased when he saw her looking at him.

Gung raised his hand and announced that Deba'l, wife of Hunak, Minister Second Only to the First, would briefly address them.

Deba'l smiled at the women before her, a smile of wisdom and warmth. Solanj'l always felt a lifting of spirit when Deba'l smiled at her. The women in the audience no longer wore the indifferent look.

"I will be brief," Deba'l said. "First, Hunak, Minister Second Only to the First, asked me to thank all who are here." She put her hands together at chest level and bowed her head, then lifted it. "It is an honour to be on this dais with people of imagination and purpose. Those here with me show how deeply they love Ramprend by their willingness to create exciting new ways to serve it. It is also an honour to be in a room filled with women of imagination and purpose. May we create even more ways to serve husbands, ourselves, all people of Ramprend." She bowed once again and stepped back.

Some women were nodding. Others looked puzzled, undoubtedly due to the idea that they had imagination, purpose, and were to serve themselves as well as husbands.

The meeting ended with Glom telling the women how to order legs. Solanj'l and Deba'l had asked that he not expect them or other Gathering leaders to take orders. Disputes would arise over which had been submitted when. All business should be handled by men anyway. He'd agreed and put Doonak in charge of creating an ordering process. Glom wanted Solanj'l and her friends to go down into the crowd so the women could see the legs in use and ask questions. Also, words should be said about the pleasure of the Private Beautification Ritual. Solanj'l quietly told him that they hadn't yet learned how to go down steps. Oh, yes ... well, they would be lifted down. Before she was, Deba'l announced there would be another Gathering of Gatherings, in one week's time. At that meeting they would establish new Gatherings.

The women became animated; they wanted to talk, they wanted to know about the legs, how it was to wear one. They wanted to know how they could get into a Gathering of their choice or start one. They didn't want to leave. They wanted to continue to be together.

The women *wanted*.

Gung was ecstatic. His hand rubbing and lip licking threatened to remove skin as he enthused over the success of his idea for a Gathering of Gatherings. Solanj'l turned from him and saw Phylli'l holding forth in a corner of the room with Casanj'l's Gathering around her. What mischief was she up to?

Glom appeared at Solanj'l's side, put his arm around her waist and said, "This is a great day, is it not, dear little wife?"

For a second she thought of calling him dear little husband, but chose to say, "Yes, it is. I hope we can meet the demand."

"Oh, we will. We will."

And we'll use that demand to make a new world. She smiled at him, but didn't share her thinking.

22. HAPPY HUSBAND AND PLEASURE WAYS

GLOM WAS A HAPPY MAN. The family businesses were doing well. The guards against Raiders were looking sharp and ready when he went for inspection. He'd followed Solanj'l's recommendation and had two trusted men take charge. They were hard taskmasters. About half of the guards had been removed and new ones brought in. Glom's greatest joy was with the success of the legs. The success might, in fact, be too much for him. Now, Solanj'l shouldn't believe it was actually too much for him, but there was such a demand and he had so much to do to keep up with everything that sometimes he got tired. Not too tired to go through frequent Private Beautification Rituals.

Surprisingly Solanj'l had been experiencing fewer headaches. Perhaps having some hope for women was giving her relief, even if she had to perform her wifely duty frequently. She and the other Firsts were creating new Pleasure Ways to test on husbands and pass on to other groups. When Solanj'l proposed putting perfume on the padding at the top of the leg, Morgani'l just about fell out of her chair laughing. Petra'l thought it a wonderful idea and thanked Solanj'l, who did not say she too found it funny. Petra'l then offered a Pleasure Way that threatened to give Solanj'l a headache. She'd lain on the floor with Metak standing above her. She had very—that was *very*—slowly, unlaced the pants, *very* slowly opened them ... revealing nothing underneath. She had slipped the pants and leg off, gotten up on her own knee and offered the leg to Metak. "Rather like a priestess offering to her God."

They stared at her until she said, "Metak really liked it." No one responded until Janka'l asked if the Pleasure Ways always had to do with sex. Couldn't a wife pleasure her husband in other ways? Yes, but the focus had to remain on the legs. Couldn't they think of ways of using the legs that would please husbands—without having to treat them as Gods? Morgani'l pointed out that is what their existence was, offering up their lives in worship to husbands. Petra'l didn't think that was so.

"What do you think our lives are about?" Solanj'l snapped. "Why else do our legs get sawed off?"

Petra'l threw her head back and said she liked sex.

"Think of how much more you'd like it if you had two legs. Think about how much more you'd like it if sometimes, once every fifth or sixth cycle of the moon, Metak did for you what you wanted. Think of how much better it would be if you weren't a servant to his master."

Deba'l said that was undoubtedly true, but they needed to accept things as they were and that meant creating Pleasure Ways of many kinds, some of which would not be well received by all. Morgani'l pointed out ways would travel from husband to husband and wives would be expected to do them, well received or not. Janka'l said she didn't see why they had to do all the work. It should be the task of all Gatherings to devise ways and pass them on. Each Gathering could take turns being responsible for creating Pleasure Ways; that would give all the groups sessions in which they could talk of other things and still take home something new. A good idea but they'd better have some in reserve for when a responsible group could not come up with a new way. They had to keep producing. It was, after all, their reason for meeting. But how many ideas could they come up with? A woman took her leg off or her husband did. What more could there be? Could they leave the leg on?

No, the stimulus was to come from kissing, licking, handling the stump. A man couldn't do that if it was stuck in a piece of wood.

What they weren't discussing in their meetings was So-lanj'l's thoroughly terrifying declaration. Even she'd hadn't been giving it serious consideration. She used work as a way to avoid it, which was easy to do as work was necessary for women to get legs. The wealthy men of Ramprend did want their wives to have special legs. It was necessary to create a staff for measuring and fitting. She was training women who would then train others. She found the viewing and handling of stumps to be so upsetting she couldn't wait until the job was no longer hers. They were so forlorn, hanging there uselessly. Forlorn and repellent. They made her think of huge penises displaced to the side of the torso. Was that part of the excitement? Fondling, licking, stroking larger than life representations of males' most prized body part? Her hands felt as if they were retracting into themselves, trying to get away from the ... the abomination. How could Phylli'l call a wood leg an abomination when she had an actual one hanging from her body?

The women she was training had been fitted for legs. Actually it was easier for them to work from chairs but she wanted all women in mills to have legs. Glom agreed to give legs to women doing the measuring because they were serving the privileged. A first step but it would not be easy to convince him all his workwomen needed legs. She'd been horrified when she first saw them hanging in harnesses like garments from hooks. Two leather straps passed down the front of the body, between leg and stump and up the back with cross straps around the torso, one over, one under the breasts one across the back. The harnesses were attached to an overhead track. If a woman needed to move she would hop to the side with the harness holding her upright. They wore padding between the leg and stump and under the straps to relieve the pressure and pain, but it had to be exhausting, hanging day after day. Workwomen needed legs more than women who weren't to do much but sit, shop, and jabber about clothing at Afternoon Breaks. And perform Pleasure Ways.

23. **GIDDY WOMEN**

GATHERINGS KEPT FORMING around the city. Deba'l created a once a month meeting of leaders. That group became so large it was divided into subgroups with a First in charge of each. Success was not complete. Phylli'l attempted to start a Gathering to Halt the Use of Aberrant Legs. Gung was pleased to report to Deba'l that he had ordered her to stop as she was not acting in accordance with the wishes of the High Priest. She attempted to meet with The Holiness and was told by a low level acolyte she had forgotten her place and her husband would be notified. Casanj'l told Solanj'l that Phylli'l was greatly taken aback and did not understand why these legs were not a corruption of the true and joyous life of women. Wasn't it Ploch who wanted women to have only one leg so they would be dependent on their husbands? How could the priests approve of a deviation from that? Solanj'l told Casanj'l perhaps she should consider breaking off contact with a woman who dared question men, particularly priests.

The time came for another Gathering of Gatherings, a three-day event. The women went to their husbands' homes each night and returned as early as they could the following morning. Deba'l had arranged for the use of the Great Hall. It was divided into spaces of various sizes because government meetings—large and small—the Silly Simples and other performances were held in it. It included an auditorium large enough to hold half the city. The entire Gathering could meet in one space or divide into smaller groups.

The women were almost giddy, a condition rare to them, though a few had attained that state when they were given the drug just before their legs were sawed off. Solanj'l had never seen women acting this way, but it was more interesting than the state in which they usually existed. They sat only when necessary, moving around when possible, some even conducting their conversations standing, quite extraordinary, given that the legs weren't, and probably never would be, comfortable.

Janka'l had suggested they have a room in which to do exercises to strengthen their flesh legs and stumps. Solanj'l asked Glom if he would find a man who would show the women how to increase strength. He thought it not a good idea until she suggested stronger women would make stronger partners in sex; they would be more mobile, more interesting. Ah, yes, possibly that was true. He knew a man who might be willing to help. Blong was eager to be of service to such an important man. Doonak, however, told Solanj'l to watch him; he might try to create trouble for the women. He had a reputation of being a wife-beater. She thanked him and said she'd ask Glom to get someone else. Someone who could be trusted.

"I don't know that you can trust any man," Doonak said.

"No man?" She smiled. "Not even you?"

"Eventually men will see what's happening. They won't like it. But you know that."

Solanj'l did not know what to make of this statement, or this man. She was not in the habit of trusting men; they were responsible for her condition, the condition of all women. She saw no reason to like or trust any of them, yet she trusted this Doonak. Why? Because he helped her with the legs? No. The carver had helped her learn woodworking skills; she didn't trust him. "What do you mean, what's happening?" she asked him.

"Women are changing. You're encouraging that. It will frighten most men and undoubtedly many women."

"And you?"

"I will continue to work with you."

"Until other men declare they don't like what is happening."

"As long as you let me work with you, I will do so." He was looking directly at her, as if trying to say something beyond the words. Another oddity, men didn't hold the eyes of a woman to whom they were not married.

She felt an almost overwhelming desire to put her hand out, put it on his arm and say.... Say what? Thank you, she supposed, but maybe something more. He'd told her to trust no one. Was he telling her that included him even though he was making promises of loyalty? They stared at each other as if questions were flying back and forth without being uttered. He was the first to look away.

Glom wanted to know what was wrong with Blong. Doonak had heard he beat his wife. Glom had made it clear from the beginning of their marriage that he did not believe in hitting wives. It was the mark of a weak man. He consulted with Hunak and as a result, another man, Furam, was brought in. He asked for permission from the Ministry and Gung to wear knee length pants and no shirt, the way he usually did when exercising. The women needed to see how muscles move. It had taken several days for the decision to come because women did not look on the skin of men other than their husbands. On the other hand, if it was one man with a group of women it would be difficult for the women to commit evil. Finally Furam was told it would be better for him to fully dress, which he did. The fabrics he wore, however, were lightweight; his body visible under them, except for his private area.

Solanj'l saw Petra'l watching him with particular interest and said, "Remember intimacy with Metak."

Petra'l looked at her with an impish smile and said, "I always remember intimacy with Metak. That does not prevent me from admiring beauty when it appears before my eyes."

Furam became a favourite, not all the interest generated by

leg or stump development. Women with marriageable daughters were issuing fervent invitations for him to call. Others were looking at him the way Petra'l did. This bothered Solanj'l and Deba'l; neither of them had ever seen women express an interest in a man who was not a husband or a possible one. Of course, they'd never been in a large group of women with a sole beautiful man. Another change in Ramprend.

Solanj'l went to his first session of each day. He instructed them in building arm strength as well as leg. Of course, women with wooden legs couldn't attempt all that men could but they were using their bodies in new ways. Solanj'l felt better for her time with him. It wasn't his beauty, but the energy she gained. She hadn't felt this good physically since girlhood. Other women were in agreement. "It's so much fun," Janka'l said. Morgani'l said it made her feel as if she could do a lot more than she'd been doing. She sounded at least slightly ominous. Women started asking if the exercising couldn't be continued when they returned to their usual lives.

When the women weren't gazing at Furam—and conditioning their bodies—they were meeting in groups, not their regular Gathering but ones that changed each day. Solanj'l had arranged this, wanting to build connections between women; they should know as many as possible, and be open to the ideas of those not in their original Gathering. They needed to learn to trust each other. It was the only way they could make *it* happen.

It was obvious by the middle of the second day women were not discussing Pleasure Ways. The Firsts had to encourage them to not completely abandon such talk. Going back to husbands with no new Ways could result in no more Gatherings of Gatherings. The women said they were running out of ideas, there were only so many ways of putting on and taking off wooden legs.

Morgani'l suggested they propose new ways to dress the legs. "We could devise different shoes and slippers, perhaps denoting certain ... things. She shrugged, and added, "Ribbons, garters, coloured stockings." Colours could indicate particular desires on the part of the woman."

Petra'l said Morgani'l needed to be more explicit. According to her women didn't have desires.

"That's why *you* should suggest new ways," Morgani'l said with a smile.

The women became excited about dressing up their legs with shoes, stockings, and ribbons. Someone said women should ask their husbands what they wanted to see on the legs. It was to fulfill their desires. A voice said, "Where's our desire?" Those who must have heard her pretended they had not. Solanj'l made note to get to know this woman. She also realized an additional value to this dressing up idea. Men could compete in the decorating of their wives legs. And, considering the legs were wood, perhaps they could be displayed in ways flesh ones could not. Skirts could be drawn up or even left open on the right side. Her idea swept the Gathering. Women wanted to show off their wooden legs.

Glom immediately saw possibilities when Solanj'l reported on the day's activities. He had an idea of his own: a man of means could provide his wife with many legs. Solanj'l picked up on that, suggesting paintings on legs, carvings on legs or private messages to be seen only by the husband. Glom was ecstatic. He picked her up and whirled around the room singing, "My pretty little wife is clever. My pretty little wife is clever." Then he "danced" her to his bed to satisfy his desires with a Pleasure Way. Solanj'l lay there hoping she was clever enough to satisfy her one desire.

24. SOME GRIM LIVES

THE FIRSTS CONTINUED TO MEET together in addition to meeting with other leaders and starting new groups. An increasingly frequent topic at individual Gatherings was the treatment women received from their husbands, some of it appalling. If privileged women lived in fear, how was it for those who hung in harnesses for long hours? Solanj'l determined they would start Gatherings especially for workwomen.

"Would they have time to come?" Deba'l asked. "Surely they have work to do when they go to their husbands' homes."

"Why do you and Solanj'l never speak of women having homes?" Petra'l asked.

"They don't," Morgani'l put in. "We don't."

"I have a home."

"It's not yours, Petra'l," Morgani'l said. "It belongs to Metak. It's all his. You couldn't even determine what food should be brought in, arrange a room as you wish, buy furniture for it if Metak wanted his steward to do it. It isn't your home. It's a place you're allowed to live in for as long as you give pleasure to Metak."

Colour drained from Petra'l's face. Janka'l drew in a sharp breath.

Casanj'l said, "I don't know why you talk of our lives like this. We have good lives."

"If you don't think about your lost leg and the fact you have no say in how you live," Solanj'l said.

Casanj'l turned toward her. "I am so tired of you complaining. Ever since you were a little girl you have been spoiled and indulged. First by father letting you build things, then by Glom who is far too indulgent. Carn says Glom sets a bad example for husbands and that you need to be brought up short. He'd beat you ... and you'd deserve it."

"You think beating women is good?" Morgani'l asked.

"It is none of our business and if you don't stop talking against men I will have to leave this group."

"Does Carn beat you?" Janka'l asked quietly.

Casanj'l's nostrils flared and her eyes narrowed. "How dare you ask such a private thing?"

"You appear to be advocating it. I wondered if that was due to the good effects it has had on you."

Morgani'l threw her hand over her mouth and gulped to hide a laugh.

"I will not be meeting with you again. And, I *will* be speaking with Gung." Casanj'l called for Carn's servant and was rolled out.

"Praises be heaped on you, Janka'l," Morgani'l said.

"How did you dare say that?" Petra'l asked.

"She is tired of Solanj'l," Janka'l said. "I am tired of her."

After a heartbeat they laughed, laughed loud and long. Petra'l even clapped her hands. Then they sobered, remembering what had been the topic that lead to Casanj'l's withdrawal.

Women were beaten with sticks. "My husband ties me to the bed, sometimes face down, sometimes face up. He uses his cane. He slams it down on me over and over. My nose has been broken more than once." This explained the disfiguring of what must have been a handsome face.

Women were beaten with leather straps. "On my back and buttocks and legs. Sometimes he makes me bend over a chair and does it in front of our children." A gasp around the room. This husband worked in government. Deba'l made note.

Women were beaten with switches. One woman pulled up

the sleeves of her bodice and held out her arms. They were covered with welts, some bright red fresh, some pinched and pulled together old.

Women were punched with fists and kicked with feet.

Women, some beaten and some not, were told they were worthless. Even stewards were allowed to tell them this in some households.

The Gatherings opened a door and stories came rushing out. The mere opportunity to talk about something other than the usual nonsense was allowing them to think differently. And to speak and to be heard. Some reported in neutral tones, as if they were speaking of what had happened in a fabric shop. Some spoke softly and slowly, straining to get the words out. Some cried. Some spoke with anger in their throats, even if the voices weren't loud, the rage could be heard. They talked and listened, and there appeared to be little fear of retaliation from husbands.

"For retaliation to occur, the women would have to talk at home," Morgani'l said. "Have any of you told your husbands about what you're hearing? Would you even consider it if you were one being beaten?"

Deba'l said she was considering telling Hunak of what she was learning. Morgani'l wanted to know what that would serve.

"Perhaps he could order it stopped."

"Do we want that?" Solanj'l asked quietly.

They looked her as if she'd lost control of her mind, become another person.

"If we are to stop the ritual we need women to be angry."

"Oh, no." Petra'l said. "She's back to that."

25. LEGS, PLOCH'S OWN, AND MATERNITY

GLOM'S GLAMOUR LEGS became works of art, inscribed with family crests, favourite objects, names of sons. Solanj'l had one with large red flowers and sunlight-yellow centres painted all around it. It was a particular favourite of Glom's. She liked it too; it looked alive and gave her a feeling that hope was possible. Whimsy was not associated with Deba'l, but she had one painted with blue vases, some tall and mostly straight, others squat and curvy. Some lopsided. It held dried flowers when she wasn't wearing it.

Men generally liked to have their wives reveal the beauty of these special wooden legs. There was a decline in presentation of flesh legs. Men had a say in the creation of artistic wood ones, the artificial becoming more desirable than nature. Slippers became a new fashion statement. Colours never before seen on feet appeared, including a startling yellow-green that could not be missed. Holes and slits were cut into the leather so the colour of stockings could peek through. Footwear became part of Pleasure Ways, removal a prelude to the Private Beautification Ritual. Some women ordered shoes that were particularly intricate in the removal, with laces and buttons and straps. The alleged motivation was to heighten pleasure by delay. Solanj'l suspected some women just wanted to put off sex as long as possible. She had a pair with two little locks on each. It was one of Janka'l's inventions, a Pleasure Way that included hiding the keys for the husband to find. Glom, who had developed an interest in footwear, never would have accepted a search of the house so Solanj'l kept the keys on a chain around her neck under her bodice. Glom had great pleasure in getting to them before opening the locked slippers.

Ribbons also became a fashion, one started by Morgani'l who tied several in different colours around the top of the wood leg so they'd hang down and slip out and in as she moved with her skirt drawn up almost to the top of the leg.

Going to the Temple became a matter of debate. Women were to be rolled into that holy place; gaining admittance on their own was not what Ploch had intended—or so it was thought. Others, Gung among them, pointed out that the date of dedicating the Temple and the birth date of the Beautification Ritual were not known with certainty. Perhaps there had been a time when women walked into the Temple. The great question was sent to the High Priest. Hunak, as usual, guided him. Let women enter as their husbands wished. Husbands were, after all, the ones to be considered. Of course, wise counsel and just what the High Priest had been thinking.

The High Priest was personally known to only a few citizens. He was called Ploch's Own, birth name not used. Solanj'l asked Glom if he knew it; he didn't. Her curiosity came with an invitation for Glom to meet with him. Glom was as excited as a little boy who learned he was to be given his heart's desire on his Arrival Day. Ploch's Own wished to know "the man of such cleverness." Deba'l suggested his motivation was of a monetary nature. Glom's new enterprise would take him to new heights of comfort, ones anyone would enjoy sharing, even men of God. Whatever the motivation, Glom was given an audience. Surprisingly he was asked to bring his wife. Women were rarely welcomed in the presence of such a level of holiness, presumably because of their potential to contaminate men. Hunak and Deba'l would also be present. Apparently Ploch's Own was also curious about the women who'd been involved in starting the Temple meetings that had become so loved by women and appreciated by husbands.

Glom rolled Solanj'l—not wearing a wood leg—into the great man's presence. She did as she'd been instructed and leaned forward until her head rested on her knee as soon as the door opened. They entered and Glom dropped to one knee and put his head down. In a high-pitched, raspy voice the High Priest said the men could stand. The women were to keep their heads down until spoken to. Solanj'l could feel the beginning of a headache after a few minutes. She had no idea of the appearance of the room in which she sat, but it smelled mouldy, old, and decayed. Did the High Priest smell this? Perhaps it was he who produced the odour.

Ploch's Own said Glom certainly was a man of distinction. "I expect your good fortune will be that of Ploch's."

Right to the money, Solanj'l thought. Glom assured him offerings to Ploch would be in keeping with earnings. Solanj'l smiled into her knee. No promises of great beneficence. Glom would pay only what he thought was required to maintain priestly good will.

"Hunak is a friend," the High Priest said, "Priests do not usually have friends, but I do think Hunak is mine. I hope it will be the same with you, Glom."

Glom's fervent murmurings of assurance brought forth an emphatic "Good."

"I would see the faces of the women who are giving much to Ploch through their work with … what are they called now? … Ah, yes, Gatherings."

Solanj'l assumed she was to lift her head. The room was dim, lit by two large oil lamps on poles about six feet high standing just behind the High Priest's tall-backed, carved, gilt chair. Draperies hung behind them, creating a danger of fire—unless they were too damp to ignite. They looked as if they needed a good cleaning to get rid of dirt and mould. Her eyes went to the priest.

Great Ploch! What an ugly man. Were priests chosen for their lack of physical appeal? Since childhood she had thought the High Priest must be an imposing man, someone of great presence, perhaps of beauty. She had been wrong. Ploch's Own was short and round with stubby arms and legs. His face was flat and appeared to flow into the area where most people have a neck. His eyes were barely visible due to fatty wrinkles drooping down around them. His mouth was a pinched O. She dropped her eyes, fearing he would see what she was thinking.

"Hunak, Glom, you are fortunate in your wives," he said. "Not only do they honour Ploch with their beauty, but also in their steadfast devotion to Him, to you, and to the citizens of Ramprend. You are to be commended in your choices. All Honour and Glory to Ploch."

"All Honour and Glory to Ploch," the two couples intoned.

Solanj'l kept her eyes down and waited to leave. She assumed the Priest would not address her. He did.

"I wonder that you have not yet had children, Glom's wife."

"We have not been so blessed," Glom said.

"Ploch's eyes are now on you. He will bless you."

Not if I can prevent it Solanj'l thought.

"You do wish his blessing of children, do you not?" Ploch's Own asked.

"Solanj'l?" Glom said, urging her to speak.

"I did not immediately respond because I did not think it my place."

"Ah, you have trained her well," the High Priest said.

"It is our dearest wish to have children," Glom said. Solanj'l nodded and gave what she hoped was an obsequious smile.

She wondered what reason Hunak had given this man for the lack of children in his home. Perhaps great beneficence curtailed personal questions. Ploch's Own had little more to say or ask. The four backed out—women with foreheads on knees.

After the interview, Hunak suggested they have a sweet and a beverage. It had been rare in recent days they could meet merely as friends. They went into a confectionery shop and ordered teas and honey cakes flavoured with spices and flowers. Deba'l reminded Hunak his Physical Attendant had warned against too many sweets. He smiled and patted her hand. The bright and warm space with tables and chairs of various woods was welcome after the unrelieved creepy dimness of the High Priest's audience room. Talk was of him. When children were mentioned, Hunak breached his usual reticence on private matters and spoke of their daughter who'd died at two years, of a disease no one understood. Deba'l had not wished to go through such a loss again and he had not insisted. Solanj'l wondered why Deba'l had never mentioned it. Deba'l's face wore a neutral expression.

Glom expressed his sympathy and glanced at Solanj'l. She assumed he was thinking they couldn't have that happen to them. She knew she would have to be very vigilant with taking *Benot*. She could not prevent the sawing off of her leg but she could take all possible measures to prevent the birth of a daughter. If that also meant no sons, so be it.

Prior to the Gatherings, birth and nonbirth was the sole area in which women had banded together, information passing down the generations. Most mothers passed on the knowledge to daughters; some left it to the oldest to do the educating of the younger. The one useful thing Solanj'l had learned from Casanj'l was of *Benot*, herbs that would interfere with the growth of a possible child if, in fact, that had been started when a husband was taking his pleasure. Innervators, women skilled in the use of herbs for healing purposes, also made the pregnancy stopper. Women who had money were relatively certain of the efficacy of the *Benot* they bought because they could afford Innervators who gathered and processed the herbs at the right time and in safe ratios. For those women with little money or who had to barter—servants, workwomen or privileged women with tight-fisted husbands—it was a gamble each time they acquired a supply. They might get a batch that did not prevent pregnancy or one that would make them violently ill or even cause death. Glom had mentioned losing more than one of his workers in this way. He always wondered why they would take such risks. Solanj'l would attempt to explain why a woman would not want another child but he seemed unable to understand. He would exclaim how fortunate they were that she did not think she had to take such things. She hoped the day would never come when he learned she'd started taking *Benot* weeks before the marriage.

Most men knew about and accepted the use of it. There was such a thing as too many children. Solanj'l knew Morgani'l used it with Bantant's knowledge. It was puzzling that he did not appear to want at least a son. Petra'l had never said whether she used it. Surely Metak would want a son and would get pleasure out of a daughter maimed, although it would be expressed in terms of carrying on the exalted tradition of creating a fine wife for a fine Ramprend man. Janka'l had told them she was taking the relatively new *AssureSon*. Deba'l said she'd been told by several Innervators that the *AssureSon* herb blend was only a guess and not a good one. It should not be relied upon. Janka'l's face had gone white. "I don't want a daughter," she'd said almost wildly. "Not now." Her friends had little to say that would help her other than a reminder of *Benot*.

26. LAMENT AND — REGRET?

I DON'T WANT TO DO THIS. *I'm not capable of doing this. Why did the idea ever come to me? I'm scared. I think I could live with being put away from people—perhaps I would like it. Few are killed for going against tradition—as far as I know. Are women ever killed? Deba'l says she knows of no cases. What I fear most is not some kind of reprisal. What I fear is not being able to do what must be done.*

Was that true? Solanj'l had been plagued with replays of these thoughts since the idea of doing away with the Beautification Ritual had come to her. The time was almost upon her, the time to put an end to the ritual. Resistance thoughts appeared practically every day.

Women had been meeting to discuss Pleasure Ways and Glom's Glamour Legs for almost five years. Well, in fact, after the first three years, they'd been recycling old ways. There were other matters to discuss: how to spend time now that they could move more easily on their own, or how to deal with husbands who terrorized and tortured. There were discussions about children, daughters in particular—wistful discussions. Poor women spoke of how work could be easier, paid and at-home work. Contrary to what Deba'l feared, women servants and workwomen were not so tired they couldn't meet in Gatherings of their own. Cresa'l, a servant in Glom's home, had shyly asked Solanj'l if she would start a Gathering for the servant women in his household and the neighbouring ones. Solanj'l was happy to do so and within a few weeks she saw Cresa'l could be the leader and was letting her do more and more of it. Glom did not want a servant being a Gathering leader. He said such women weren't capable of the thought needed to do so. It was obvious women like herself and Deba'l could be leaders of women, but not those who had to work for money because they had to marry inferior men. Solanj'l felt the back of her neck tingle. Inferior men? Who kept "inferior" men— and women—in that position? Men like the one to whom she was married. Never letting them rise; treating them worse than they treated their wives. But not worse than they treated their daughters. Nothing was worse than that.

She carefully explained she'd seen Cresa'l leading the group, that she was perfectly capable, and that she, Solanj'l, and women like her could not lead all the groups that wanted to meet. Even servant women wanted to discuss Pleasure Ways and they wanted legs. Had he considered making Glom's Glamour Legs that were less costly for the husbands of women like the ones who worked in homes and mills? No, he had not. She thought he should. There was money to be made.

Cresa'l became a Gathering leader, and within six months of the initial suggestion a less expensive leg was available for husbands of women like her. When Solanj'l asked Doonak about the quality of these legs he said they were a version of the original ones, only lighter as all legs were now hollow, except at knees and where the adjustable feet and ankles attached. Glom was offering them at a lower price than he did to rich men, who wanted their wives to have legs with carvings and paintings, plain no longer sufficient.

Several months after Solanj'l got her red flower leg she learned Doonak was the creator of most of the artistic features of the Glamour Legs and he had done the actual painting of hers rather than leaving it to one of the mill people. He had also painted Deba'l's blue vase leg and Petra'l's with multi-coloured gillyflowers. He should have been an artist, but that was not possible, his family being one level too low. Glom was ignoring the fact that low-level people, those even lower than Doonak, were painting and carving Glamour Legs even though they were known to be incapable of doing such fine work. When she told Doonak she knew he'd done these painting his face lost colour. For a moment she didn't know why, then realized he'd think Glom would be upset over his presumption. She assured him Glom didn't know, she wouldn't tell him and she thought the leg exceedingly beautiful. His face broke into one of his rare smiles.

"Thank you," he said. "I would like to paint another one for you. One with legs on it. Legs with various paintings and carvings and ribbons. You should have a leg of Glamour Legs."

Solanj'l felt a surge of pleasure. "I would like that. I'll ask Glom if he would order one. I think he'll like the idea. He won't know who did it, but I'll know it's from a friend."

A scowl flashed across Doonak's face, then he said, "A friend?"

"Yes."

"We are of different sexes and levels."

"Glom thinks of Kracak as a friend. They're on different levels."

They both knew perfectly well that Glom might think of Kracak as a friend but that was not the case. Kracak was a hireling, no matter how well treated, but with talk of friendship she was so bold as to ask if Doonak had found a woman he would like for a wife. He said it was too late. Solanj'l, who had never before felt even the slightest urge to find a mate for a man, thought of women who might have appropriate daughters. She knew women of different levels; surely she could find someone. She gave a huff-snort laugh and Doonak looked offended. She quickly explained she was not laughing at him but herself. She told him what she'd been thinking.

"I thank you for the thought, but the woman I want is married."

"But, why deny yourself completely? It's a man's right to

have a wife." Why was she pursuing this? What did it matter if he was married or not? Did she want him to be?

"I have gotten along without one until now. I assume I can continue to do so…. I see the woman I want from time to time. And, for now, that is good."

Solanj'l wondered if she should be having this conversation. She did not ask him who the woman was. She was not that bold, and she didn't want to know the answer in any event. It might be she wouldn't like what she heard. Doonak was a good, honourable man. He was steady, smart, able to paint beautifully, and probably capable of much more. He was assured but did not have the arrogance she saw in Glom and men like him. Even Hunak, whom she liked, had an air of being so right that it could be off-putting. Doonak was different from the men she'd known all her life. With a clutching in her mid-section, she realized she might feel different as a woman if she were married to someone like him. How extraordinary. How sad.

It crossed her mind to tell him about her plan to do away with the Beautification Ritual. Telling Glom had never occurred to her, yet she was thinking of speaking of it to this man. But she couldn't. It would be his obligation to tell Glom, and all the men he knew. Although she had used men to give women legs, she would not be able to use one for her next action. No man could be asked to take part in doing away with the Pretty Little Spots to fondle and lick.

Maybe she could get the Raiders to help. They continued to make appearances, slipping past guards no matter how or where they'd been placed. The Visitors, as Solanj'l had come to think of them, had taken a few more machine parts, nothing of great value that couldn't be replaced easily. It was the audacity of it that galled Glom, Hunak, and other powerful men who maintained the Ramprendian way of life. How dare these ruffians come into Ramprend to steal and embarrass? To Solanj'l they were encouragement. If they could befuddle the men of Ramprend, perhaps the women of Ramprend could do so as well. She asked Doonak if he had ideas about what these visitors were up to. He didn't, but said they weren't taking materials that would easily become weapons so he assumed they were not getting ready to wage war on the people from whom they were stealing. He added they might be people who lived in the city. She said she'd wondered if that might be true and that she'd also suggested to Glom that someone go into the mountains and talk with people there, find out if they actually were coming into Ramprend.

"An interesting idea," Doonak said. "I'd volunteer if that were to happen."

"I'd like to go. Me, a lowly woman.... They'd never let us go together."

He threw his head back and laughed. She joined him. It was a good moment. Later she was surprised at her boldness. Women did not suggest to men that they go off together, particularly to do something completely out of both of their experiences.

As she went back toward Glom's house she thought of Doonak, her father, and her husband, and how no man would be with her on her next attempt to do something different. She was thinking this and feeling ... regret. Regret? How could she be feeling regret? She lived her life with men telling her what to do, where to be, where not to be, what she could and could not know, how to be a woman and she was feeling regret over the absence of a man? She must be losing control of her mind. Men and regret were not words she had ever put together, other than regretting she lived in a world in which men maimed her kind.

Perhaps it wasn't regret. Fear. Fear of taking on a task with no man helping. She'd never done that. She knew no women who had. Her father and his steward had helped her build her little house. Glom and his steward and two other men had helped her with the legs. What made her think she could do this without a man easing the way? That might be the real fear; not opposition from men, but of doing it without the approval and aid of at least one. Glom would never accept an end to the ritual, nor would her father with his set ways. No help from any man. Could she function without a man?

Twinges—then stab, stab, stab—announced an approaching headache. They'd been rare of late. When she walked through the door of Glom's house her head split open, as if it'd been hit with an axe as heavy as her first wooden leg. The headache that stopped her ability to do anything went on for days. Tears ran down her face. Never before had she had one like this. She bit down hard on the inside of her lip to move the pain and looked at Glom in despair. He called in the Innervator Plaka'l, whom he did not know was Solanj'l's helper in the matters of preventing birth. She arrived on two legs, one wooden, and props, carrying a basket filled with herbs and cloths and instruments of various shapes.

Solanj'l alternately stood and sat. Lying down brought unbearable pain, a kind that could turn her into a killer if it didn't stop. Plaka'l put her hands on the top of Solanj'l's head, causing her to cry out, down the back of her neck and up on to her face causing another cry. She asked about the history of the headaches, their intensity, duration.

"Do you know what causes them?" she asked.

"Living."

"Living?"

"As a woman."

Plaka'l nodded, ordered warm damp towels and a large glass of berry juice from Cresa'l who so wanted to do something for the woman she now called Mistress, an honourific not usually attached to women. She step-dragged off with her wood leg to do as bidden. Plaka'l took some packets of powder out of her basket.

"I'm giving you something to make you sleep, you must get away from this pain. I'll tell your husband and his servants to let you wake when you're ready." She held up a packet. "When you do so, take this powder in berry juice, any will work. If the headache returns, send for me."

Cresa'l returned and Plaka'l prepared the drink and gave it to Solanj'l. She wanted Solanl'l to lie down but when she leaned back she cried out and sat up, panting. Plaka'l arranged pillows around her, wrapped her face and the top of her head in the towels, instructing Cresa'l to remove them when they cooled. Solanj'l would be asleep by that time and should be eased down.

She was alone when she finally woke. How long had she slept? She slowly sat up. Even though the headache hadn't completely left her, remaining as a nagging reminder that it could slam her into agony, she could move and tears did not flow. She looked around trying to remember what it was she was to do when she woke.

"Cresa'l," she called. Her voice was weak but it didn't matter because Cresa'l appeared immediately, having stationed herself outside the room when Kracak didn't need her.

"Oh, Mistress, how are you feeling?"

"Better. I'm supposed to do something."

Cresa'l said she'd be right back with berry juice for the powder Solanj'l was to take.

She'd slept for three days. Deba'l and Morgani'l had visited twice. Janka'l and Petra'l had come, too. They all asked to be notified when she was awake and arrived within minutes of each other. They came with flowers and cakes, which was rather silly given Glom's baker, but they hadn't known what else to do.

How was she? Was she well? What had caused the headache? Everyone was alarmed. Gung had even sent a Temple servant to inquire. Even though she still felt weak, she was glad to see them. Friends. People who were with her. Would they stay with her for the next step? The axe touched the top of her head reminding her it was there, ready to cleave. She put thoughts of the ritual aside.

Morgani'l had a strange story to tell, a mystery to divert her.

"Yesterday one of Bantant's servants thought he saw a Raider in the street. Had to be a Raider because of the cloak. There was only one so he went out to make a capture. He called out a halt and the person turned. It was a woman. He was so stunned he just stared at her. She turned and walked away, as a man walks, with two flesh legs.

"He was certain it was a woman?" Solanj'l asked.

"He insists he knows the difference."

Petra'l wanted to know if he was drunk.

"In Bantant's house?" Morgani'l said and raised her eyebrows. "Either a Ramprend woman has managed to keep both her legs or the Raiders include women."

"Maybe they're all women," Janka'l said.

"Wouldn't it be interesting to visit women in the mountains, women with two legs?" Solanj'l said.

Petra'l clasped her head and groaned. "Now she wants us to go travelling. Do we do this before or after..."

"Be quiet," Deba'l said.

They stared at each other, remembering they could not talk freely in Glom's home. Petra'l broke the silence with another story. Metak's sister, Roto'l, who was in one of her Gatherings, had come to see her. She wanted to know how other Gatherings worked, if they discussed different topics. She'd heard women in a shop talking about something happening at the next Gathering of Gatherings.

"What?" Morgani'l almost yelled. "What did you tell her?"

"I said I didn't know anything special."

"Tomorrow," Solanj'l said. "Tomorrow we talk. I need one more day of sleep."

27. PLANNING AND TROUBLE

THEY'D WORKED SLOWLY, dropping hints to selected women, starting with wishes—all a variation of, "I'd like my daughters to have legs that work better than what we have. Have you thought about that?" Some women readily said yes, others looked pensive. There were those who scowled as if such a thought couldn't even enter their minds. The initial response determined whether a woman would be approached again. Ones who readily said yes were asked how they felt about having a leg removed now that they had two—more or less. Hints, suggestions, more often than not presented as questions, were dropped judiciously.

Solanj'l wanted to tap into the women's rage but another emotion could hinder it. Shame. All their lives they'd lived with shame, and generally not being aware of it. But, it was there, like a blemish on the skin not seen because it was part of you, or an ache in a joint you'd learned to live with, not-feeling until something caused a twinge or stab. Solanj'l had no idea why she'd always been conscious of worthlessness and shame. How could women feel anger if shame had become the natural state? But the anger appeared—gradually, but it came. When a woman realized another might be angry she could consider it and examine her own feelings. Rage started bubbling up in the Gatherings—in a reverse kind of way. Women spoke of how awful the legs were, how awkward, how uncomfortable, how clumsy. Some would pound on the leg as they spoke.

Many talked of not wearing them any longer. They complained and threatened and Solanj'l smiled to herself. Most women would not give up the leg no matter what was said. Increased mobility, even the idea of it, was opening their minds to what else might be.

Some men didn't like what their wives were becoming and ordered them to stop wearing the legs. These women begged their Gathering leaders to intercede. Please ask Solanj'l and Deba'l to ask their husbands to speak out. Glom and Hunak did, at a Gathering of Gatherings. Hunak stated the legs had enriched their lives by making it more interesting and exciting. How fortunate they were to have a man of vision who could bring this about. The implication was men had a duty to have two-legged wives.

Solanj'l wondered about his ready acceptance and approval. Ramprend men wanted their wives maimed; it was *the* way to sexual excitement and satisfaction. She suspected he was motivated by something beyond a new way to do sex but she hadn't been able to figure out what it was, nor had she asked Deba'l. It was pure superstition but she feared mentioning it would cause the loss of his support.

Glom gave one of his exuberant speeches about the beauty of Glom's Glamour Legs, of how much pleasure, no, more than pleasure, joy had come to the men of Ramprend and Glom's Glamour Legs also gave joy to women who were pleasing their men by wearing them. Solanj'l knew it would be a long sex scene that night. He had his glow-look. She'd give herself a night off of attending to what was happening to her and think of running in the fields with Spirry, and of all the women of Ramprend running with her.

Hunak's and Glom's speeches were printed and distributed to all households. The message was received by naysaying men and their wives once again wore Glom's Glamour Legs. There were men who continued to resist; the loss and rage felt by their wives would be fuel for ending the ritual. Would it work to their favour if all women were denied legs? A possibility, but women must be able to get around on their own to do what was to be done. The Firsts couldn't do it alone.

They, with the exception of Casanj'l, had held together. Solanj'l had worried about Petra'l, who kept making resistance noises. One day Deba'l suggested she go without her leg for one week's time. Go back to being carried. Just one week, then tell them if she was with them or would step out. Petra'l had stared at her, saying nothing. The others waited.

"No," she finally said. "I don't want to be without my leg.... There's something I haven't told you. I'm carrying a child. It could be a girl." Tears slipped out of the corners of her eyes and down her face onto her neck. "I think I keep saying these things because I'm afraid. But I think I'm more afraid of a daughter having her leg sawed off. The way mine was." She put her head down on her flesh and wood legs and sobbed. Deba'l stroked her back. No one spoke until she lifted her head. Janka'l handed her a handkerchief. That was the day they started their serious planning. It would take them two years to get to the point of believing they could move to implementation.

* * *

Just when they felt ready, Phylli'l appeared again, with supporters. She was once and for all going to put a stop to this disgusting business with the legs. What people were doing was obscene. She'd sniffed out a jealous priest who thought Gung was getting too much attention from the High Priest and other men of power. It was perfectly clear to Lumok that the legs were not of Ploch. The city was adrift in error and it had to be stopped. Phylli'l established an anti-Gathering group with the priest's support and was attempting to create more. Gung had tried to stop her but, not surprisingly, the High Priest took the easy course and let the two priests battle. Lumok had convinced the minister Sixth to The First that life was not as it should be in Ramprend. Hunak could have had this minister removed but decided to leave him alone for a time, hoping he and those with Phylli'l would end up looking like the fools he considered them to be. Glom had tried to change his mind, but he said The People for What is True and Right As Ordained by the Great God Ploch should be given the opportunity to fail by their own initiative. Deba'l told Solanj'l she thought Hunak was right. Mothers who wanted their daughters maimed could stiffen the resolve of those who wanted the Beautification Ritual stopped.

Phylli'l and her group commenced the real battle when she and cohorts attempted to disrupt one of Solanj'l's Gatherings. The door flew open and Phylli'l was rolled in by a large, angry-looking man. Other women followed along with their pusher/rollers.

"You have fallen into decay!" Phylli'l yelled.

The Gathering members looked at each other and shook their heads.

"You are not following the ways of Ploch and Ramprend. Join me while you can."

One of the outspoken Gathering members, Bemla'l, said, "What are you going on about? Why in the name of Ploch should we join you?"

"The legs are an abomination. They are not pleasing to Ploch. You are polluting all that is true and right. You will be punished."

"If we were doing wrong the High Priest would have told us," Bemla'l said. "Go away."

Bemla'l was one of Solanj'l's strongest supporters; according to Deba'l she'd fight one of the mountain cats to protect her. Phylli'l didn't know this and kept yelling about decay and error. Bemla'l took out a tablet and started asking for names of the intruders, some of whom readily gave them until Phylli'l told them to stop.

"I have enough to give to Gung, who is responsible for these Gatherings," Bemla'l said holding up the list. "He'll give it to the High Priest. What is your name?" she asked Phylli'l. "I certainly want to put it at the top."

Phylli'l motioned to be rolled toward Solanj'l, who'd locked her leg for standing.

"You will leave or I will send for a deputy to remove you," Solanj'l said.

Phylli'l moved her mouth. Bemla'l yelled, "She's going to spit," grabbed Phylli'l's chair and yanked it to the side, causing the spit to flip back on its owner. Bemla'l locked her leg, stood, grabbed Phylli'l's chair from the man and started pushing her toward the door. The pusher/roller didn't dare touch Bemla'l and followed. The People for What is True and Right As Ordained by the Great God Ploch squawked protest but had themselves rolled after their leader, who continued yelling about evil and punishment. Bemla'l shut the door and leaned against it.

"If she wants people to agree with her, she's going to have to do better than that," one of the women said while shaking her head. There were murmurs of assent, then laughter. "What is wrong with her?" "What a fool." "Was that man her husband?" They agreed Phylli'l was funny—and a potential problem. Solanj'l was fairly certain this group would be with her in the move to stop the ritual—which would start at the next Gathering of Gatherings.

28. DECLARATION

BUZZ, BUZZ, BUZZ. The first day of the Gathering of Gatherings was so energy-filled one could almost hear it, a humming of excitement and delight. At any Gathering of Gatherings life felt richer, more possible; being alive was enjoyable in and of itself, beyond anything felt while being of husband use. And this Gathering was special. There was going to be a declaration. Of what? When women tried to get an answer, all they heard was it would be good for "our daughters." Petra'l was the most enthusiastic respondent. "You will love it. It is so exciting! (A clap of her hands.) I wish I could tell you how wonderful it will be, but you'll know that when you hear it."

The leaders of the individual Gatherings had been asked to a special meeting a week before. They needed to be readied to support—it was hoped—what was coming. When the declaration was read there were great intakes of breath, and if eyes gave off light the room would have become brighter as they snapped open wider.

The Firsts had had trouble with the wording of the declaration. "...Sawing off the leg" was so awful.

"Why say it that way?" Petra'l had asked.

"Remove would be better. Wouldn't it?" from Janka'l.

"Why?" Solanj'l almost yelled. "Our legs were sawed off. Sawed off and thrown into blood-stained buckets and tossed in a waste pit where scavengers ate them. That is what will happen to your daughters, to all girls. Sawed off and eaten. Sawed off and eaten."

The faces turned to her were ashen. She was right, but who wanted to be reminded? Someone suggested "Beautification Ritual" could be used.

"It isn't beautification," Solanj'l snapped. "Naming it that says we agree it is. We'd defeat ourselves."

The debate had gone on and she finally won, probably by sheer force of desire and repetition.

The Gathering Leaders sat stunned upon hearing what The Firsts had agreed on. Some nodded as they thought about the hints that had been sent their way. But what did The Firsts think they were doing? Surely they didn't think they could stop the Beautification Ritual by making a declaration. It was an established tradition. It had been a part Ramprendian culture for longer than anyone's memory. Who would marry their daughters if they had two legs? The men would be enraged and stop them from gathering. Women would be beaten, maybe some who had never been beaten before.

Solanj'l and the other Firsts kept reminding them that many women—most of those present—had expressed a desire for their daughters to keep both legs. Well, yes, but no one thought that would ever happen.

"It will happen if women make it happen," Solanj'l said.

"No, this will stop all we have gained."

"The legs will be taken away from us."

"Life will go back to what it was."

"How can you even think about doing this?"

"Because we have learned we are people," Solanj'l said.

"What does that mean? Of course we're people."

No one has ever said we aren't people."

"But we aren't," Solanj'l said. "Men don't have their legs sawed off. We do. Men control the city. We don't. Men control us. *They* are people. We are what they want us to be. We are things to be used for their pleasure. We are nothing if they want us to be nothing. We have learned to be not-people. But we *are* people. That is what we've been learning in the Gatherings."

The women shook their heads. This was too much for them to take in. Morgani'l pointed out that there was no demand for immediate cessation. This was a call to men to join women. It had to be forcefully stated or the men would not take it seriously. Individual women didn't even need to say they agreed with the declaration. They could merely say it had been presented. They could engage their husbands in discussion.

"I can't lie to my husband," one woman said.

"Who says you have to?" Morgani'l asked, then smiled. "Haven't you ever?" She gave the woman a conspiratorial wink.

The woman looked unhappy and said nothing.

"Phylli'l will make much of this," another leader said. "She'll make much trouble."

"Our existence is an affront to Phylli'l and her acolytes," Deba'l said. "It won't matter what we say or do."

Nods of agreement around the room. The talk went on through a midday meal and afternoon. When the sun neared the horizon and it was time for the women to go to their husbands' homes, it was agreed that talking about the ritual *might* be a good thing and a declaration *could* start the discussion. But they didn't need to include men in the statement. Did they? That was very presumptuous. It might be dangerous. Janka'l pointed out there would be no movement forward if men weren't asked to join.

Some flatly stated you couldn't change men. You couldn't change life. Ramprendians did as Ramprendians had always done.

Solanj'l said in a quiet voice. "We have changed. Rather easily I think. We didn't have wooden legs a few years ago, now they are considered a regular part of our lives. We are capable of change."

"But it was a man who did that."

The Firsts cut their eyes at each other. It hadn't been agreed as to just when all women would know it was Solanj'l who'd created the legs—her idea, her execution.

The meeting ended with the leaders promising to think about the declaration and to tell no one about it; that could be dangerous. During the following week The Firsts talked to the individual leaders; some were approaching acceptance, but there were those who still thought it a bad idea. The Firsts hoped they wouldn't turn their Gathering members against it, but it would be foolish to think all women would come to accept such a "radical," "outlandish," "outrageous" idea. All they needed were enough. Enough to take the actual step toward stopping the ritual at the Gathering of Gatherings after this one, only a year away.

* * *

The Declaration was to be made the second day of the Gathering. Many women were staying in the Great Hall to help The Firsts, and because they liked the novelty of being away from their husbands' homes. The Firsts had encouraged as many as possible to do so. It was necessary for the women to see staying together as an important part of major Gatherings. Many who had chosen not to stay, or hadn't been allowed, wished they were because the ones who did were having such a good time.

Gung had tried to push himself into the entire proceedings, but Deba'l and Petra'l managed to keep him under control by appealing to his vanity. Petra'l gleefully told the others she'd used all her skills of flirtation. "As a priest you should be honoured, not taking part as a worker ... or a woman." She dropped her eyes, then looked up, her tongue peeking through her lips. "Yours will be the first speech, the honoured one. That is all *you* need to do." Petra'l honoured him with her little girl pouty smile. His tongue circled his lips, then flicked in and out. He agreed to one speech, then absence.

Day Two started with "Our Past and Future." Deba'l had suggested after the first Gathering of Gatherings that a statement reminding the women of what had been, and what could be, would strengthen a sense of connection. Then participants could recount their best memory for the year, offer a new Pleasure Way or make suggestions for the future Gatherings.

Solanj'l was very brief in this year's statement. For memory she told a personal story, of how Glom had presented her with a Glom's Glamour Leg of Legs. She didn't mention it was Doonak's idea. She stepped to the edge of the stage and lifted her skirt to display the special leg. Clapping and even cheering. How appropriate that she had such a wonder. Later she was asked repeatedly to show it, each woman wanting to know if a leg like hers had been painted on it.

Solanj'l told them she would not speak of the future because that would be addressed later.

The women then spoke of their memories—and wants. They actually spoke of wants. Oh, yes.

Ramprenders could change. At least the women.

They broke for a festive lunch in the large courtyard in the center of the building. One Gathering had volunteered to decorate the trees with bits of coloured papers that fluttered in a gentle breeze. Tables resplendent with red and yellow flowers were piled with meats, breads, vegetables, cheeses, fruits. Glom had hired extra staff to help Crusak, his baker, make cream cakes for all. Their reputation had preceded them and women could hardly wait to put their teeth into one. As they oohed and ahhed over the cakes, The Firsts announced they would stay outside for The Declaration. Janka'l had suggested such a statement should be made in fresh, open air.

Just as Solanj'l was about to read, there was a flurry of activity at a courtyard door to the outside. Phylli'l and cohorts had arrived. Bemla'l and others tried to prevent their entry. Deba'l motioned to let them come in. They might as well hear it now. Phylli'l was rolled, not by the mean-looking man, but a woman servant. She tried to get near the head table. A group of women spontaneously stood and blocked her passage. Phylli'l glared, the women stood impassively, and Bemla'l, who'd taken a particular dislike to Phylli'l, said, "You will have to stay near the door." The servant took a step toward her, but Phylli'l held up her hand and shook her head. Her acolytes were rolled around her. Morgani'l and Petra'l laughed behind their hands over the fact that these women were being rolled by other women. Did the Phylli'ls see the irony in that?

The Firsts stood next to Solanj'l, shoulders almost touching. Deba'l held up her hand and waited for complete silence. "Solanj'l, First of The Firsts (Solanj'l glanced at her with a little scowl) will make The Declaration."

In a loud, clear voice Solanj'l slowly read, "We, the women of Ramprend, declare the practice of sawing off the legs of our daughters must cease. We declare the men of Ramprend should join us in our resolve to stop the practice."

Silence. Women turned and looked at each other. They cocked their heads and scowled. "ABOMINATION," screamed Phylli'l who was motioning for her servant to roll her to the head table. Once again she was blocked. She continued screaming. "Abomination. Death to the Daughters of Filth. Kill them. Kill them." That brought other voices.

"Who's talking about killing?"

"What's going on?"

"What do The Firsts mean?"

"Who's that women screaming?"

"Kill who?"

"What did Solanj'l say?"

Solanj'l held up her hand, but the women weren't yet ready to be quiet. They needed to give vent to their confusion so The Firsts waited. Phylli'l kept yelling. Many of her followers looked unhappy. She'd gotten some control of herself and there were no more cries for death to the filth but saying it had been enough to be off-putting. She undoubtedly would have to do some clever talking to keep all her toadies in line. Once again Solanj'l held up her hand and the crowd quieted down, except for Phylli'l. Bemla'l step-dragged to her, leaned down and said something that caused Phylli'l to shut her mouth. Later Bemla'l reported she told her to close her mouth or she would stuff a rag in it. It was such a shocking statement Phylli'l had been stunned into silence.

"We know this is an unusual statement," Solanj'l said. "We know you will want to discuss it. We suggest you meet in your Gatherings and do so."

"But what did you say?" one woman called out. "I don't think I heard you correctly."

There were nodded heads around the courtyard. Solanj'l started to read the declaration.

"Filth."

"Traitor."

Deba'l rang a bell she'd put near her place at table and Sheriff's deputies appeared and herded Phylli'l and her followers out of the courtyard. Hunak knew nothing about a declaration but because Phylli'l was an opponent of the Gatherings, he'd agreed to have deputies posted around the building to prevent any trouble she might try to make.

"Now that we have order," Solanj'l said, "I'll read the declaration. Leaders will be given copies so you can read it in your Gathering. She paused, then declared in a voice probably heard beyond the courtyard, "We, the women of Ramprend, declare the practice of sawing off the legs of our daughters must cease. We declare the men of Ramprend should join us in our resolve to stop the practice."

Women, talking, talking, talking went to their individual Gatherings. Solanj'l collapsed onto a chair, her wooden leg of legs sticking straight out until she leaned forward and let the calf drop. The other Firsts also sat and adjusted their wood legs.

Petra'l said, "I think that went rather well," and went into a fit of laughter. Morgani'l, then Janka'l and Deba'l joined her. Peals of laughter. Solanj'l smiled, but her eyes were pensive.

29. AGITATION

GLOM CAME RUNNING into the Great Hall demanding to know where Solanj'l was. She was going from Gathering to Gathering, attempting to allay fears and encourage support. Glom found her in a hallway.

"What do you mean by this ... this?" He was flapping his hands as if trying to shake something off them. "Declaration? What exactly did you say?"

"We, the women of Ramprend, declare the practice of sawing off the legs of our daughters must cease. We declare the men of Ramprend should join us in our resolve to stop the practice."

"What are you saying? What are you thinking? Hunak didn't approve this. Gung either."

"Deba'l is talking with Gung. How did you hear about it?"

"I would have expected to hear about it from you."

She smiled and shook her head.

"You're my wife. It's your duty to tell me everything."

She glanced down the hall and saw Deba'l, Petra'l, and Gung coming toward them. She made a motion with her head. Glom turned and saw them.

"Glom," Gung called out, "just look what little women will do when we let them have meetings." He was attempting to sound jocular.

"You didn't know about this did you?" Glom asked.

Gung shook his head. "Deba'l sent for me and here I am."

He was rubbing his hands together and licking his lips that were even more red and moist than usual.

"Hunak?" Glom said. "What does Hunak say?"

"I've sent word to him," Deba'l said.

"How could you do this?" Glom almost yelled. "Did someone tell you to do it? Did something come over you? Are you ill?"

"I think it's a good idea," Petra'l said with a beguiling smile.

"What? What are you talking about? The Beautification Ritual is part of Ramprendian life. It can't be stopped."

"It could," Petra'l replied, the open-eyed ingénue.

Glom threw his arms and hands into the air. "What is happening to you women?"

"As Solanj'l has said," Petra'l replied, "we've discovered we're people."

Glom and Gung looked at each other. People? What were they talking about? Of course they were people.

"I declare this Gathering to be over," Glom said.

"You don't have the authority," Solanj'l said.

He turned and glared at her. "These Gatherings were started for the purpose of promoting Glom's Glamour Legs. Not beautifying women would mean the end of them."

"Ah yes," Solanj'l said.

"Hunak has approved the Gatherings and given us the space," Deba'l said. "His is the authority."

"Well, we know he'll stop this nonsense," Glom said. "First the Raiders, now this. What is happening to Ramprend?"

Gung declared the High Priest had approved the Gatherings; he had as much authority as Hunak.

A Sheriff's deputy came down the hall to inform them a crowd was outside demanding the Gathering be stopped, as well as all future ones. It hadn't taken Phylli'l long to re-rally her toadies.

"Is there talk of killing?" Janka'l asked.

The Sheriff's man looked puzzled and shook his head. "No. Who said anything about killing?"

"Pay close attention," Deba'l said. "Phylli'l, wife of Fulm, was demanding it earlier."

"We'll have none of that," the deputy said.

They stood and looked at each other until the deputy asked, "What are you going to do? Is the meeting going on?"

"Of course," Solanj'l said.

"Hunak will decide that," Glom said.

"Is there a danger of the crowd becoming agitated?" Gung asked.

"That'd be less likely if you went out to talk to them, Priest," the deputy said. "There's one out there already, but I don't know what he's doing."

"Come along, Glom," Gung said. "We'll go out and quiet them. Then we can determine what is to be done with these naughty women in here."

The "naughty" women followed them, slowly step-dragging down the corridor.

Phylli'l's priest, Lumok, was with her. As soon as he saw Gung he ran up the steps to confront him. What was a priest doing in this group of deceitful women? How could he be involved with such wickedness? Gung said he was taking care of the situation but that couldn't happen until the rabble had been removed from the front of the building.

"Rabble?" Phylli'l shrieked from below. "How dare you suggest we are rabble. We are the true Ramprendians. We are The People for What is True and Right As Ordained by the Great God Ploch."

"How dare you declare what is true according to Ploch?" Gung said. "How dare you, a mere woman, take on the authority which belongs only to the High Priest. Lumok, how can you let a woman presume to act as if she were a priest, a *man*?"

Lumok looked befuddled, then turned toward Phylli'l and said she was not to speak. She opened her mouth but he slashed his hand in a way that told her to be silent. He demanded to know what Gung was going to do. Gung explained everything was under control, that he and Glom would be meeting with Hunak and the High Priest to determine the best course of action. No help was needed or wanted from people assembled outside. The implication was Lumok was not wanted. He rocked back and forth, uncertain whether to go or stay. Apparently, he decided he'd lost the confrontation because he ordered the crowd to disperse. Phylli'l kept shrieking about vileness and tradition and Ploch as she was rolled down the street until he said something to her. Glom and Gung followed shortly after, off in search of Hunak.

The women of the Gathering were fearful, some so much so they'd left, presumably in the hope their husbands would not be too angry with them for being present for such outrageous talk. Many who remained hoped The Firsts had been playing a joke on them, even if that made no sense. Deba'l told them the Gathering might be ordered cancelled. They would have to decide whether or not to comply. Buzzing again, now indicating confusion rather than energy. The Gatherings and the future were taking a direction not envisioned. They were in an experience beyond their imagining.

"I would like to speak." Casanj'l was sitting next to an aisle in the auditorium, her group beside her.

"Oh, my," Janka'l said quietly.

"Brace yourselves," Morgani'l said.

Deba'l motioned toward Casanj'l who said, "I have no idea what has possessed you to present us with this truly appalling declaration, but I am proposing we get new First Leaders. We need women who will lead us in the right direction. We need women…"

"Does that mean you?" someone called out.

"Well," Casanj'l said and waited for affirmation—which did not come.

Bemla'l stood and said, "The Firsts have given us the Gatherings. The Firsts have given us legs. The Firsts have served us well. They will continue to do so."

There was clapping from women sitting near her.

"Now wait a minute," came from the back.

Solanj'l held up her hands and waved them crisscross over her head. Silence gradually came. "If you want new leaders, you are free to find them. We, however, will go on with our plan to stop the sawing off of our daughters' legs."

"Stop saying that," Casanj'l yelled out. "It is the Beautification Ritual."

"Your leg was sawed off," Morgani'l said. "You don't remember the terror? You don't remember the tears? You don't remember being able to walk and run? Do you remember the despair? Do you remember pain? Do you want that for your daughters?" She was yelling so loudly at the end you could imagine the words being torn from her throat.

Eyes were shifting back and forth, fear in some, tears in others.

"Do you want that done to your daughter?" Petra'l, who was openly crying, echoed Morgani'l.

"NO!" Bemla'l yelled and women awkwardly stood and yelled, "No. No. No."

Casanj'l and others looked around. What was going on? Women didn't act this way.

Solanj'l waved for silence again. "We all need to consider what has been declared. We need time to think. We suggest we have our evening meal and wait until morning for further discussion."

"Many of us will leave and not return," Casanj'l called out.

"How unfortunate," Morgani'l said so only those around her would hear.

Women looked around, then started moving out of the auditorium. Bemla'l came to the stage and said, "Good work. Don't worry. You'll see tomorrow." She nodded repeatedly to reinforce her point, probably her own belief in it.

Solanj'l thanked her, hoping she was right. Other women looked toward the stage as if they wanted to say something, but eventually turned and went out. The room emptied.

"I wonder what the men are doing," Janka'l said.

The others merely nodded. Eventually they'd find out what the men were doing.

30. HUSBANDS

HUNAK WANTED TO SEE DEBA'L at home. She left without eating. Kracak arrived to declare Glom wanted Solanj'l. She left with him, ignoring the smug look that said this woman was finally going to be put in her proper place. Solanj'l had anticipated this day, as had all of them, the day of explaining to their husbands why they could no longer go along with the mutilation of their own children.

Glom was in the Sitting Room. "Have you eaten?" he asked. He appeared relaxed and composed, a man ready to spend a quiet evening at home. She shook her head and said she wasn't hungry, but he made a gesture to Kracak that food should be brought. They sat and stared out the window until bread, cheeses, fruits, and a bottle of dewberry wine were brought in by Cresa'l, who bobbed her head in Solanj'l's direction but said nothing.

Glom poured wine into two glasses and handed one to Solanj'l. He cut a piece of bread, put it on a plate with a slice of cheese and handed it to her. She was the one who should have been doing this for him. He prepared a plate, placed it in front of himself and leaned back.

"Given your declaration I assume you expect to be waited on by me," he said.

She had not expected an attempt at sarcasm.

"No," she said, "I do not expect to be waited on by you, but I thank you."

His eyes narrowed but all he did was pick up the bread and cheese.

"I assume you have some explanation for your inexplicable behavior."

Tiredness descended. She and her friends had barely begun and the idea of trying to explain felt like a weight pressing her into the chair.

She took a big breath and said, "Glom, someday we may have a daughter. Do you want her to have her leg sawed off?"

"It is for beautification."

"How is an absent limb beautiful?"

"A stump is beautiful. It is our way."

"We can make new ways. Glom's Glamour Legs are a new way for us."

"And they would cease to exist if you had your way."

She cocked her head. "You care more about the money from them than you would about a child?"

"It is what girls want."

"It isn't what I wanted. It isn't what Deba'l and Morgani'l and Janka'l and Petra'l and every woman I know wanted. It wasn't even what Casanj'l wanted. She seems to forget that she was terrified before her leg was sawed off. She was like the rest of us. We were all so afraid." She looked into a corner of the room, remembering Casanj crying for days as the hour of maiming approached. "We were so afraid."

Glom was looking at her as if he'd never seen her before.

"You see, Glom, I do mind not having my leg. I mind very much."

He became very busy placing another piece of cheese on bread, carefully putting both on his plate and then taking a drink of wine.

He finally looked up and said, "I thought you were happy."

"Men think all women are happy."

"I thought you liked your life with me."

"Men think their wives like their lives."

"I conclude you do not."

"I would like it more if I had two legs."

"I see."

"What I want, Glom, does not have to do with us, with me, or you. It's too late for me. What I want is something better than I, all women, have had."

"We men have given the best we can. You have our protection and care. I don't know what is wrong with you. I feel like I'm living with a woman I don't know."

He was, but she didn't say so. He thought he knew her because she never before had done anything that would make him think differently. Women had gone along with life as it was, acting as if they wished it. They'd been almost as unimaginative as the men of Ramprend. But one change was undoing hundreds of years of mindlessly following tradition. Whatever happened, there was no return to the Ramprend of their birth.

"Glom, you gave women the gift of surrogate legs. Think of what it would mean if you helped to give women the gift of their own legs. Think of the honour in that."

He leapt to his feet. "And what of sex? How can we have sex if we don't have the excitement of the stump?"

He glared down at her. Her stomach turned over and she put down the bread and cheese she'd been holding.

Seconds passed in silence until he said, "I order you to have nothing more to do with this disgusting idea."

She shook her head, barely moving it back and forth. "I can't do that, Glom. It's become my reason for being alive."

"You're a wife. You'll do what I say."

"Have you talked with Hunak?"

"No. I have not. That doesn't matter. I determine what happens in my home."

She nodded her head and said softly. "Yes, your home."

"It is your responsibility to do what I say."

"How can you expect me to be happy when I can't do what I think is right?"

"You're a woman. You don't have the mind for deciding what is right."

She lifted her wood leg, locked it into standing position and stood face to face with him. "I did all the deciding that created your surprise, the surprise that became Glom's Glamour Legs. I think I have a mind for thinking and deciding much."

She started to leave the room, having no idea of where she was going.

"You'll not leave until I have your word that you will have nothing more to do with that declaration."

"I can't do that."

"Then I'll lock you in this house."

She turned and looked at him. "Do you think the Gatherings with the creation of Pleasure Ways and a demand for Glamour Legs will continue if you do that?"

His eyes shifted to the side and his mouth tightened, his assessing profit and loss face.

"Why don't we wait until we hear from Hunak," she said.

He said nothing

"I'll go back to the Great Hall."

"No," he said. "You'll stay here. I have missed our nights together."

I suppose I should have anticipated this she thought and step-dragged to the Master's Pleasure Room. Her body was the instrument of proof that Glom ruled.

When he flipped her skirt up and saw the Leg of Legs he smiled. "The best leg in the city. Don't you think so, pretty little wife?"

"Yes. It is beautiful." She wondered how she would feel if Doonak were looking down on the leg and her. Probably not like she was feeling now. Glom was pulling on the laces that held the leg-pants together. He became frustrated and told her to undo them so he could remove the leg.

"And undo the lacing on both your bodices. I want you bare tonight."

Nothing, she thought. A nothing in nothing.

He removed the leg and moved as if he were going to throw it down, then placed it carefully against the wall. Such fine goods should not be damaged. He turned back, took hold of her skirt and tried to yank it off. She reached down and removed the buttons from their holes and the skirt was off. He dropped his mouth to her Pretty Little Spot and licked it as she finished opening her bodices. He looked up and said, "Take them off." When she'd done so he put his hands on her waist and pulled her flat on the bed. He dropped on her and rubbed what was left of her right leg. Rubbed it and rubbed it, while he kissed her mouth, running his tongue as far in as he could. He suddenly reared up, grabbed her hips, lifted them up and rammed himself into her all the while saying, "Pretty Little Spot, Pretty Little Spot, Pretty Little Spot."

Solanj'l left to run in the fields with Spirry.

The next morning her entire body was sore, from the pressure of him on her, from rubbing, licking, kissing, and being driven into again and again. He ate the morning meal and left without saying a word, not even ordering her to stay in. She soaked out as much pain as she could in a bath, dressed and set out for the Great Hall. The day was beautiful with a clear blue sky and gentle white fluffy clouds idling along. She was certain the day's events would not reflect such beauty.

31. DEATH TO THE RITUAL

A S THE COACH CARRIED SOLANJ'L to the Great Hall, she looked out at women "walking" or being rolled in that direction. Women with two legs, one flesh, one wood. Would the declaration take everything from them? Would the self-hating convince them they deserved their contemptible condition? Would men, even mild ones, turn against women for upsetting their world? Would fear overtake women, leaving them in thralldom? She shook her head. These were not new questions; they'd been discussed over and over in meetings of The Firsts.

Glom's coach stopped in front of the Hall but some distance from the doors because of a crowd. Solanj'l saw Lumok and assumed Phylli'l was present. The driver got off his seat, opened the door, and held out his arm for her to steady herself as she got down.

"There she is," a voice shrieked. "There's the hater of all that is True and Right."

She raised her hand, smiled and waved.

"Demon."

So be it. She continued to smile, partly out of amusement. Many calling her demon were standing there on their wood legs. How rich. She looked up and saw Deba'l and Janka'l standing at the entrance with two Sheriff's deputies. She moved toward the five steps to the doors. People did not try to stop her but words worse than demon were yelled. "Termer." "Wallower in

Filth." She kept walking and came face to face with Casanj'l.

"Look what you've come to," her sister said.

"Are you with them?" Solanj'l jerked her head toward the crowd.

"I'm here to try to talk some sense into you."

Solanj'l started step-dragging again. "You never could talk me into anything, Casanj'l. Don't bother trying now."

"Our parents are devastated. You are an embarrassment."

"Oh, I'm sure I'm something more than that."

They arrived at the steps to the entrance door. All The Firsts were now waiting.

"Have you decided to come back to us," Morgani'l asked Casanj'l.

"I have nothing to say to you."

"You never did."

One of the deputies, with her permission, helped to steady Solanj'l as she hitched her way up the steps. Hunak had ordered that service for the Gatherings. The Firsts started into the building but Janka'l turned and said. "Please come with us."

"You're as mad as my sister."

"Please join us, Casanj'l. Think of your daughters."

A look of distaste crossed Casanj'l face. She looked at Solanj'l who had paused in the doorway. "I only wanted what was best for you," she said.

"I know. But we never agreed about what is best. As Janka'l has said, think of your daughters. Remember how terrified you were before they sawed off your leg. Remember the itching, the pain. Remember the unrelenting months of trying to comfort a leg no longer there. It still bothers you. Admit it. Don't make your daughters give up a leg so men can have pleasure."

Casanj'l said nothing, merely staring in the direction of her sister. Solanj'l entered the building and Janka'l followed, after putting her hand out to Casanj'l, who ignored it. They went to The Firsts' Special Room, the others were already there. They looked at Solanj'l with "well?" in their eyes.

She shook her head and said, "I don't know what he's doing. Last night he ordered me to have nothing more to do with the declaration but left this morning without a word."

Eyes turned to Deba'l. Hunak had requested a recitation of the declaration, then asked if she planned to support it, and what she expected men to do about it. She answered the questions with what were the obvious answers—to The Firsts. He said men would need time to consider. He would ask the husbands of The Firsts to not do anything as yet.

"That's all?" Petra'l asked.

"I asked what he thought about it and he said he, like other men, needed time to think. I have no idea what's in his mind. I usually have a sense of his thinking, but there was blankness last night. That may have been due to tiredness. On both our parts."

"I guess we might as well move forward," Morgani'l said. "Talk to the women about making The Declaration a reality."

The auditorium was not filled, but more women were present than Solanj'l had thought would be. When The Firsts entered, the women in the auditorium clapped. Bemla'l started to chant, "Death to the Ritual. Death to the Ritual." The women in her group joined in, then others. Many remained silent; that was to be expected, some were there out of curiosity more than commitment.

"I like that," Janka'l said. "Death to the Ritual," she called out.

Morgani'l joined her, then Petra'l, Deba'l, and Solanj'l. They linked arms. "Death to the Ritual. Death to the Ritual." Women started swaying and chanting, "Death to the Ritual. Death to the Ritual."

"Should we march them outside?" Deba'l asked.

"Why not?" Morgani'l said.

So they did. March-dragged out of the room, down the hallway, onto the entry steps, chanting all the way. "Death to the Ritual. Death to the Ritual." Their opponents were taken aback; they hadn't expected to be confronted in this way.

The Firsts agreed to go down and meet them face-to-face. Morgani'l led off by stepping down with her own leg while Petra'l held onto her, then swung her wood leg down next to the real one. Then Petra'l held by Janka'l, went down a step, then Janka'l held Deba'l, Deba'l held by Solanj'l alone at the top. Janka'l and Deba'l reached up to hold Solanj'l as she went down. It was a laborious process, stepping down, swinging the cumbersome wood leg to join the real one, but as soon as the other women saw what The Firsts were doing they followed. The steps were broad enough that several women could go down at one time. Their opponents below watched in silence after a few nasty shouts. Solanj'l also watched and thought how brave they were, it would be so easy to lose balance and fall. The Firsts later learned some who'd been listening to Phylli'l and Lumok joined the ranks of Death to the Ritual that day.

It took a quite a span of time but many women at the Gathering finally lined up facing their opponents, The Firsts didn't know what to do other than chant. The Phylli'ls called out insults but had no effective counter chant and finally stood and looked at the traitors of all that was True and Right—some relatives or friends. Women who'd always gone along with established life, behaving as they ought, were facing each other in opposition. How could this be?

Lumok stepped in front of Deba'l. "You are an insult to womanhood."

Deba'l wrinkled her nose, looking as if she smelled something rotten. "Tell that to my husband, Minister Second Only to the First. He has not declared me so, nor has the High Priest."

"The High Priest will speak."

"He sometimes does."

Phylli'l rolled next to him and started a rant. Bemla'l started the Death to the Ritual chant again.

"Join us," Solanj'l said to Phylli'l, who responded with a kick that hit Solanj'l's wooden leg, causing her to lose balance. She went down flailing her arms. Gasps and cries from women on both sides as she hit the street with a thud. Bemla'l moved in front of Phylli'l and slapped her across the face. "How dare you?" Lumok grabbed Bemla'l by the hair, almost causing her to fall but the deputies intervened, making him let go and demanding a space be made between the groups. The lead deputy asked Solanj'l if she was hurt. She shook her head. He called for a colleague to help him raise her to her feet, a wooden leg being more encumbrance than aid to rising when lying on one's side. She assured everyone she was fine except for a pain in her left shoulder and elbow. She moved her arm to show it was working.

Nothing more could be accomplished with this ridiculous confrontation. She suggested they go inside. What a process that would be. Most women had never climbed stairs—of course many hadn't gone down either. Why hadn't they thought about this? A temporary madness had taken hold of them. Chanting had carried them out and down; now they had to go up and in, which would be more difficult.

"I know," Bemla'l said. "We can use the platform in the back. One of the women who stayed on the steps can unlock the door at the back."

The Great Hall, a square with the interior courtyard, was three floors tall with a flat roof. A pulleyed platform was used to carry supplies to each level including the first that had no steps at the rear. Bemla'l and three others took their slow step-dragging way to the side, then rear of the building. The others waited, giving the Phylli'ls the opportunity to call out insulting words, although not as vigorously as before.

"I never thought I'd see women acting that way," Petra'l said.

Morgani'l laughed. "Well, I never thought I'd see women acting the way we are either."

"That's true," Petra'l said and they grinned at each other. These two, who started as mild antagonists, had become friends, even if they frequently needled each other.

The woman who'd unlocked the rear door appeared and said Bemla'l and the others had raised and lowered the platform. They knew how it worked and several women could be lifted to the first floor in one trip.

* * *

"This is what we propose." The Firsts were now taking turns as primary speaker and it was Morgani'l's turn. "We, all of us, need to talk to anyone, women and men, any who will listen, about the necessity of stopping the ritual."

"Death to the Ritual," someone called out,

"Do you think this is really going to happen?" another asked.

"It will if we make it happen," Morgani'l said.

"The men are going to stop us."

"They haven't yet and won't if we don't let them."

"That's brave talk, but what if we are beaten into submission?"

"What if we're locked up?"

"What if the High Priest orders us to stop?"

"If the High Priest has something to say we'll hear it. Right now, we need to do two things. One is to talk of how to help each other in speaking about the ritual. But," she sighed, "we also need new Pleasure Ways to show husbands we are still interested in keeping them happy. We have some to suggest." There were soft groans in the room.

"Let's get it over with." Bemla'l said. "Then we can get to what's important."

The Firsts offered Pleasure Ways to start the discussion. In one, wives or husbands were to be smeared with sweet butter or jams and jellies to eventually be licked off—the Biscuit Way. There was the Teacher Way, in which the wife instructed the husband in what he was to do—a woman teaching a man was considered radical by most. An expansion on an earlier one was called The Carriage Way in which the wife would "gallop" in a slow clomping way, around the patio making snorting noises like the coach beasts—considered downright stupid to The Firsts—even though Petra'l told them Metak said it was fun. He liked the unhitching part, that being the removal of her leg. Others, equally messy and ridiculous were offered. Women laughed, snorted derisively or nodded their heads. Some ways got all those responses.

What was really happening was not consideration of Pleasure Ways, but waiting for the men. When would Hunak, Glom, and Gung, and who knew who else, arrive? When enough Pleasure Ways had been created or recycled, the women went into a meeting of their own group to discuss how to advance Death to the Ritual. They talked about how it would be to see a daughter, an adult daughter, walking on her own two legs. Would they see that? Would any woman ever see that? They talked, yearned—and waited for the men.

The men did not come, not that day, nor the next, the last day of that Gathering of Gatherings.

32. SILENCE AND PLOTTING

MONTHS PASSED WITH MEN SAYING nothing, women not asking. Glom, Hunak, Gung treated The Firsts as they had before the declaration, as if nothing out of the ordinary had happened. No word came down from the High Priest, undoubtedly a blow to Phylli'l's belief in the ways of Ploch's priests. She kept trying to agitate against The Declaration but to little effect. Why should women do anything if the men were ignoring it? Deba'l tried to discuss the declaration with Hunak. He'd either say he had to continue considering it or change the subject. They'd discussed ideas, decisions the entire time they'd been married and now when it was most important, to her at least, he withdraw. She repeatedly spoke of this to Solanj'l who was sorry to see her friend so upset. It had to be galling to be cut off from someone with whom you had reciprocal respect. She'd decided to follow Glom's lead and said nothing. She doubted attempting to talk about it would result in anything more than him being dismissive. Their sex activities continued. She occasionally suggested trying a new, or not recently used, Pleasure Way. She disliked offering any of them but absolutely refused to suggest The Carriage Way. Pretending to leap and snort around the patio would be chokingly embarrassing and she hoped Glom would not request it.

They did discuss Glom's Glamour Legs. Sales had slowed, which was to be expected. Men of wealth continued to buy decorative legs for their wives, but not at the rate of first fascination. Men of lesser means had been buying for their wives but that market would slow as well. Glom wanted Solanj'l to think of something new that would increase sales, at least for a time. She suggested he encourage owners of mills to provide all their workwomen with legs. He didn't like that idea. Workwomen might get ideas about being almost as good as women like herself. Solanj'l assumed he'd do it when sales slowed enough.

Morgani'l and Janka'l had made it their responsibility to find a way to get women servants and those who worked in mills to join them at the next Gathering of Gatherings. Janka'l was concerned about them. What would happen if they lost their work, didn't earn money? How would they live?

"How will we live?" Morgani'l asked. "We could find ourselves homeless. We too could face hunger. As well as other awful things."

Awful things. Each of the Firsts spent sleepless nights harrowing herself with grim fantasies. Imprisonment. Torture—even though the concept was hardly understood. Ramprend had not been torturing people in anyone's memory so what that would entail was not known. It was interesting that the word lingered. Did not knowing what it meant make it easier or worse to contemplate? Would they be banished, maybe sent to the People From Across the Lake to have their second leg sawed off? Would they be turned out as termers, having to let men do whatever they wanted to them? They said they'd die rather than suffer any of this. Perhaps the only punishment would be isolation in their husbands' homes, allowed contact only with him. A rich husband could afford to build a prison on the property and keep a wife in it for the rest of her life. That wouldn't be so awful, unless they were allowed nothing with which to occupy their hands and minds. After recently discovering what they could do, that would be intolerable. Solanj'l said she was going to ask Plaka'l for a poison to be carried in a stoppered vial and worn as a pendant at the next Gathering of Gatherings. Each of her friends wanted one as well.

They had to get the women to confront their fears and be willing to overlook them, as much as possible. The shame carried inside needed to be turned against the ritual that had made them the butchered creatures they were, inside as well as out. Gathering leaders were asked to lead their groups in reliving the terror and pain of the ritual, on themselves and their daughters. The layers of not-thinking about what had been done to them needed to be peeled off one by one, leaving raw rage.

* * *

The apparent indifference of the men allowed The Firsts, Bemla'l, and others committed to Death to the Ritual to do what would have been more difficult if they'd been watched, the stockpiling of food. The Gatherings had grown beyond what the Ministry could hold and the Great Hall was now used by most groups. This gave Bemla'l and friends the opportunity to explore the basement. Rooms that looked as if they hadn't been entered in eons could be used for storage. It was so difficult for women to go up and down stairs no one would suspect they would go below even once. After the initial exploration, Bemla'l had an idea for reducing the number of food trips. She attached ropes to baskets to hang over the stair railing. Foodstuffs could be lowered in the baskets. Once a week two women would laboriously go down and hide whatever had been deposited.

They were able to smuggle some food from homes in which there were lax stewards and sympathetic women servants. Deba'l was able to contribute in that she was Hunak's agent for charity. It was good for a Minister to give food, clothing, furniture to the poor. She increased the charity food orders. No one questioned her; it was assumed Hunak was being even more generous than usual. She would also triple or quadruple order for the upcoming Gathering, but they had no way of knowing if it would be enough.

They should have thought about this earlier, perhaps hiding food during previous Gatherings. Having to think this way was so new to them. Women had no training in planning ahead. Going along was what women did, whether rich and idle or poor and bone-tired from working. Solanj'l's mind drifted to Doonak when she had a problem to solve. She hadn't yet gotten past thinking—and feeling—that men had to provide help. But she and her friends were doing so. And they were thinking about problems no man had ever had to solve.

They were worrying when they'd didn't know if there would be a next Gathering of Gatherings. What if it was ordered cancelled? They were busy planning for an event that might not occur.

Petra'l offered a way to stop cancellation. "We could lie. Tell them The Declaration was obviously a silly idea. You know how women are. Silly Simples. They'll let us meet and we'll carry on."

"I hate lying," Janka'l said.

"Even to save Petra'l's daughter's leg?" Morgani'l asked.

Petra'l had given birth to a little beauty, not surprising given her mother. Firsa had her father enthralled, and he didn't know Petra'l had created Firsa's name to denote first with two legs of her own. She wished she could be more obvious about naming her but it was good to know she was able to do that much. Metak was pressuring her to get pregnant again. He wanted a boy. She was avoiding it with Plaka'l's formulation of *Benot*.

Janka'l smiled sadly. "I can lie to save Firsa's leg."

"We'll lie." Morgani'l declared and grinned. "Honesty is good ... but not always."

Her friends nodded. What choice did they have?

33. WHAT IS GOING ON?

TWO THINGS HAPPENED in one week. Glom announced he would run the next Gathering of Gatherings. There was a raid more spectacular than previous ones. Glom's news was somewhat welcome because it meant there would be a Gathering. He was playing coy about it. "It will be a surprise. You gave one to me. Now I will reciprocate." Upon learning this, Morgani'l slit her eyes and said, "How vindictive can he be?" Solanj'l had never seen him vicious, but the only thing she'd ever done that was alarming was being involved with the declaration against sawing off girls' legs.

The Raiders had everyone talking. They'd come in greater numbers than previously, raiding not just on the northern side of the city, but the east as well. They'd taken gears, metal, and wood rods, more harness strapping, and a few of Glom's Glamour Legs as well as Silly Simple costumes from a recreation center—all in an hour's time. A bone hair comb with a cat's head carved on it had been found in one of the mills. How puzzling; men didn't wear hair combs. Glom was in a dither. Something had to be done. Why couldn't guards remain alert? Did Solanj'l have any ideas? Once again she suggested going to the mountains in an attempt to talk with whomever was in power. Once again he questioned her sanity.

Doonak arrived at Glom's house the day following the raid, not to talk about legs but of the Raiders. What he had to say caused Solanj'l's heart to skip beats. He thought at least some

were women. He'd been taking an evening walk near the recreation center and seen three cloaked people do something to
the lock then enter. He followed them in. He could hear talking
and judging from the voice quality he was certain at least
two of them were women. He couldn't understand what they
were saying, even though it sounded somewhat familiar. They
went on the stage, then behind it. He took his boots off and
followed. The Raiders wandered around, at first just looking
at things. Then they came to the closet where costumes were
stored, exclaimed in an excited way, and took several items.
They left and went down the street, were joined by four others
and entered an alley. He waited a bit before following; when
he did, they had vanished.

Solanj'l and he were in the guest room. She poured him a
cup of tea and moved the biscuit plate closer to him.

"It's hard to believe," she said. "What do you make of it?
The Raiders being women."

"I don't know that all of them were."

"Did they walk like women?"

He raised an eyebrow.

She gave a snorting laugh. "How silly of me. Of course they
wouldn't walk like the women of Ramprend. I should have
said girls."

"Maybe the day will come when we'll know the way Ramprend women walk."

It was her turn to raise a questioning eyebrow.

"If your declaration has the effect you want."

She looked at him for a bit, then realized she was rubbing
her hand up and down her leg, her flesh leg, slowly up and
down. It felt like comfort and excitement merged. How would
it feel if Doonak were doing it? She shook her head and clasped
her hands.

"What do you think of the declaration?" she asked.

"I understand why women would make it."

"Do you?"

"It seems fair.... The ritual is brutal."

Solanj'l's heart seemed to pause. Was it really possible there were men who would support Death to the Ritual? She stared at him and he stared back.

"Would you support it? Help us?"

He stood and walked to the window, "You started something extraordinary out there in that workshop of yours."

"It wouldn't have gone as far as it has without your work."

He turned, "Ah, but you are the creator. Ramprend hasn't seen a creator like you in memory. Glom receives the credit for the legs and people say he is unique in our history. Can you imagine what would be said if they knew a woman was responsible for it? They might be stunned into accepting your declaration, into giving up the ritual."

She got up and joined him at the window. "Are you saying we should tell the truth?"

"It would put Glom in a difficult position."

"It would make it impossible for him to support the declaration."

He turned and looked at her, looked at her in a way other men did not, as if he were seeing a person rather than someone's property. There was something else in the look. Longing? Solanj'l had no idea of what was on her face. She was finding it increasingly difficult to remain guarded with him. Ramprendian women generally avoided becoming involved in any way with men who were not their husbands; the consequence of discovery was too great. Occasionally one did hear of a woman found betraying her husband and being sent out of his home to the world of the termers. Her daughters found it difficult to marry a husband of their station. Solanj'l's desire to stop the ritual might put her in a position equal to that of women who dared to be with men not their husbands. Why not? What was she thinking? She couldn't be distracted from Death to the Ritual.

"What does Glom think of the declaration?" Doonak asked.

"I don't know what he thinks. I suppose he's hoping I'll forget it."

"If that's so, he doesn't know you."

She silently agreed with him. "You haven't made clear if you'll support us."

"What do you want done?"

"I don't know. Yet."

She turned and pointed to the table. "Let's have another cup of tea. I'll ring for cakes. Crusak will have finished making today's batch. Wouldn't you like a few of his famous cream cakes?"

"Yes, I would. Who can resist the pleasures of this house?"

34. **RAGE AND FOCUS**

"WHAT DO YOU THINK we should do?" Glom asked. He hadn't been able to finish his plans for taking over the Gathering. He would speak, as would Gung and Hunak. Gung was attempting to convince the High Priest he should be present. Hunak told Glom he'd advised the High Priest to not do so.

"What we do is discuss Pleasure Ways, being good wives and mothers," Solanj'l said. "Why not just let us continue?"

"Now, Solanj'l, I am certain you know the answer to that. We can have no more of that silly idea about doing away with the Beautification Ritual. I do not know who put such a foolish and dangerous idea into your head, but we will have no more of it. A Silly Simple is being prepared to illustrate just how foolish you women have been."

Solanj'l felt something in her chest, like a living thing growing at a fairly fast rate. The surprise! That was the surprise! She felt the thing expanding into her throat, making it hard to breathe. She was going to explode. How dare he? She clamped her teeth together to keep the rage from roaring out of her. How dare he? She got up and started step-dragging around the room—teeth still clinched, breathing heavily—air in, bursting out.

"What are you doing?" he asked. "I would prefer to talk to you sitting down."

She sat and stared at the wall behind him. A Silly Simple. A specific ridicule of specific women. A denigration of her and her friends' desire to stop the mutilation of their own kind.

"Do you have any ideas about what else we can do?" he asked again.

"No."

"You always have ideas."

They sat staring at each other. He appeared patient, waiting for her to create an idea for him to claim. Her mind was flipping from one point to another, not fastening on anything. Legs. Silly Simple. Rage. Women gathering. Pain. Women wanting. The end of her stump hurt which had been happening whenever she felt anger. As if headaches weren't bad enough.

Wait. Perhaps she did have an idea, men's contempt could be used against them. "Is the Silly Simple being performed just for the women?"

"Yes. You are the ones who have to learn what is right." He shook his finger at her, attempting to be playful. "You have been very bad."

She wanted to grab the finger and break it off. Rage keeps growing once you take it as your own. Accepting him as her lord and master was becoming increasingly difficult. And he wasn't bad as a husband. Great Ploch!

"Why not invite the husbands?" she asked. "It will be something new and different for the Gatherings. And it will reinforce your message." It would also be doubly insulting to the women. Feed the rage.

Glom clapped his hands. "Of course. Oh, Solanj'l, I am so blessed to have you as a wife. We men will speak. The Silly Simple. That will do it." He leapt up and started walking around the room. "Having the husbands present will show you how foolish this idea is. The men will tell their wives how ridiculous they are. You will stop being silly and return to what you should do."

He stood, came to where she sat, bent down and kissed her. Could she go on with this until she died—or was ... whatever.

Night after long night her body pawed, mauled, invaded. How had she tolerated it? Could she continue to do so?

"Come," Glom said. He was glowing.

She got up and followed him to the Master's Pleasure Room. She looked at his back and thought of his mindless pursuit of *his* pleasure, of his mindless use of her body—and her mind. Years of living like this. Years of mindlessly going along. She still had the lump in her throat, a lump of anger, choking her. If she didn't need him she could drive a knife into that back. But she did need him. She also needed the anger.

Tonight she'd stay focused on what was being done to her. Very focused. She wanted to remember it all. She wanted to carry it into the Gathering of Gatherings, into the special Silly Simple, into the revolt that would come. She wanted to carry it every day of her life. She needed to hold the rage, swallow it, keep it in her chest and belly blazing away and not let it go. Until the time was right. Only the rage would carry them through what could come.

Glom commenced his pleasure by watching her unlace her bodice. She was wearing only one over a simple chemise that could be pulled over her head—at least she didn't have to unfasten two garments. He stood next to the bed rubbing his hands up and down his thighs. She looked at his thighs, thought of rubbing her own, how good it could feel. Doonak came to mind. No. Focus on here, now—this.

When the bodice was unlaced she smiled and asked if he wished to remove it. No, he wanted her to do so. She slipped it off and let it drop to the floor. He leaned forward and slid his hands under the chemise onto her breasts. He pushed, then squeezed, but not so hard she had to clamp her teeth. He pushed and squeezed, pushed and squeezed. She thought of the cooks working dough. He stopped, grasped the bottom of the chemise, pulled it over her head and tossed it on top of the bodice. He stood and stared at her above-the-waist nakedness.

"Why do we have no children, Solanj'l?"

A clutching in her stomach. She shook her head. "I don't know. I guess it's not yet a time to be so blessed."

"I find it strange that none of The Firsts have children."

"Petra'l has a daughter. Don't you remember?"

"Ah, yes, Petra'l. That is true. I did forget. Even though she's sometimes too friendly with men at dinners she is a good wife. I have never heard Metak complain."

"It will happen, Glom. When the time is right." *May it never be right.*

He told her to stand up and remove her skirt. "Pull it over your head," he said when she had unbuttoned it. She did, which was a bother, all that fabric to manipulate. And it left her blind. It was so much easier to slip if off lying down. She almost fell twice. She stood in her underskirt of the same fine white material as her chemise. He put his hand under it and ran it on her abdomen, down to the delta and then moved it first over the flesh leg, then the wood one.

"Take off that skirt. I want to see you in the leg with *my* Glamour Legs on it."

She step-dragged to the cabinet where the legs were stored and removed the one he wanted, returned to the bed and sat down to unlace the pants that held the plain leg on her. She leaned back against the headboard and pulled it off. It was the first one she'd created that she could more or less comfortably sit in as well as stand. She propped it against the bedside table and started to put on the one with legs painted on it. She looked at Glom who was watching her intently. She realized he'd never seen her put on a leg. Could there be a Pleasure Way involving that? She inserted her flesh foot in the leg-pants with the wood leg attached and pulled them up to the stump which she eased into the wood leg, then pulled the pants to her waist and laced them closed. She looked at Glom. He told her to stand and walk around the room.

"I have never seen you walk before, walk without your clothing," he said.

She did the hesitant step-drag walk back and forth at the end of the bed, stopped, smiled and struck a pose she thought Petra'l would admire, left hand on hip, head back, right hand feigning the covering of her breasts. Glom laughed and lunged. He grabbed her by the waist, spun around, lifted and dumped her on the bed, her head narrowly missed the headboard. He leaned over her and started unlacing the pants.

"This leg is my favourite," he said. "I wonder who painted it. It's fine work. I'm surprised those people can do work like that." He eased the leg off her and put it against the wall. He threw off his clothes, dropped on top of her and went to work on producing his pleasure, kneading her breasts, then rubbing her stump.

"Oh, Solanj'l, I so love doing this," he said after a few minutes.

He started licking her Pretty Little Spot and pinching her right nipple. It hurt, it always hurt. Where had he gotten the idea that it felt good to have part of your body pinched? She'd like to pinch something of his.

"The pinching hurts, Glom."

He stopped, jerked up and looked at her. "You've never said anything before. I thought you liked it."

"I may be particularly sensitive tonight. It may hurt more, but it always hurts."

"I see. You should have said something."

She remembered a time shortly after he'd taken her as his wife. He'd rammed himself in and she'd cried out. With time she learned to relax to a degree and disappear into her own head, but as a new bride his sudden entrances hurt like nothing she'd ever known with the exception of the time she broke her wrist. And of course nothing hurt more than the clutching, gnawing, stabbing pain in her absent leg lying outside the city in a trash heap, slowly rotting or being devoured by wild animals. She couldn't help but flinch a bit. He'd asked her what was wrong and she'd told him. He said she should go to a healer to determine if there was something wrong with her.

Wives were to receive pleasure from their husbands' entrances into their bodies. She had not complained again; going along was the better course.

He put his hands on her breasts and moved them in circles. This was not flat out painful, but it certainly was annoying. As much as she hated having him lick her she thought doing so to her nipples might be better than this swirl action. She suggested it and he went at it. It would be so much easier to go away to the field with Spirry. No, she needed to hang onto the rage.

He kissed her mouth then said he wanted to see her standing. She sat up, wiggled to the edge of bed, twisted around, grasped the headboard and stood, almost falling as she finished the twisting turn to face him.

"I've never seen you standing on one leg," he said. "You can't move can you?"

"I could hop if I held onto something but it would soon become tiring."

"Yes. You can't go far without two legs."

No. She couldn't go far.

"But that is the way it is to be for women. It is our tradition. It has become what we all desire, will continue to desire."

Even though her leg was stronger than it had been before Glom's Glamour Legs, she found it tiring to stand, muscles were being asked to do something different from what they were used to. She asked him if she could sit or lie down.

"Here," he said. "Let me help you." He put his hands on her waist and put her down onto her stomach. He lifted her up so she was supporting herself on her elbows and one knee. She found it difficult to remain in position as he inserted himself and moved back and forth. She wouldn't have been able to if he weren't holding her waist.

"Ah," Glom said, "this is good, is it not?"

She found it ridiculous, stupid and uncomfortable—at best. She murmured a yes, then clamped her teeth together to keep from screaming with rage.

35. LIKE NO OTHER GATHERING

"IT'S NOT LIKE A GATHERING." The Firsts heard variations of this from the first hour. Gung was officiously running hither and thither, acting as if he had originated and run all previous Gatherings, as well as created Glom's Glamour Legs. Glom was officiously running hither and thither acting the same, which made some sense in that he was closer to having created the legs. Hunak put in an appearance at the first formal meeting to give greetings and sing the praises of Glom and Gung. Deba'l looked at him as if he were someone she didn't know. She'd said little about him for several weeks.

Phylli'l was present with her acolytes and Lumok, which annoyed Gung but there was nothing he could do about it. Phylli'l should not have been in attendance as she neither led nor was a member of a Gathering, having left Casanj'l's, but it was decided to ignore her—as much as possible. At the first opportunity she said to Solanj'l, "I hear your husband has finally put you in your place and that will be very obvious with the special Silly Simple." She produced a smirk. Solanj'l had never before wanted to hit a woman, but the urge came on her with this fool sitting before her. There was some satisfaction in looking down at her. She said nothing and swung past, giving Phylli'l's chair a jolt with her wood leg. She was getting rather good at anger.

She later saw Phylli'l talking to Glom. It looked as if she were trying to flirt with him. Where was Petra'l? She'd love to see those eyelashes and that insipid smile. Glom was smiling po-litely. He'd told Solanj'l that he'd had the opportunity to offer marriage to Phylli'l but decided against it in that she seemed so stiff. Solanj'l had to give him credit for being gracious.

Phylli'l and the Daughter-haters, as The Firsts had come to think of them, were busily attempting to convince the attendees of the evilness of even thinking of doing away with the Beauti-fication Ritual. It *was* the way in which women showed their true worth. Nothing, absolutely nothing should subvert it.

"Women with two legs are of no use to men. They wouldn't get husbands."

"Women are to bring pleasure to men. A stump enhances the husband's pleasure."

"Without a stump a woman has nothing to give a man."

"It is the will of Ploch."

"Without a stump women are nothing, nothing at all."

Morgani'l, who'd been grumbling about the stupidity of some women, told The Firsts she'd asked Phylli'l if stumps were so wonderful why not saw off both legs, like in the Land Across the Lake? Phylli'l had jerked back in her chair and said, "We are not barbarians."

Gung gave the first speech. They feared he'd want to make several. He licked his lips and praised the women of Ramprend for "their unwavering devotion to their husbands and children. Nay, their incredible unwavering devotion to husbands. Think on the beauty of Pleasure Ways. I dare say there are no other people in the entire world who have their women willingly give up a leg and then create new ways to bring pleasure to their husbands." After several lip-licking repetitions of that theme he admonished, "Do not allow new ways of thinking to carry you away. Do not be deceived by silly ideas. Tradition and the ways of Ploch are to be maintained. To the glory of Ploch."

"To the glory of Ploch," the women mumbled.

Gung left off praising the virtues of one-legged women and began the repetitious praising of Glom and his Glamour Legs.

Such imagination and ingenuity. Such foresight. Such understanding of women. Glom glanced at Solanj'l. She smiled at
him. Was he feeling guilty for taking credit for something he
wouldn't have thought of in a hundred years? Doubtful.

Glom's speech was a surprise only in that it was short. He
had not asked Solanj'l for assistance in constructing it so she
had no idea of what he would say. It was a condensation of
his previous utterings. There was a new ending, however. "We
men of Ramprend are grateful for the women of Ramprend.
They have served us well for generations and we know they will
continue to serve us as we pass our traditions to our sons and
daughters. Our daughters are here to learn the truth, beauty,
and joy of being a Ramprend woman. Nothing will be allowed
to draw us from what is good and true and right."

Great Ploch, Solanj'l thought, he sounds like Phylli'l.

* * *

The daughters had been a matter of debate among The Firsts.
Were they to be part of the Gathering of Gatherings? Petra'l
had immediately said yes, not wanting to be separated from
Firsa. Morgani'l wondered about putting them at risk if there
was an attack. Solanj'l declared they were at risk no matter
where they were and those perilously close to the Ritual needed
protection. Janka'l said she could see both sides. Deba'l also
could, but agreed with Solanj'l.

Glom was delighted with the idea of daughters being present.
Even though their ages would prevent them from attending the
Silly Simple, they would hear the talk of how wrong the women
had been to think the Beautification Ritual should be stopped,
and they would also be introduced to the joys of discussing
the bringing of pleasure to future husbands through the use of
Glom's Glamour Legs. Solanj'l didn't ask why they couldn't
see a Silly Simple but could hear about Pleasure Ways. Hunak
had no objection and Gung also thought it a wonderful idea,
the very thing he would have suggested if those clever little
wives hadn't said it first.

The girls arrived aflutter. Being allowed to engage in women's matters before they lost their legs was so exciting they were beside themselves with pleasure. Well, not all; some wore a look Solanj'l recognized. She could feel her face settle into it, the look she'd worn knowing her leg was going to be sawed off and she would no longer run with Spirry. The Firsts were known to the girls; most were in awe of these women who had created the Gatherings and Pleasure Ways. They really wanted to meet Solanj'l. She was so pretty. They so hoped she would speak to them. Maybe she'd tell them about all the beautiful Glamour Legs she had. It was said she had the largest collection in Ramprend, in the whole world. Of course that was only right when her husband had created them.

Petra'l was originally put in charge of the girls. She was the youngest, definitely the most playful, and she had a little daughter of her own. She didn't know what to do with them.

"Get them to talk." Morgani'l said. "They are given little chance to do that, other than about clothing and getting husbands. Let them talk about what they want. Ask them questions to get them started."

Petra'l looked into the distance for a few moments, then said, "I don't know if I can do that. I'm not a questioning person. I blurt, not question."

Morgani'l laughed. "I guess that's right. We could make a list for you."

"You can do it," Petra'l said.

"We need your liveliness, your sense of fun."

The two of them led the first meeting after an opening statement from Solanj'l. "We are happy to have you join us at this Gathering of Gatherings and hope you find it exciting. You, of course, know about the wooden legs." She lifted her skirt to show the leg of legs, "This is my most special one." The girls pointed and oohed and aahed. "You probably look forward to having legs of your own. We hope to give you ones even better than this. I am now going to let Morgani'l and Petra'l lead you in talking about your hopes and wants."

Fashion—skirts, bodices, fabrics, slippers—the usual topic of female desire was used to start the girls talking, but after some minutes Morgani'l abruptly changed it all by asking "How would you like to live as you grow older?" There was no response. The girls turned to each other and looked confused. This should have been anticipated. How could you answer a question girls were not to ask, thought incapable of asking? Women weren't supposed to have thoughts about wants other than the usual. But it had happened with The Firsts and then the women attending Gatherings. Deba'l had said after the last Gathering of Gatherings she thought seeds of dissatisfaction had been lying in women and girls for a long time, just waiting for something to bring them to life. Were the seeds in these girls? Would they come alive?

Morgani'l took another approach. "What do you like best about your lives?" The answers were to be expected. The girls would have gone on and on about bodices and necklaces and the dear little purses to be found in shops if Morgani'l hadn't cut in. "What do you like beside fashion?"

Silence.

Morgani'l turned to Petra'l and asked, "What did you like when you were a girl?"

Petra'l looked around at the girls and smiled ruefully. "I loved clothing, ribbons, purses and jewellery. I still do, but I wish I had wanted something more. Dressing up and being pretty isn't enough." She paused. "I wish I had wanted two legs ... and I wish I'd tried to keep mine."

There were scowls; puzzlement was increasing. Why wish for something that couldn't be? That was just dumb. A girl close to "beautification" said in a voice touched with anger, "I heard about doing away with the Ritual. Are you going to help us keep our legs? Both of them?"

Petra'l picked up Firsa and held her close, looked at Morgani'l then back at the girls. "We'd like to." Then she started to cry.

No one had anticipated what happened. The majority of girls started to cry, some silently, others sobbing. It was as if a shared nerve had been struck. The seeds of dissatisfaction were there. Morgani'l and Petra'l looked at each other, wondering how they could use this. The crying continued but there were those not in agreement with keeping both legs.

"That's not right."

"Ploch wants us to have only one leg."

"It's our tradition."

"How would we give pleasure to men?"

The crying lessened. Girls wiped faces and blew noses. They looked around. The mention of men and giving pleasure to them recalled them to their lessons for being a woman. You could not please a man if you had two legs. Were these Firsts saying they should live without men? Women couldn't do that. Surely The Firsts didn't mean that.

"Why must women be one-legged for men to have pleasure?" Morgani'l asked.

The answers were some form of because that is the way it is. Some mentioned Ploch, but the majority position was because it was tradition. There would be no Ramprend if you didn't follow tradition. Ramprend had to have the Beautification Ritual. Without the Beautification Ritual, Ramprend wouldn't be Ramprend.

"I don't know how well that went," Morgani'l said later.

"We forgot what it was to be young," Janka'l said.

"But we were so terrified before it happened," Solanj'l said. "Why wouldn't they be overjoyed at the thought of not facing that fear? And the outcome."

"I think it should not have surprised us," Deba'l said. "They have not known what it is to lose a leg. Nor have they known the joy of almost regaining one."

Morgani'l and Petra'l were charged with working out ways to deal with the girls as the days went by. If they asked their mothers to let them go home to get away from the mad idea of The Firsts, the mothers might want to leave as well.

"We could be foiled by those we seek to help," Solanj'l said.

They got help from one of the girls, Majana, who told Morgani'l she didn't know women could think the way The Firsts did. She'd never hoped. Morgani'l, not given to touching people, wanted to hug her but resisted the urge, sensing it would not be appreciated. Majana said she would talk to girls she knew, try to get them to think about life with two legs, and avoid talking about no husbands.

"I think I've meet another Solanj'l," Morgani'l told The Firsts.

36. HUMILIATION LEADS TO...

THE SILLY SIMPLE WAS HELD the second evening, the apparent goal being to so demoralize the women that they'd return to what they were supposed to do at Gatherings: create more Pleasure Ways. Why the men thought demoralized women would be eager to do so was not understood. The Firsts did not ask.

"This may be the best thing that could have happened," Deba'l said. "Men seem to have no idea women have changed and will no longer readily accept ridicule. We may be temporarily downhearted but it won't last." She was only partially right. Downheartedness was not what the women experienced.

Men stood, with women standing or sitting, outside the auditorium waiting for the call to performance. The men talked with enthusiasm; the women, however, were quiet for the most part. The men said this was good; it indicated the women knew they were going to get what they deserved. Phylli'l, acting as if she were the one who had created and was in charge of the Silly Simple, moved from group to group, encouraging the men in this thinking. Morgani'l reported with satisfaction that men were looking at her as if her presumption in talking to them was as bizarre as the idea of doing away with the Beautification Ritual. Also, many women were looking at Phylli'l with distaste, or even loathing.

The time to begin came and passed. There was a problem. All the women who usually played the female roles had become ill.

It was strange that only the female members of the troupe had fallen to a stomach condition. Men were being asked to take female parts and they were not about to do that—self-respecting men did not play at being women. Glom appealed to their sense of duty, this was after all to show women how silly they had been. The men set their mouths and shook their heads. Gung appealed to their love of Ploch. The men, apparently having insufficient love for their God, continued to refuse. Glom asked Deba'l to speak to the actors. The wife of the Minister Second Only to the First would be heard.

"Glom," she said, "you know they aren't going to hear what I say. If a man of your position and eloquence can't convince them, I will not be able to do so."

He wanted to know when Hunak would arrive. She didn't know.

"Why not have women here play the parts?" Solanj'l asked. "I think some of us would volunteer."

"An excellent suggestion," Deba'l said. "I'll volunteer."

She and Solanj'l looked at each other, knowing the other's thoughts.

"I'll volunteer," Solanj'l said. "If I may make a suggestion, have everyone come into the theater, explain the difficulty, ask for women to help and while they're learning what it is they're to do, the troupe can provide some kind of entertainment, singing or juggling. Promise a longer show."

Though this meant the troupe would have to be given extra pay, Glom heaved a sigh of relief and went to where the actors were huddled together in their stubbornness and told them the solution had been found. After several declarations of "Impossible," the actors agreed and the plan was set into operation. Two of the actors and the manager instructed The Firsts, Bemla'l, and two other women in what they were to do and say. This was not difficult. The Silly Simples were essentially the same story over and over, not much coaching was needed.

When the women were left alone for a few moments, Bemla'l

said, "I hope we can make this as awful as possible."

"Look incredibly abject," Deba'l said. "We want optimum upset."

Laugher, occasional roars of it, came from men during the opening performances. The male actors had hit upon the idea of showing how silly women could be by acting out their perceptions of women. Apparently they thought if they told the audience what they were doing they wouldn't actually be playing women. Female laughter could be heard from the audience but it was weak. Other than the Phylli'l contingent, women were finding it increasingly difficult to laugh at being made fools of. After prodding from husbands, more female laughter was heard, but it sounded unreal, as if the women opened their mouths and uttered high-pitched huffs.

The Silly Simples were finally ready for presentation. Female laughter declined when Janka'l fell on her back and flopped around trying to roll over and get up. Deba'l crawled to her and tried to help her up. Morgani'l and Bemla'l enacted a fight over a man both wanted for a husband, shrieking and pulling hair until their chairs got tangled up and they toppled to the floor. Solanj'l peeked out past the curtain covering the space beside the stage. The men wore eager, amused faces. Most female faces, however, were drawn and hard. Eyes were being cut from side to side as if looking for someone with whom to share a flash of sympathy. Or anger.

It was time for the grand finale, the one Glom thought would turn women back into who they had been before The Firsts came forth with that fool declaration against the Beautification Ritual. He was running around declaring how well the evening was going; and he wasn't even taking credit for having solved the problem. "I am so blessed," he declared. "I have a Pretty Little Wife who has ideas." He grabbed and kissed her, right in front of everyone off stage, pulled back and smiled as if the world were truly a wonderful place. Solanj'l felt rage roiling in her guts—and was glad.

The original idea for the special Silly Simple was to illustrate how absurd it was for women to have two legs. Glom had stopped that; it could carry the message women shouldn't have wood legs. Women had to fail at something else. Creating and running a business would be just the thing. Solanj'l had the key female role. She and her partners in humiliation knew she had to do it but she wasn't certain if she could keep the rage in check as she made herself into a fool by acting out something akin to what she'd actually done. In the role of Giddi'l she officiously gave orders to her husband's steward and other men who became involved with her project, which was to create a chair women could wheel themselves. She stabbed her right index finger in the air or flapped her hands up and down while shrieking directions that made no sense, thoroughly confusing the men, who would gather at the side of the stage from time to time in an attempt to interpret what she wanted. This included shrieking, flapping their hands and pointing fingers at Giddi'l that brought roars of laughter from men in the audience. All Giddi'l ideas were failures. She tried pawing the ground with her foot in an attempt to propel herself forward, resulting in her barely moving at all, almost falling out of the chair and ending with her throwing herself against the back of it, panting and waving her hands in front of her face to cool down. A roar from the audience, at least the men. She suggested an animal pull her, as they did coaches. It was obvious coach animals couldn't be used, so a make-believe cat from the mountains was brought in, which tried to attack her, salvation coming when a man shot it with a make-believe arrow. The final solution offered by her involved having knobs on the wheels. When they neared the bottom of the wheels and she was bent forward she fell splat onto the floor, breaking her fall with her arms. She was hauled up and dumped into her chair. She tried again, then again until she curled into a fetal position and collapsed into wailing sobs. When one of the men tried to pick her up she screamed like a terrified child, "I want my husband." The husband came striding in demanding to know what all the fuss was about. Giddi'l awkwardly got to one knee. With one hand she kept herself from keeling over, the other she put in front of her face and dropped her head.

"I have been so foolish, husband," she said through gulps. (Calls of yes from men and Phylli'l followers.) "I will never again do such a foolish thing as to believe I could think like you. Only men can think. I am *sorry*."

The husband looked down on her with contempt. "I hope you've learned your lesson, you foolish thing."

"Oh, yes, husband. Please forgive me."

"You have behaved worse than a child. You shall be punished."

"Yes, husband." (Clapping from the male audience.)

"I will be merciful." ("No," called out some men.) "I'll beat you only once, not for five days as you deserve. Crawl over here so I can administer the beating."

"Yes, husband." Giddi'l crawled.

Solanj'l thought, if he hits me, I will attack him.

The steward presented the husband with a rod that he raised as the curtain closed. The husband popped back on the stage, threw his arms up in a gesture of frustration and said, "What would they do without us?"

Men leapt to their feet. There was clapping and cheering. Solanj'l could see from the side of the stage where she'd crawled that women were not joining the men in their enthusiasm. Husbands were urging their wives to clap, which they did as if their arms and hands were barely able to move. With the exception of the Phylli'ls, the women's faces were blank. They looked as wooden as the legs they wore.

Glom helped Solanj'l into the chair with knobs. "Listen to the audience. I must acknowledge their appreciation. They're calling for me. You must come with me." He rolled her onto center stage and motioned for the curtain to be drawn up. The men continued to clap and started to call out, "Glom, Glom, the Glamour Man." Solanj'l glanced to the side and saw Deba'l

and Hunak standing at the edge of the stage just out of audience sight. Deba'l was smiling at her, holding her hands out
clapping. Hunak was clapping also but Solanj'l didn't know
how to interpret what was on his face. He wore a smile that
could be interpreted as amused. But at what, and by whom?

37. THE DAY AFTER

CONGRATULATIONS TO US, the men of Ramprend thought. Women had been put in their place, shown how nonsensical it was for them to have ideas. You could see how shamed they were. Those faces. Their silence. Oh yes, they knew they'd been wrong. It was good the women actors had not come, and how very clever of Glom to have used his wife as the major Silly Simple. All The Firsts had been so humble when it was over. They'd all come on the stage and stood with their heads down. Ah, yes. The Silly Simple was a success. Glom reported all this to Solanj'l and said he and Gung decided it was not necessary for them to be in the Hall any longer. He shook his finger at her and said, "I don't know what came over you with that silly declaration, but now you can return to what you're supposed to do, think of ways to advance Glom's Glamour Legs."

The men of Ramprend were wrong. Shame was not the dominant feeling. Anger filled the Great Hall. "I had doubts when you proposed stopping the Beautification Ritual, but now I will do what you ask." The woman standing before Solanj'l reminded her of her mother in age and solid build. Her spirit was not that of Luranj'l, who went through life like a bad actor, reading lines and assuming positions with no feeling conveyed. The eyes of this woman, Hopa'l, held a smouldering anger. There were others like her. The women could talk of nothing but the Silly Simple.

"I just wanted to cry."

"Cry? I wanted to hit someone."

"How dare Glom make fun of Solanj'l."

"It was so awful."

"I used to laugh at Silly Simples. I'm ashamed of that."

Anger simmered, bubbled, almost ready for the eruption that would come later that day.

Solanj'l wanted to run away and hide. She wasn't capable of leading these women into a battle that could endanger their welfare, perhaps their lives. Doing away with what made Ramprend Ramprend. How absurd. Better to hide. Well, she was hidden. She was standing in a closet, listening to women pass by, hoping no one would open the door and find her. How ridiculous she'd seem standing there looking at brooms, mops, dusting rags, and buckets. It smelled dry and dusty. This room that held cleaning supplies needed to be cleaned and she, a First, some said the First Among Firsts, was hiding in it. Why had she been brought to this? Solanj the girl might understand what she was attempting. Solanj'l the woman wasn't certain. A feeling of futility had dropped on her after the performance last night. She felt the failure of Giddi'l with her "silly" desire to make something new. It was difficult to breathe. Too much dust in her nose. Too much trouble in her heart. Had Solanj the girl hidden in closets trying to avoid the mutilation? She didn't think so. She didn't remember doing it. Thinking of that time always brought a clutching in her stomach and the stab of an approaching headache. And now the end of her stump started to itch and throb.

Don't remember. Act. Open the door.

What would she say to anyone out there? I'm looking for a mop? Why would one of The Firsts be looking for a mop? She gave a snorting little laugh. How silly she was being. Being a Giddi'l, a Silly Simple. She realized tears were running down her cheeks. She really was scared. Very scared. And so sad. A band was tightening around her head, right through her eyebrows. She pulled a handkerchief from her pocket, wiped her cheeks and blew her nose. She had to step out of this space. She needed to move. It might prevent the headache from gripping her.

Morgani'l was walking past. "Looking for something?"

"Peace."

"Are you all right?"

"I feel the start of a headache."

"Bantant recently found an herb for headache. I'll have some brought here. It might help."

* * *

Women looked to the right, to the left. A babble of talk broke out. Why hadn't they been told this before? They needed clothing. They needed to arrange for their children. They needed…. They needed to do many things. They couldn't stay here an indefinite period. What about food?

They'd been brought to this confusion by Deba'l's announcement, "We will not be leaving today. We will stay until the men agree to Death to the Ritual."

She let the talking go on for a time, then tapped her knuckles on the table until silence fell. She explained there were facilities for cleaning clothing. For those who had gone home each day, additional garments would be provided. Food was stored in the basement. Stewards and other servants could take care of sons.

The women continued in their disbelief. What The Firsts were proposing just wasn't possible. How could they think staying in the Hall would bring the desired result? This was absurd.

Solanj'l stepped to the edge of the stage on which she had been humiliated the previous night and held up her arms. I look like I'm trying to imitate a priest, she thought. "We know this sounds unbelievable. Why weren't you told? Why weren't you allowed to get ready? Stop. Think. Could we believe that each and every woman in the Gatherings would not tell someone? Surely the Phylli'ls would talk. And perhaps some of the rest of you would have told a mother or sister who is not in a Gathering. Perhaps even a husband. We couldn't tell you."

One of the Phylli'ls had herself rolled toward the exit. Bemla'l blocked her way.

"Anyone who wants to leave will be able to do so," Solanj'l called out, "but not ... yet."

"You can't keep us here," Phylli'l roared and started toward her follower.

Hopa'l joined Bemla'l in blocking the door, a formidable pair in their quiet, arms crossed over the chest sturdiness. The babble of talk and complaint continued until Bemla'l shouted, "Be silent and listen."

"There is something you need to know," Solanj'l called out.

Body movements and eye-shifting said too much was happening. Last night, now this. Should they listen? Leave? What was it they were supposed to do?

"What I have to say might help you decide what to do," Solanj'l said.

Quieting in the room.

Here goes, Solanj'l thought and said slowly, "The Great God Ploch did *not* order the Beautification Ritual. Nowhere in *The Book of Ploch* is there *any* mention of the Beautification Ritual."

Silence—louder than the shouted questions and accusations that would follow. She looked at the stunned faces, remembering the day she'd sat for hours trying to absorb what she'd learned. There was not even a suggestion of the Beautification Ritual in the book. It was also true that Ploch had no specific sex, never being referred to as he or him.

"Liar," It came from Phylli'l. "She's lying."

"Read the book," Solanj'l shouted and held up a slim volume, a copy of which probably had never before seen by many in the room, Ploch being an author not much read in Ramprend. Kracak had searched closets, then gone to the Temple to get the copy she'd read and now held up.

"We have a copy for each Gathering leader," she continued. "We suggest you take turns reading to each other. It's a small book. It won't take long."

After The Firsts had recovered from the initial shock of Solanj'l's revelation to them, copies from family and friends had been borrowed, requiring searches like the ones in Glom's home. It would have been easier to ask Gung for copies, but he could have become suspicious—assuming priests knew their holy book any better than the other citizens of Ramprend.

"This is an abomination," screamed Phylli'l.

"The abomination," shouted Morgani'l, "is that we have been lied to. For Ploch's sake, read the book."

A day is not a long time but much can happen. Solanj'l had worried that women learning something of such magnitude would be stunned into inaction. That was true for only a few hours—then eruption. Anger spewed as the readings of *The Book of Ploch* concluded. They wanted Gung. He had to explain the lie. The High Priest had to explain the lie. Deba'l said no, bringing even one man in would be a great mistake. The women talked and talked. There had to be an explanation. There must be another *Book of Ploch*. They were informed the copy Solanj'l had was from the Temple. The books they'd just read were all the same. The Firsts had checked each one. Phylli'l declared this could not be. Even women not associated with her agreed. It could not be true. No. Something was very wrong. More explanation was needed. They needed to hear from leaders, Hunak, Gung, the High Priest.

"Why?" Morgani'l challenged them. "Leaders have lied to you. Or ... they don't know. How can you trust leaders who lie or don't know what their holy book says?"

No ready answer for that. It was all too confusing. More time was needed for consideration. They needed to hear from Hunak and Gung. They needed to hear from their husbands.

"Why?" from Morgani'l again.

Petra'l stood next to her. She had gained in respect with motherhood. She was the one First who had a child, a girl. Her desire to stop the Ritual gave her special status, particularly given her reputation for being a light-hearted lover of fashion and parties. She was considered by many men, and women, the epitome of what a Ramprend woman should be—if you overlooked the sometimes too flirtatious behaviour.

She held up her hand. "As you know I have a baby girl.... She is so beautiful.... Do you know what I most like to watch her do?" She paused and those close to her saw tears glazing her eyes. "I like to watch her wave her arms and kick her legs in the air. And smile. She is so happy when she can wave her arms and kick her little legs. So happy. I want to know that all her life she can lie down and kick both those legs if she wants to. I want her to walk down the street beside me without having to drag a wooden thing to do it. I want her to run." She motioned toward Solanj'l. "Solanj'l often talks about the joy she felt when she ran as a girl. She would like to run now. I would too. All of The Firsts would. I think all of you would." A pause so long there was rustling in the room. "We can't run. Running and jumping and dancing were taken from us when our legs were sawed off and thrown away. I ... do not ... want Firsa's ... leg sawed off." Tears flowed through gulping sobs. Morgani'l put her arms around her and held her close.

Bemla'l, with the help of friends, climbed on a chair and called out, "Death to the Ritual. Who is with The Firsts? Who will stay in the Great Hall? I will."

Silence again, then one, two, three, then more and more women got to their feet and yelled, "I will." Solanj'l would remember the pattern made by the standing and the seated. Death to the Ritual standing on two legs, the tradition-bound, the fearful, the self-haters sitting. A sad and glorious sight, like a dead field sending up hopeful shoots, as happened each spring, even in arid Ramprend.

The Phylli'ls and others demanded to be released. The great doors were opened and they went out, some yelling about what The Firsts intended. There was so much freneticism about them the few deputies standing around did not take them seriously and none tried to enter. Phylli'l continued her accusations that all who stayed in the Hall were an abomination and unnatural. Just before she was rolled out by a female servant, Morgani'l stood in front of her, leaned down, put her hands on the armrests of the chair and said, "You think sawing off legs is natural? You are a fool, a pus-filled sore on the ass of Ramprend." Those who heard her were initially stunned. Women didn't talk that way. After a second or two they erupted into laughter. "Pus-filled sore on the ass of Ramprend" became the way to describe anyone or thing that was troublesome. Petra'l was particularly fond of saying it.

Casanj'l was among the last to leave. "I don't know what is going to happen to you," she said to Solanj'l. "The mortification of having you for a sister may kill me." She struck her chest with her open hand. "Our parents. Have you no consideration for our parents?"

"They had none for me, or you, when they had our legs sawed off."

Casanj'l opened her mouth then snapped it shut it. It was the last time Solanj'l spoke to her.

The doors were closed and barred. All other doors on the outside had been barred and the delivery platform raised so no one could use it to enter the building. Few windows existed in the walls facing outward. Their shutters was closed and barred. They could be breached but it was the best that could be done. Janka'l had wondered if they would have to hit men on the head with something if they tried to get in. "Probably," was Morgani'l's response. She later asked Solanj'l if she could hit Glom on the head. "Maybe with a leg." This sent them into gales of laughter but gave rise to the idea of using legs as weapons. The Great Hall was as secure as they could make it.

The Firsts, Bemla'l, and Hopa'l rode the platform to the roof and hung a banner from the effigies that ringed it. Bemla'l broke into raucous laughter. "The fathers of Ramprend, who decreed our mutilation, will carry our message around their necks."

THE MUTILATION OF GIRLS WILL STOP

ALL WOMEN WILL BE TWO-LEGGED

WE WILL NOT LEAVE HERE UNTIL YOU AGREE

38. THE MEN COME

WHY IT TOOK SO LONG for the men to respond was never understood. The Firsts expected at least Hunak, Glom, and Gung to be at the door shortly after the banner was hung, but no one appeared until the morning of the next day. A thundering on the door. The Firsts went to the roof.

"Have you accepted our demand?" Solanj'l called down.

Hunak, Glom, Gung, the Sheriff and what looked like all his deputies were standing on or around the steps. Hunak, Gung, and Glom went down the steps and looked up. How shocked they must be. Their Ramprend casually and repeatedly raided, and now these women attempting to destroy what was held so dear, what made Ramprend what it was. Were they scared?

"Have you gone entirely mad?" Glom shouted up. His face was red and Solanj'l could see his eyes were opened very wide and bulging, the way they were when he was angered by some foolishness of one who worked for him.

"I want our daughter whole," she called down.

"Daughter? Are you carrying my child?"

"No. If I ever do I want her whole."

He turned to Hunak and said something. Bantant and Metak were coming toward the Hall. A gathering of husbands of The Firsts. Doam would undoubtedly arrive soon.

"Let us sit down and talk," Hunak said.

"We can talk," Deba'l said, "but we will stay up here and you down there."

"Deba'l," Hunak said in the way of a man disappointed and sad, a tone Solanj'l had never heard him use with his wife. She felt sadness settle around her like a shroud. If she was feeling this, what of Deba'l, who had appeared to have as good a life as a maimed woman could with a man who wanted her that way.

"Solanj'l," Glom shouted. "I want you home."

"I'm sorry, Glom" she said, surprised at the sorry, "but I can't come out. Not until we have assurances our daughters won't have their legs sawed off."

"It is the Beautification Ritual."

"I wonder if you'd call it that, if it were done to you."

"Petra'l," Metak called out, "get down here right now. Get Firsa and come with me. I will not have you acting this way. I have been far too lenient. Get down here."

Petra'l looked down at him with her head cocked, as if questioning something. She said to the women with her, "That man is a bully. Why didn't I see that?"

"You did, but you didn't want to admit it," Morgani'l said.

"Petra'l," Metak yelled. "Did you hear me? Get down here."

"No! Not until I know Firsa will not have her leg sawed off."

The men looked at each other and formed a circle. Doam had joined them and after looking at the women on the roof, dropped his head to listen to those around him. The women looked at each other. They did not form a circle; their organizing talk had been done.

"It's a beautiful day," Janka'l said. "We should encourage the others to come up here and enjoy nice days. It will become oppressive inside."

"Deba'l," Hunak called up, "if I could just have a private time with you."

"No, Hunak, I'm afraid that can't happen. We have agreed to not come out until the girls of Ramprend are safe."

"Safe?" yelled Gung. "What do you mean? The girls of

Ramprend have always been safe. We keep them safe."

Solanj'l so wanted to tell Hunak there would be no more communication until that slimy little man was removed but knew she could not. He and perhaps the High Priest would have to be involved in a decision of this consequence.

"Having your leg sawed off is not safe," Solanj'l called down.

"Solanj'l," Glom said in a despairing way.

"Ploch is very displeased," Gung called up. "You women will be punished."

"Have you read *The Book of Ploch*?" Deba'l asked.

He said nothing and she repeated the question. He sputtered and mumbled something the women couldn't hear.

"If you have you know there is no order for the Beautification Ritual. No mention of it at all. Nothing is said about sawing off girls' legs. Nothing, in any part of *The Book of Ploch*."

Several men said, "What?" in unison and all looked puzzled, with the exception of Hunak. He knows, Solanj'l thought. He's always known. She looked at Deba'l whose face seemed to have slipped down, making her look like an old woman. This was betrayal that could not be ignored.

"Deba'l," Glom said, "this can't be true. Why are you saying it?"

"Why have you become a liar?" Gung added.

"For Ploch's sake, read the book," Solanj'l said in a voice filled with contempt.

The deputies and those who'd gathered out of curiosity were in urgent discussion. What madness was being uttered? Glom and Gung started waving their arms and talking to Hunak who stood like a pillar. Solanj'l could imagine him as one of the effigies the women were standing between. How many ministers had known the truth? Did they pass the knowledge to their successors? Glom and Gung stepped back almost in unison. Hunak must have said something quite startling. The truth about Ploch? The men looked up at the women.

"What you say does not matter," Gung said in as much an

authoritarian voice as he could muster. "It is the tradition of Ramprend and it has been accepted by Ploch. Women are to serve men."

Morgani'l went into a fit of laughter that didn't stop until Deba'l slapped her, bringing her back to herself.

"That isn't in the book either," Solanj'l said. "You don't know what's in it, do you?"

"There he goes," Petra'l said. "Look at that."

Gung's tongue was moving so fast around his lips it was as if he had no control over it.

The men around Hunak were talking, several at once. He finally chopped his hand in the air and said loudly enough for the women to hear that discussion was not useful at this time and it didn't matter because the women couldn't stay in the Hall. They would run out of food.

"We have food," Deba'l said. "We have a lot of it."

"Have you?"

"Yes."

"You have planned this."

"Yes, we have. I, for one, learned from a master."

"Thank you."

Metak and Doam demanded their wives come out.

Bantant asked Morgani'l if she was resolved to stay. Yes she was. "You have been a good husband, Bantant, but I have always hated this world."

Glom flapped his hands back and forth, then grabbed his hair and pulled it. "All this talk doesn't matter. We need the Beautification Ritual."

"Why?" Hunak asked. All eyes went to him. "Why we need it is never discussed. Perhaps it should be."

"You don't expect us to talk of ... private matters?" Doam asked. "It would shame our wives."

"It appears they feel shamed by what has been done to them." Hunak looked up. "Exactly what is it you want us to do?" he said to the women.

Deba'l looked straight ahead rather than down and spoke as if she were addressing the city. "We want a decree from the First Minister and High Priest that the Ritual will be stopped immediately, that all girls will keep their legs. We want a penalty, loss of all property, if a man has the legs sawed off his daughters. We want any such girls supported by the Ministry. We want the decree brought to us. We want to hear it read before this Great Hall. We want to see broadsides distributed in the city. We want your word of honour, Hunak, that all this is real, not a pretense to bring us out. We want the word of honour of the High Priest also."

Solanj'l was certain this one statement contained more wants from a woman than had been uttered in generations.

"Is that all?" Hunak asked.

"No. We want no penalties against us or any women with us."

"We will discuss it," Hunak said. "You are certain you have enough food?"

"We are fine," Deba'l said.

"Petra'l," Metak yelled, "I want you down here. Now. I want my daughter."

Petra'l merely shook her head. Hunak said something to him and turned to lead the men away. Glom looked up. His face was no longer red and his eyes were in more or less normal position. Solanj'l could see him take a big breath. Just before turning to walk away he said, "I thought you were happy."

39. INACTION AND THREATS

"WE CANNOT ACCEDE to your demands." So said Hunak two days later. He, Glom, and Gung with the Sheriff and multiple deputies, had returned and pounded on the great doors, not thunderously, just to announce they were there. "I'm certain you understand why it is impossible."

The Firsts and a few others looked over the parapet between the effigies and said nothing. "You cannot expect the citizens to give up centuries of tradition. One that brings them much pleasure."

Deba'l stunned her friends by coming out with a shout of laughter, following by rolling peals that went on and on over the roof and street. They feared she was losing control as Morgani'l had done. She abruptly stopped and said, "Not for us, husband. Not for the half of the population that is female. Why is it so difficult for you to understand that?"

Gung butted in with, "Women are opposed to you. You know that. Phylli'l...

"A curse on Phylli'l," Debal said.

His mouth dropped open.

"What he says is true," Hunak said.

"We are aware of that," Deba'l replied. "But if the Ritual is not stopped the daughters of Phylli'l and her toadies will someday curse all men, all citizens, for hating girls and women so much they wanted them maimed for life. The daughters of those who want the Ritual stopped will also curse them."

"Why have you gotten this idea in your head?" Hunak asked. "Why now?" He sounded weary, probably thinking, why now when I'm the one governing?

"I'd hoped for more from you, Hunak," Solanj'l said. "I thought perhaps you understood."

Perhaps he did, but that didn't matter. Change took time. Ramprendians were not given to change. Except for advancements in the making of goods and increasing food production, there'd been little change in memory. People were set in their ways. Women had been happy until this current situation. The people could not be asked to suddenly stop a practice that defined them as a people. Furthermore, with an increase in the raids, the men of Ramprend had enough to deal with.

"There've been more raids?" Solanj'l asked. These people who'd appeared shortly before she'd started working on the legs had become a talisman, something new and different in the life of the city. Why couldn't there be two new happenings—changes?

"They took legs, many, many legs from one of my mills." Glom was obviously upset.

"It is thought they have seen the wisdom of our ways," Gung said, "and are about to start the Beautification Ritual amongst themselves. They may have also heard of the Pleasure Ways. It is not the time to stop the ritual, when we can teach others of beauty and rightness."

Solanj'l felt she might throw up. Her friends also looked sickened.

"That is speculation," Doonak said.

To Solanj'l's surprise, he'd appeared shortly after the main contingent. Apparently, given Glom's reliance on him, he'd been granted enough status to speak with his betters.

"Why else would they take the legs?" Gung snapped at him.

"Perhaps as a symbol of the difference in the ways we treat girls and women."

"Surely you don't agree with these women."

"I can understand why they want to stop the ritual. I think I would if I had a son who was going to have his leg sawed off."

"Maybe there is hope," Janka'l said.

Petra'l asked, "Does he have a daughter?"

"He isn't married," Solanj'l said.

"Where was he when I came of marriage age?"

The men were in a discussion, voices rising and falling. Doonak was under attack from Gung and Glom. Solanj'l feared he would be out of work. And out of her life.

Suddenly Petra'l called out, "How many men agree with you, Doonak?" He said he hadn't been asking. "Why don't you do that? Why don't all you men go around the city and ask how many share Doonak's view? Why don't you ask before you tell us it's not possible?"

Morgani'l clapped.

"I think she speaks for all of us," Solanj'l said. "Find out what the men think."

Glom claimed men had been coming to him, demanding a stop be put to the nonsense. Men were also talking to Hunak, not in support of women. The Temple was being besieged according to Gung.

"What of the men who haven't come?" Deba'l asked.

"Why don't you come out," Hunak said. "Come out and start working to change people's minds. With time you might convince them. We can agree you will be free to talk of this idea."

"That could take years," Solanj'l said, "You know that. We aren't willing to sacrifice that many girls."

"I don't understand,' Glom said, "why you keep talking as if you're saving girls. It's as if you think men don't care about their daughters."

"That is exactly what we think,' Solanj'l said. "Why don't we start sawing off the legs of sons so they can give pleasure to the daughters of other men?"

Silence—as if the men had been struck mute. Deba'l asked if they'd completed what they had to say.

"Yes," Hunak said. "We must ask you to come out and resume your lives."

"That is not possible."

"We don't want to break in."

"I'm sure you don't. Abuse of those beautiful old doors would be unfortunate."

"We can come through the windows."

"That, too, would be a desecration of a revered building. The ornate glass is almost impossible to replace."

"Sheriff's men could scale the walls," yelled Metak.

"Women would push the ladders and men away," said Deba'l.

"Women wouldn't do such a thing," from Gung.

"It has been discussed and the women are resolved to do so if necessary," Solanj'l said.

"Evil!" Gung shouted.

Solanj'l looked to the north and saw people moving around. Was she seeing cloaks on them? Undoubtedly an illusion, a distraction from what was actually happening. Raiders came at night when people weren't working. It would be funny if they came by day while the men of power were distracted by the impossible behaviour of Ramprendian women. She might be able to get rid of the men by telling them a daytime Raid was occurring, but if they were Raiders she didn't want them caught. Not her symbol of hope. Let them take what they could. Legs included.

There was nothing more to say but the men remained. The women could have left the roof but didn't. Not knowing what lay ahead left them stuck, unable to move on because "on" had no clear meaning. Solanj'l felt as if she could stand there an eternity, waiting for deliverance from what had brought her to this place. But—deliverance would not arrive on its own. It was in her hands and those of the women around her. They could go downstairs, gather the women, and shamble out of the Hall back to the lives they'd led, leaving their daughters to lives just like theirs. Or, they could stand fast until the girls were freed of mutilation. Or they were defeated. Defeat would be a form of death, but to surrender, give in, go back to life as it was, would also be a death.

"It appears we have nothing more to discuss," she said. "We're going inside to attend to the lessons of the girls."

Gung started buzzing in Hunak's ear.

"The priest requests you release the girls," Hunak said. "You're subjecting them to harm. You're confusing them. That is not in their best interest."

"And sawing off their legs is?" Solanj'l said. "They will remain."

"You will starve to death," he said, turned and walked away. After a moment the others followed.

"Does that mean he wants the girls to starve as well?" Janka'l asked.

"He's trying to scare us," Deba'l said. "How disappointing."

40. RAIDERS AND YEARNING

A S THE STAND FAST DAYS WENT BY, the childhood image of women and men running together kept flashing into Solanj'l's mind and every time it brought tears to her eyes. She'd never been one to cry, in fact her family had spoken of how hard she could be, but now she was fighting tears regularly. Sadness would almost overwhelm her when she was alone. She'd find tears falling off her chin. Was this intuition about the future or the past catching up with her? Several times she thought of asking the other Firsts what they were experiencing then decided she didn't want to worry them. They all needed to think she was strong, holding fast.

She'd go onto the roof alone and just stare out, not at anything, just out. It was usually toward the mountains, toward a place where the women kept their legs. She'd go up at night and look at the stars. When sleep eluded her she might as well look at the beauty of them rather than walls that were becoming increasingly oppressive. Bemla'l or one of her Gathering members would patrol the rooftop each night, watching for approaching men. Other women watched during the day.

A few nights after Hunak had told them they would starve, she heard something below, went to the parapet, and looked down. Doonak was below. He looked up and said, "Solanj'l." The moon was almost at full, bright enough for them to recognize each other.

"Doonak? What are you doing here?"

"I walk at night. I came here."

He went to one of the benches across from the Hall and sat. It gave him a better view of her without tipping his head far back.

"Do you really have enough food?" he asked.

"That depends on how long the Stand Fast lasts."

"And if you run out?"

She didn't know how to respond and said, "Tell me about the Raiders."

He got up and walked to one side of the building and looked down the street running next to it.

When he started toward the other side, Solanj'l told him they had a lookout on the roof at all times. One she trusted with anything he said.

He'd been walking home five nights past when two people in hooded cloaks stepped out of an alley in front of him. There was some trouble in communicating but the languages were sufficiently similar that he and the two women finally came to an understanding. They had a need for nuts and bolts. The women explained they had become tired of dodging the "dolts," their word, who were supposed to be catching them. They knew he was working with a woman, something a Ramprend man usually did not do. They thought he might help. When asked why they didn't buy what was needed, they looked at him with contempt. Ramprend men did not do business with women. Why didn't men attempt to do so? Because the women were making a surprise for the men. The idea came after some of the men had started stealing materials for their own purposes. A couple of the women had hoped to talk with Solanj'l a couple of times. They'd seen wood and other materials going into her workshop and she was the only one going in. They thought her unusual for a Ramprendian woman. Perhaps she would have helped them. They gave up because of Kracak prowling around.

"You were right about them being women," she said. "What are they making? Why a surprise for men?"

They were making a cart that could be drawn by one person to be used for general hauling purposes—tools, materials, anything needed in places where it was not easy for draft animals to work. They had wood, but not enough metal parts to make several. As to why they wanted to surprise the men, it was an expression of appreciation for not wanting to mutilate women the way the men of Ramprend did, or even worse the men in the Land Across the Lake. They wanted to lighten the work that men usually did.

Solanj'l felt the familiar sadness settle on her. Wanting to say thank you for not being like men in Ramprend. "How extraordinary," she said "Did you get them with what they want?"

"I told Glom I wanted to experiment with the legs and bought the materials from him. Said I might fail and didn't want him to lose money. It's in a shed behind my home. The women will take it when they can. They are quite extraordinary. They know what you're doing. They never imagined the women of Ramprend would do such a thing. They wish they could help but don't know how."

Solanj'l's heart did a skip. She opened her mouth but saw a deputy coming down the street. She pointed and slipped out of sight. The deputy approached and asked Doonak what he was doing.

"Out for a walk, thought I'd look at this place of foolishness." He said it loudly enough for Solanj'l to hear, then went off with the deputy, presumably talking about the stupidity of women.

Solanj'l went inside filled with sadness and longing, thinking of Doonak helping them, of him being like the men in her childhood tales to herself or those who lived in the mountains, not wanting to maim girls, and of women wanting to give something to the men because they appreciated them. How fine it would be to live in a world like that. There was also that vague yearning when she was with Doonak. Never felt before. Her body reaching out to touch and be touched. A uniting. She'd come to think her body automatically rejected the touch of a man. What Glom thought of as uniting she experienced as invasion. How could she even imagine desire when men's desire came out of women's mutilation?

41. THE TUNNEL

BEMLA'L'S TRIPS TO THE BASEMENT to store food had yielded information that might help them get more food. She, Hopa'l, with Majana and other girls, had explored the basement. It would have been more difficult to do without the young, two-legged helpers. Given the opportunity to actually do something other than sit and babble banalities, these girls were eager to investigate. Moving around in hallways and rooms with limited light from oil lanterns didn't bother them. Getting dirty, which it was impossible not to do, didn't bother them—as long as Bemla'l, Hopa'l, Morgani'l, any of the women down there were within ear range. Morgani'l said she thought of these excited, eager, two-legged girls every time her spirits flagged. "They're wonderful." The other Firsts thought them wonderful as well. Girls were proving to be extremely helpful with all work that needed to be done. The decision to keep them in the Hall was fortuitous.

The basement was not as large as the entire Hall. "Thank Ploch," from Bemla'l. The walls, of hard Ramprendian earth, weren't completely smooth and squared. The explorers wondered if it had been dug out after the building was erected. They found rooms that they came to call chambers. There was something not quite of the present world about them. The chambers were empty—for the most part. Majana found one on the third day of exploring that contained something that caused her to come to where Bemla'l and Morgani'l were standing and look at them with sad eyes. When asked what was wrong she motioned for them to follow. They entered a chamber that contained a wooden table with alternating light and dark blotches. Four metal clamps were affixed to the top, two at one end, two at the other, at just the right position to hold arms and legs. Two rusty saws lay on a bench nearby.

"Was this the first beautification room?" Majana asked. Morgani'l put her arm around her shoulders and said she didn't know. Majana thought it was. When Solanj'l learned of it she said it should be blocked up. Deba'l differed; it could be used as a reminder if resolve wavered. Whether The Firsts wanted it or not, the news of the discovery spread. Women and girls became agitated in a way they hadn't been previously. There was something about an ancient dark, dingy chamber where girls had their legs sawed off that was almost as horrific as the reality all females of Ramprend lived. How terrified the girls must have been down there. Were they given a drug to dull the fear and pain? Did some of them die? Were there healers to take care of the stumps? The women's faces became determined and set. Deba'l had been right. Women were hardened in their resolve to kill the ritual.

Sharp-eyed Majana made another discovery in the basement. There was a door near the ritual chamber. It hadn't been seen right away because dirt made it blend in with the wall. It wouldn't open; the handle wouldn't even turn. Solanj'l suggested oil be poured on and rubbed into it, a technique she'd learned from Doonak. The handle turned but the door wouldn't budge. They couldn't even tell if it moved in or out. Bemla'l suggested they all push against it while Majana kept the handle turned. Nothing. Try it the other way. Majana turned the handle. Bemla'l held her waist, Morgani'l held Bemla'l's and they all pulled. It slid a tiny bit but Bemla'l and Morgani'l almost fell over. What was needed were two strong legs on the pullers. Girls were called in to do the job. The door slid a bit more. Bemla'l asked Sasa, a friend of Majana's, to get down on her knees and examine the floor in front of the door. She found a buildup of caked dirt. It was so dry down there, what would cause the dirt to cake that way? Bemla'l and Morgani'l thought of wooden buckets carrying out bloody legs. Under their direction girls dug and scraped at the dirt until the door could be opened enough for two girls to grasp the edge and pull. It opened onto darkness. Bemla'l took an oil lantern and went in and in and in. "It was scary watching her go away from us like that," Majana later reported. Bemla'l returned and said it seemed they'd found a hallway. She thought it her responsibility to find out where it went. Not before consulting with the other Firsts, Morgani'l said.

The Firsts and any other interested women gathered to discuss what to do with the new information. Morgani'l and Bemla'l were certain the tunnel went in the direction of the Temple but it might terminate anywhere under the city square. The only thing to do was investigate. They'd take a lantern holding two hours worth of oil and turn around if it got to the halfway mark, but certainly they'd come to something before an hour passed. They hoped so because they might find themselves pushing the limits of endurance. Two hours of step-dragging? Could they do it? Morgani'l had always had trouble with the wood legs. Something about her stump made it impossible to create a degree of comfort. Cresa'l raised her hand and shyly said she would volunteer to go. She was a servant; she'd built strength in her flesh leg all her adult life and fortunately she'd been able to adapt to the wood leg. It made sense for women like her to do the exploring. It was generally acceded she had a good idea. Several other servants and workwomen said they too would go. The Firsts debated this among themselves. It seemed at least one of them should take the risk, if there was one, and they might recognize something the other women wouldn't. Bemla'l reminded them she'd assiduously worked on strengthening her body, spending hours walking around her husband's property and going through the exercises Furam had taught them. She thought she could go quite a distance without tiring.

She and Cresa'l led out. A human chain, of sorts, was set up. After a count of three hundred, a workwoman followed them, then Majana after the count and so it went in an alternating pattern of servant or workwoman and girl. If there were a problem, all would be within hearing distance of another and there would be swift-footed girls in the tunnel to get back to the Hall quickly if necessary.

"It seemed like forever," according to Majana, but the lantern indicated it wasn't quite an hour when Bemla'l and Cresa'l found a door that opened fairly easily. They stepped into a room. They sent a message down the chain to stop and hold. They knew they were beneath the Temple because the room and the tunnel just before the door into it were damp. The Great Hall's basement wasn't damp. It was doubtful other basements were. The room opened into a hallway with other rooms off it. The arrangement was similar to that under the Hall. They debated about how far to go. They certainly didn't want to be caught and the oil would run out before they got back to the Great Hall if they explored more. They went back into the tunnel and sent out the word to return.

Gung, ever ready to talk, had once told The Firsts when they'd complained of cold in the Temple, that there were rooms below so bone-chilling damp no one had any interest in exploring them. If rooms hadn't been used in memory what was the need to go down there? None, absolutely none. The Firsts had always wanted to tell Gung to go away but were glad they'd not had the power to make that happen. If the basement was unexplored, the existence of the tunnel must not be known.

Janka'l offered to go with Bemla'l for another exploring visit. She thought she could be on her legs for that length of time. She had a surprising physical capacity once she started training with Furam. Majana said she thought she should go with them. There'd be stairs to go up and she could do that more easily.

There was reticence about sending a girl into possible danger. She said she was in danger in any event. Her mother agreed. But, if one girl was going, they'd send a second. A girl should not explore alone. Nalani volunteered. The four set off with a chain forming behind them, this time composed entirely of girls. They went at night because few, if any, priests were in the Temple after dark. Priests didn't spend much time in the Temple at any time of the day. Their function, or lack thereof, was a common topic of conversation.

Majana and Nalani went up stairs to first floor of the Temple. They found several rooms. The description of one was recognized by Bemla'l and The Firsts. It was the original Gathering spot.

Now the women Standing Fast had a possible way to get out of and into the Hall without being seen. Perhaps food could be brought in through the Temple. Solanj'l thought of Doonak bringing in "donations" for charity food.

The tunnel could also expedite the possible final act of the Stand Fast, the one The Firsts avoided thinking about as much as possible.

42. TALK, TO NO AVAIL

IF IT WEREN'T FOR DOONAK, they wouldn't have known much of what was happening outside. Morgani'l was downright gleeful over a man being a spy for them. Some of the information could be passed freely. Some Doonak sent up in notes in a basket lowered from the roof when no deputies or other men were around.

Hunak had a committee discussing the matter of the women, some arguing for a charge on the Great Hall, others for letting the women starve, not believing they'd gotten food inside. How could women do that? The fathers of sons objected to the latter, too many dead girls would mean their sons couldn't get appropriate wives. Gung asserted no one would starve, the women would come out when they got hungry, pampered things they were. Hunak wasn't certain of any of this. Women were engaging in behaviour thought not possible. He knew how steady his wife was and suspected Solanj'l was the same, although Glom didn't seem to know it and kept talking about the women coming to their senses. He'd even suggested the Raiders might have put something in the water to make the women have strange ideas. After all, the women of the mountains had two legs. What was wrong with the men up there?

Pressure kept mounting. Men wanted their wives home, and they wanted them now. Many said it was all Glom's fault, him with his Glamour Legs, putting ideas in women's heads. That nonsense should never have started. Glom pointed out how eager men had been to get legs for their wives. If it was such a bad idea, they should have seen it and not bought the legs.

If the committee didn't act soon, men would take matters into their hands and do real damage to the Hall, and perhaps many women, particularly The Firsts. Hunak issued an order that the Great Hall should not be touched unless it was done by Sheriff's men under Ministry direction. That did not solve the problem of what to do with the women and their demands.

Hunak, out of respect for his advisors, did not initially ask Doonak to be a participant in the committee talks, but he did speak with him privately about his work with Solanj'l. What he learned reinforced his view. She and Deba'l would stay unless forced out. Would Doonak be willing to act as his representative? Because of their work together Solanj'l might be more willing to speak with him than to those who could now be seen as enemies. Surely a compromise could be found. Also, could Deba'l be convinced to talk privately with Hunak? Doonak agreed, being careful to not look eager about taking on the task.

He asked Solanj'l if she could envision any compromise. She merely shook her head. He would so report. Deba'l agreed to talk with Hunak, but with him on the street and her on the roof. The result was a message that the Minister Second Only to the First did not stand on streets yelling at his wife. She replied that he'd done so before, another time shouldn't matter. Two days passed with no further word from him.

On the second night he appeared and called out that he wished to speak to Deba'l, a First of the Gatherings. Solanj'l was on the roof, thinking Doonak might appear. She called down she'd get Deba'l and kept out of sight when Deba'l asked her to stay.

"Can we not have a private talk?" Hunak asked. "Speak face to face. I promise I will let you return. Have I ever broken a promise to you?"

"No, you have not and I have always greatly respected you for that, Hunak, but I am Standing Fast with my friends and will not break my promise to them. I hope you can respect that."

He told her the Stand Fast could not go on. It had to end at some time and there was limited time he could keep men from charging the Hall and wreaking havoc on the women they were growing to hate, if they had not already arrived at that emotion.

"All you have to do is order the stopping of the Ritual," Deba'l said.

"It isn't so easily done, Deba'l. You know people don't make sudden changes."

"There was a rather sudden change in adopting the wood legs. Ramprenders can change. It's time they did. Think of how grateful the girls of this and all following generations will be. But, then, I suppose that doesn't matter because they're female. Only men are worthy enough for you to accept their gratitude. It has taken me all this time to realize that women aren't included when you say people. I no longer accept that."

"Of course women are people and not all people agree with you. Look at Phylli'l..."

"I'd rather not."

Hunak laughed. "No, I suppose you wouldn't. But, she and her followers are opposed to you. Not all women, people, feel as you do."

"But think of how many do. I have thought about Phylli'l and her self-hatred. She wants her daughters maimed because she was. If she's so worthless that she had to be maimed, then her daughters must be worthless as well and should suffer the same fate. It's sheer loathing of herself that makes her defend the ritual. She disgusts me. I disgust myself when I think how I once was the same."

They stood in silence for a time. She'd lived with a man who showed her more regard than any Ramprend woman could expect and now they were standing apart calling to each other, and the space between them might never close.

"Are we at an impasse, Deba'l?"

"It seems we are."

"We will take action to bring you out."

"It won't be easy and some, perhaps many, will die."

"Oh, Deba'l, don't say that."

"Goodnight, Hunak."

43. THEATRE

LETHARGY DESCENDED. DAYS LOCKED in a building, even if you've locked yourself in, drains energy. The Firsts began to fear women would demand they be allowed to leave merely because they were getting bored and thus dispirited. This was puzzling to Petra'l. Those who weren't servants or workwomen had never done much of anything. What was it that kept them feeling alive in their lives of inaction? What had kept her interested in her life?

"Flirting," Janka'l said with a smile.

"Predictability," Morgani'l said. "That's what's missing. We knew what was going to happen day after day. Some of us didn't like our lives, but we knew where we were, what we could do and not do. It's not inaction that bothering us. It's the nagging little fear about the nature of tomorrow."

The Firsts had assumed—hoped—the men would not be quick to attack. Ramprendians did not make war, and given the difficulty of growing food on the land surrounding the city, others didn't attempt to take anything from them. Fighting, attacking, was not their nature or necessity. Oh, yes, some men did attack women in their families, but to do so to a large group was outside their experience. That and the shock of women acting in such an incredibly abnormal way would slow response. None of The Firsts thought it would allow them to stay in the Hall indefinitely. If, when, an attack came, any women who wanted to could surrender.

Others undoubtedly would die. How strange to consider that. Solanj'l was stunned when she realized how many women appeared to be willing to do that. Once committed to the rightness of Death to the Ritual they were ready to confront their own death.

Petra'l arrived at a morning meeting of The Firsts with an idea. She was so excited about it words tumbled over each other and it took some time for the others to understand what she was suggesting. Have the girls and women put on a play, maybe with music. She didn't know how many of them had any talent,

"How could we know when females aren't encouraged to develop any if they have it? And it'd be so much fun and it'd be something to focus on, to keep us busy and interested and it'd be so exciting because it's new." She looked around. "Isn't it a good idea?"

"My word," Morgani'l said. "Not a good idea, a great one."

Petra'l sat taller and looked most pleased with herself. The other Firsts were equally impressed. Bemla'l, who'd essentially become a First, said she thought it was absolutely outstanding and she'd be glad to create sets and make props, not that she had any experience, but Solanj'l could certainly give her tips with her knowledge of making things. They quickly decided to call a meeting, present the idea, and let those who were interested go to work. They needed writers to create a play, the only existing ones about women being those that humiliated them. They needed people to write songs. They needed workers to help Bemla'l. The workwomen had much to offer if they wanted to do so. They needed actors. They needed people to help the actors get ready. They needed someone to keep things organized.

As was to be expected, there was a mixed response. Some immediately became excited and started sharing ideas. Others scowled and didn't know what to make of it. Women didn't create plays. Women didn't act in plays—except to be Silly

Simples. Women didn't know anything about putting on plays or musical performances.

"Just ignore them," Petra'l said. "When they see how much fun the others are having, they'll join in."

She was right. The women and girls became so enthralled with theatre it was all they wanted to do. The Firsts had to become rather sharp in giving reminders about getting meals prepared and served. Not for the first time. The privileged women had assumed servants and workwomen would do the feeding chores and were taken aback when told they all would take turns, including The Firsts. Cresa'l and other food servants had a lot of training to do but everyone got fed more or less satisfactorily.

There was such eagerness to get some performance on stage, it was decided to rewrite a Silly Simple so a woman won her point. That could be done almost immediately. New entertainments could be started as well. Several people, women and girls, started writing alone or with one or two others.

"You can almost feel energy coming out of rooms where people are working," Morgani'l said. She paused, staring into the middle distance. "There's no going back."

"You just realized that?" Solanj'l asked.

"A heightened understanding."

"What do you...?"

"What do I what?"

"Nothing."

"What do I think is going to happen? I try not to think about it. I'd either create disappointment, or terrify myself. Or both."

* * *

Glom arrived a day after the Stand Fast became a place of theatre. He demanded to see Solanj'l, not with her on the roof, but to actually see her when he talked. From the roof she told him he was seeing her and she was not coming down, nor was he coming up.

"I demand this nonsense be stopped," he said. "Everyone is tired of this and if you and the others don't come out, there will be violence. I do not want you hurt. I want you home and I want you helping me with the legs. I am beginning to lose patience."

"You know our conditions."

"You have completely lost your mind. What has happened to the good little wife I had? Solanj'l, you were such a delight. I miss you. I miss.... Well, I can't talk about that while I'm yelling at you."

"We aren't yelling. There is merely a slight elevation of voices."

"You are being facetious. That is not a good thing in a woman. I don't know what's happened to you. I don't know who you are. It's as if you've been taken over by someone else. Who did this to you?"

"The Beautification Ritual did it to me."

Glom stamped his foot. Only once before had she seen him do that, when a mill caught on fire and been severely damaged. It appeared she had moved into catastrophic status.

"Great Ploch, Solanj'l, the Beautification Ritual is one of Ploch's greatest gifts to men."

"No! It is not. You know that. The Ritual was devised by some men who were bored with women the way they were. They got it into their heads that women would be more interesting if they were maimed. And not able to move freely."

"How can you say such a thing? That isn't written anywhere."

"And there you have it. Nothing written anywhere. Choose the story you want. You have yours and I have mine. Accept it, Glom, life will never be what it was. I don't know what it will be, but it won't be what it was."

He stared up at her and said nothing. Finally he shook his head and turned, but didn't walk away. She looked down at him. How easily he could turn back toward her or leave. Step out, or not. How dare he think women didn't want that kind of choice?

He turned back. "I wish you would change your mind, Solanj'l. I do miss you. Perhaps we could arrange our lives so you could be happy. I always thought you were."

"I haven't been happy since I fully realized what was going to happen to me. That isn't going to change."

As she rode the platform to the first floor she thought of the theatre work going on and how what had just happened with Glom was a Silly Simple in reverse. The woman walked away with her dignity. She was certain Glom felt his seriously damaged. He wasn't crawling and begging but he certainly wasn't getting what he desired. Perhaps Hunak would understand the perverse humour in that. Doonak would. Glom? No. She knew she'd been about as fortunate as a woman could be in her world. She gotten a husband who did not beat her and would let her do things most men would not. The fact that he had no sense of what another person might think and feel was unfortunate, but understandable given their world.

Nalani, her beautiful neighbour on the edge of puberty, came running up to her. "Solanj'l, Solanj'l, I can sing. Petra'l says I can sing."

"Let me hear you. Sing a bit of something."

Nalani opened her mouth and out poured a ditty sung by boys when they were throwing and chasing balls. "I'm the greatest, I'm the best. I throw a ball in your nest." This had never made sense to Solanj'l and she suspected Nalani didn't understand it either but the girl did have a strong, true voice.

"You can sing. Can you write a song?"

"I don't know."

"Why don't you try? Ask Morgani'l to help you. She understands music better than anyone else I know."

Nalani went off skipping and singing, "I'm the greatest, I'm the best."

"Yes, you are. Believe it, believe it," Solanj'l said.

44. GET THEM OUT

"THERE ARE MEN OUTSIDE. There are men outside!" Hopa'l, who'd been standing watch on the roof sent one of the girls to The Firsts. How many men? She didn't know, but there were a lot and they looked mean. The Firsts went up to the roof, after telling Bemla'l to keep others from following. When The Firsts looked over the parapet they saw a mass of men below and flowing off to their right. Metak was standing in the front with Gung and Lumok. Interesting they were together. Solanj'l then saw the women in the group. Phylli'l and several of her acolytes were right behind the priests. Solanj'l looked toward the mountains, which did not have their usual friendly look. Blackish-grey clouds scudded across the tops. Maybe that meant rain. They could always use rain.

Phylli'l was screeching something.

Metak called out. "Petra'l, I'm ordering you to come out. Come out now with my daughter. This is your last warning. This is the last warning to all women. We have had enough of this. It will end now."

"On whose authority?" Deba'l asked

"On the authority of the men of Ramprend."

"And the women of truth and decency," Phylli'l called out. "The women who love Ploch."

"Come on, Phylli'l," Petra'l called out. "You know Ploch has nothing to do with … anything."

Phylli'l appeared to puff up, as if air or water were being pumped into her.

"Do you have Ministry approval?" Deba'l directed at Metak.

"We are not waiting for the Ministry," Metak yelled. "They are doing nothing,"

"Yes, that's right," came from a man. "Get them out. Get them out." This was taken up by others. Some started banging on the door with sticks. "Get them out. Get them out."

"The Ministry will be very unhappy if the doors are damaged," Deba'l called down to them.

They paused and looked at Metak. Gung put his hand on Metak's arm and said something, looked up at the women and said. "We are ready to be lenient. The punishments will be light, but we cannot have the women of Ramprend violating the laws of … Ramprend." He turned to Lumok, who nodded.

Phylli'l started an urgent whispering at Lumok, probably trying to get him to take control. Some of the men at the door started banging away again. Gung told them to stop.

The Great Hall was built to withstand much. At one time there must have been a need for a fortified space in the city. Getting into it would not be easy without doing much damage and Ramprendians were proud of their Hall. The thick beautifully carved doors shone almost like glass. Every twenty-eight days they were cleaned and oiled. Attacking those doors without Ministry approval was foolhardy but it seemed there were other men as angry as Metak.

Solanj'l said to her friends, "We need to keep them talking until the Ministry knows what's happening and orders the Sheriff's men here."

"Tell us why you want the Beautification Ritual to continue," Janka'l called down.

The men scowled and shuffled their feet. What kind of question was that? Everyone knew why it was wanted. Even women wanted it. Women were right there with them.

"It is for the glory of union," Phylli'l said.

Lumok and Gung, who weren't supposed to be having union with women, nodded with enthusiasm.

"And just why is it," Morgani'l asked, "that half of the partners in union have to be maimed?"

"It is the way of Ploch," Phylli'l said.

"You still haven't read the book have you?" Morgani'l said in her most contemptuous voice. "But, if you insist it agrees with you, bring it here and show us where it says girls are to have their legs sawed off so men can get their penises to work."

Gasps from below couldn't be heard on the roof but Solanj'l imagined them, given the shock on the faces looking up. Women did not speak of … male things.

Petra'l gave one of her trilling laughs. "Oh, you bad woman." She put her arm around Morgani'l, who smiled and shook her head as if surprised at herself.

Deba'l called down, "It is sacrilege to speak lies about Ploch."

Solanj'l smiled. She knew Deba'l didn't care about Ploch and sacrilege anymore than she did.

"We'll give you proof when you come out," Metak said.

Men started banging on the doors again. It wouldn't be long before dents would be made in the carvings of the early fathers of Ramprend.

"I remind you of Ministry prohibition on damaging the Great Hall," Deba'l yelled down over the sound of wood beating wood.

"Let's break the windows," someone called out.

"That will bring equal displeasure," Solanj'l called down. "The windows of many colours are as prized as the doors."

"Who are you to speak for the Ministry?" Metak said. "Women have no authority. In anything."

Men started to hit the window to the right of the great doors, which were still under attack. The glass and the wood of the shutters behind it were so thick, that it would not be easy to break in, but it would happen sooner than the doors coming down.

"Go tell the women to get ready to hit anyone who comes through a window," Deba'l said to Majana. Take the platform only to the second floor. We don't want men getting control of it."

"Oh, my," Janka'l said. "Is it going to come to that?"

Gung and Lumok were trying to get the men to stop the attack, to little effect; a few men stopped but others continued. It appeared some had no more respect for the representatives of Ploch than did The Firsts.

Where was the Sheriff? Solanj'l wondered. Had the Ministry decided to let the Hall be damaged, perhaps irretrievably? How strange she was thinking of the Hall rather than the women. Perhaps because she knew the Ministry held the Hall in higher esteem than it did the women of Ramprend.

"Here they come," Janka'l said and pointed east.

Yes, here came the Sheriff and his men. Two of them were carrying Ramprend banners, ones used for ceremonial purposes only. Serious matters were afoot. The Sheriff walked to Metak and the priests and started talking. Phylli'l started to speak. The Sheriff looked at her, said something and pointed. She spoke to Lumok who shook his head. She was rolled back. The Sheriff made a shooing motion and she was pulled farther away. The Sheriff spoke, Metak waved his arms around as he spoke, the priests joined in. Occasionally fragments would drifted to the roof.

"We have the right..."

"They need to be..."

The Sheriff, a tall and heavily muscled man shook his head at whatever Metak was saying. After a few exchanges between them, he went up the steps and apparently told the men who'd been attacking doors and window to leave because they did.

He called out, "You are to disperse. Now. This is an unlawful action. Men who do not leave immediately will be arrested and taken to jail. This is by order of the Minister Second Only to the First."

Someone called out, "What does the First Minister say?"

"You, as a citizen of Ramprend, know the Second always speaks for the First. Leave. Pass the word."

Men turned to leave but couldn't because of those behind them. Deputies started herding them and the Phylli'ls up the street to the north where fewer men were gathered. Metak and the priests stayed to talk to the Sheriff, who was examining the doors and writing on a tablet of the type used by the Ministry—and paying little attention to them. They finally left, Metak throwing one last angry look at the roof.

"Women," the Sheriff called up, "the removal of the men does not mean the Ministry endorses what you are doing. It is to protect the Hall. Shortly you will be given your final ultimatum." He walked off.

"That wasn't bad," Petra'l said.

"I guess we wait some more," Janka'l said.

What could they do other than that, guard the roof, feed themselves, and create plays. Making up make-believe. Ironic. They'd lived in a world of make-believe all their lives. The horrible danger came, the leg was sawed off, and then there was the long pretence that life was worth living.

"What are you thinking?" Deba'l asked Solanj'l. "You look troubled."

"Merely considering dangers, past and present. Perhaps the greatest danger was seeing life as it is."

"You've known that for some time."

"Yes.... How will this end?"

"In joy, with singing, dancing. And running."

Solanj'l smiled sadly. "Remind me daily."

"I'll do that. As much for myself as you."

45. WAITING AND TEMPERED RESOLVE

S OLANJ'L FELT ENGULFED BY PEOPLE. Being self-sufficient by nature and having had privacy for most of each day in Glom's house, it was difficult to live with people always present. Even when they weren't speaking with her, they were present—across the room, down the hallway, on the other side of the wall. People who wanted something, even if not expressing it at the moment. Surprisingly, she'd like to go to the Sitting Room in Glom's house and be quiet. Those days were over; she doubted she'd ever again sit there enjoying the birds or little animals that romped on the patio. And no more watching for Raiders—Visitors, hoping to see one, perhaps a woman, on the edge of Glom's field. How strange the Raiders included women. Could she get to the mountains if the need arose? She would move too slowly. Could she steal a draft beast? It would have to be by stealth and she doubted she could do that either.

Times on the roof were precious. She took a watch every other night. Doonak came frequently. Hunak's hope for the women being talked out gave Doonak license to visit and pass on information that might encourage, or scare them, into giving up. Increasing dissatisfaction over Ministry inaction was resulting in plot-making. Storming the doors was about as clever as anyone had gotten, but there was the concern about Ministry retaliation. The citizens couldn't understand why the Ministry was being so inactive. It was known the Ministers didn't agree with the women. So what were they waiting for? Even Glom was becoming impatient with Hunak.

One night Doonak signaled for Solanj'l to lower the basket. His message was: Store water. Engineers are trying to find a way to cut it off to the Hall without stopping it in the Ministry and Temple and businesses.

This was not a surprise. There was a tunnel to the Temple. Water connections must exist somewhere between buildings. Bemla'l had put the basement squad of girls to work on finding additional tunnels. They tapped on the dirt walls with sticks and finally found another door at the far corner of the basement closest to the Ministry. This one they would block; its existence might be known to the Ministers. The question was how? Empty food crates wouldn't be enough. They needed the tables from upstairs, perhaps not all of them but they would be difficult to get into the basement, even by two-legged girls. The solution came from Majana. "Why don't we use some wheeled chairs? Those who walk fairly well or who are willing to use props could do without chairs. For awhile."

And so it was; women gave up their chairs to be turned over and stacked in front of the door. It was a difficult job, one the women couldn't help with very much. Two girls, one in front, one in back, bumped a chair down the stairs, wheeled it to toward the door, turned it over and pushed it against the ones already there. It took a good part of a day, but the basement hallway to the Ministry tunnel door was filled with upended chairs. It would take great effort to move them sufficiently to let men through and then they'd have to climb over the chairs. It was possible they'd be able to do so, but it was the best the women, the girls, could do. One tunnel was like a gift, the second could be their defeat. They had no idea of what to do about water, other than store it as Doonak had suggested.

Two days after his warning Doonak arrived during the morning and said he had a message to be read from Hunak, Minister

Second Only to the First to The Firsts of the Gatherings. The Firsts gathered on the roof, looking down between the effigies. He gave a slight bow before reading. "The Ministry is losing in the attempt to calm those who want to force you from the Great Hall. It is imperative you leave within one day of this reading. If you do not, the Sheriff's deputies will enter and bring you out. It will not be possible to prevent men who want to assist them. These men will not be under Ministry control. We fear women and girls will be injured. You have one day."

That night a new banner was hung from the Great Hall's effigies.

THE MUTILATION OF GIRLS WILL STOP
EACH WOMAN WILL BE GIVEN HER OWN HOME
IF SHE SO WISHES
EACH WOMAN WILL BE FREE TO RAISE HER SONS
TO RESPECT ALL PEOPLE

* * *

The theatrical event was scheduled for the evening of the day they were to vacate. The Hall was filled with energy, equal parts fear and first experience jitters. Women who weren't involved in the performance were at work creating a special meal to be eaten prior to the show, and tasties for after. Cresa'l was an outstanding orchestrator of kitchen work. Solanj'l wondered how much Kracak owed her for his reputation as an excellent steward.

Listening. No matter their work, each woman and girl was listening for the pounding on the doors or windows. Busy and yet suspended. Waiting. Listening. Wondering. What would happen to them? If forced out many would face husbands who'd viciously beat them. Others might have nowhere to go, husbands being unwilling to even acknowledge being married to such vile creatures. It was feared The Firsts would be attacked or even killed for having led this revolt. Deba'l might survive because few would want to face the wrath of the Ministry. If not for the food and theatrical preparations, the tension in the Hall could have broken many spirits.

Simla'l, one of the women standing guard on the roof, sent down one of the girls to report women were being rolled to the Hall. Deba'l and Solanj'l went to the roof. The Phylli'ls formed a line in front of the building, almost as if they were trying to protect it from attack by men.

Phylli'l called up. "I wish to speak to all The Firsts. I'm here to convince them of their sin. I am here to save them, to save you all. You must return to Ploch and to the ways of Ramprend."

Deba'l said, "Phylli'l, you have nothing to say to us. You are free, of course, to stay out there." She paused. "But, as long as we are here, let me ask you. Have you read *The Book of Ploch?* Have you learned your mutilation has nothing to do with God?"

Phylli'l shifted in her chair, then cried. "It is our way. We believe all that is true and right."

Female willingness to accept their own maiming, and that of their daughters, had been discussed in Gatherings. How had the first mothers been persuaded or coerced into accepting the barbarity? Why did generation after generation continue to acquiesce? Women assisted with the mutilation. How could they do that? Was something missing in them that produced docility? Would they allow removal of both legs like the women in the Land Across the Lake or were those women more deficient than the Ramprend women? Were women generally so deficient they deserved maiming? And what of guilt? Of shame? Did they carry such a load of shame for being deficient, and guilt over what they'd allowed to be done to girls that they'd been rendered incapable of action? Questions yielded more questions. Had it always been that only one woman's voice raised in opposition would result in bringing a halt to the crippling of body and spirit? One woman had raised her voice and women had broken through to imagining a different life. Could men imagine daughters with two legs, their sons married to two-legged women? Solanj'l thought Hunak might be able to make the leap. Doonak had. Could the two of them bring men to the women's demands? Doonak would be willing to try. Hunak was holding back. Why? Fear of revolution? Loss of position?

The day passed with no banging on the doors, no men taking position outside. The Phylli'ls were rolled off in late afternoon, having gotten no more response from the women inside. If they were on legs, Solanj'l thought, they could create greater mischief. Did Phylli'l understand that?

Enough of them. On to the performance. She had no idea of what was coming. Her friends and Nalani had sworn all others to tell her nothing, let her see nothing. That was fine. A surprise would be good. Tension was so high she didn't know if they could get through the evening. It didn't matter where they were in the building if Hunak made good his threat, but gathering together to engage in playacting hardly seemed an appropriate response to peril. But, what else were they to do? Not everyone could go on the roof, ready to push men away if they tried to come up on ladders? Standing by the great doors and windows or entrance to the basement was equally useless. They might be able to fight off a few men but an onslaught could not be countered. There really was nothing to do except hope the men didn't come, or the doors and windows held fast, which they might, assuming Hunak didn't order their complete destruction.

Practically everyone made an effort to be cheerful during the evening meal. The women who'd had little or no experience in cooking were quite pleased with themselves. Under Cresa'l's direction they had put together a flavourful feast of roasted bullock and vegetables and breads—the last of the bullock, of most of the meat. Soon the beans and grains would be gone and they'd have to get food somehow, but tonight was special and no one spoke of the impending problem. Laughter rang in the dining room, some of it edged with hysteria, but better that than silence or low-level mumbling.

The performers left the tables to get themselves prepared for their debuts. The women who had prepared the meal sat with cups of tea while others cleared tables and made the kitchen ready for the next meal. The Firsts also sat with cups of tea, saying little. Deba'l did say it was too bad they didn't have some of Solanj'l's unbelievable cream cakes. Now they've become my cream cakes, Solanj'l thought. They used to be Glom's.

"I can't stand it anymore," Petra'l finally said. "Deba'l, why do you think they haven't come?"

Deba'l slowly shook her head. "I have no idea. The husband I thought I understood has become a stranger. He is not one to engage in idle threats. Maybe men are getting ready to scale the walls right now."

Solanj'l felt an almost irresistible urge to go to the roof to see for herself what was happening around the building but didn't. Bemla'l had a group up there. If they didn't see climbers she wouldn't. It was time to go into the auditorium and enjoy themselves. Or try to. She heard many a woman taking in a gulp of air and letting it out in a a long sigh.

After a brief introduction by Morgani'l the show began. Lafa, a girl of on the edge of puberty chanted and hopped back and forth to a ditty all girls learned.

I am a girl but
Soon a lady
I run and play but
Soon a lady
I am a girl but
Soon a lady
I run and jump but
Soon a lady
With one leg
I'll be a lady

After a pause she chanted something of her own.

I don't want
to be
a lady

A moment of silence, then an eruption of applause. Other
familiar compositions were read or chanted, most with qual-
ifiers like Lafa's. Then something new came from Majana,
who reminded Morgani'l of a future Solanj'l. What it lacked
in structure and style was compensated for in content.

A day will come
Soon too soon
When I will cease to be
You will see me
You will hear me
You will touch me
But I will have left
with the leg
no longer mine
Belonging now
to hungry cats
How can I live
if what held me
straight and firm
is eaten by
creatures
not like me
Creatures with four legs
Don't they have enough?

I want my leg
I want my leg
I want my leg

Silence. Majana stood—sad and slightly puzzled—how was she to interrupt this response? The others had gotten applause. Solanj'l started to clap and was quickly joined. The girls and women stood and clapped and cheered through tears. If there had been pounding on the doors they would not have heard it.

Finally they settled enough for the show to continue. Nalani put in her appearance— dressed as a boy! Gasps. Few, if any, had seen a girl or woman in male clothing. She swaggered onto the stage, an excellent imitation of a man or boy feeling very good about himself. Several girls called out, "Nalani," and clapped. She put her hands on her hips and started sing-songing the boys' nonsensical, "I'm the greatest, I'm the best. I throw a ball in your nest." She bounced a ball and threw it into a basket at the side of the stage. The ball went in almost every time. Clapping. Cheering. She skipped off, calling, "I'll be back." After a short absence she returned wearing a skirt, looking like a girl. She ran and jumped around the stage, tossed the ball in the basket and chanted but this time with new words. "I am great. I am good. I've two legs, as I should." She came to the edge of the stage, stood very still and slowly sang in a high sweet voice. "I am great. I am good. I've two legs, as I should." Once, twice. She motioned for others to join her. First the girls with two flesh legs stood and sang, then women on their real and wooden legs. "I am great. I am good. I've two legs, as I should. I am great. I am good. I've two legs, as I should." Over and over and over until throats were raspy.

Morgani'l step-dragged onto the stage and said there would be a break while all was made ready for the final presentation. The hall became quiet, thoughts and feelings kept inside. What could be said other than they had to stop the Ritual? They already knew that.

A Silly Simple in reverse form was the finale, women were the ones of power and the men made to look ineffectual. It was a tribute to The Firsts and particularly to Solanj'l, the creator of Glom's Glamour Legs who made the initial demand to do away with the Ritual. It was a compliment to have her work publicly acknowledged but Solanj'l knew the heart of the evening was in the performances of Majana and Nalani, all the girls. That was right. Girls would give the women the resolve to face whatever was coming.

46. THEY'RE NOT COMING — YET

THE NEXT EVENING Doonak brought word the Raiders had struck again, which had interfered with the assault on the Great Hall. They'd appeared in several places in the city but nothing was missing. Because he'd been designated as Hunak's messenger, he was now attending some of Hunak's committee meetings and could report Raider action was being interpreted as an act of sheer irritation, coming for the sole purpose of annoying the people of Ramprend. Given the ease with which Raiders came and went, and the rebellion of their own women, it was obvious the men of Ramprend were too soft. Glom was extremely angry. Even usually phlegmatic Hunak had sounded agitated when he spoke. More guards and deputies were needed to patrol. Therefore, the plans to bring the women out were delayed. Hunak was pacifying the disgruntled with talk of danger from outside. Furthermore, he was arguing, if the women were driven out through hunger they would be more docile than if they were forcibly removed. Gratitude to husbands would be more likely. The waiting for the arrival of the Sheriff and his men would also erode the resolve of the women; some might demand they be allowed to leave. More was to be gained by waiting than taking vigorous action. Grumbling by men continued but Doonak thought nothing would happen for at least a day or two. He didn't know why Hunak had changed his mind; perhaps he had not, the threat being a test of the women's resolve, or a pacifier to men while he considered alternatives.

Doonak told Solanj'l some things Hunak did not know. The Raiders had not been engaged in general irritation. They knew what the women of Ramprend were doing and had deliberately created a distraction in the hopes of easing the focus away from what was happening at the Great Hall. Solanj'l felt her heartbeat flatten out then hop into its usual rhythm. How extraordinary. The Raider woman had taken the materials from Doonak's shed. He'd gone out to speak with them. They were getting better at talking by speaking slowly and using hand gestures. They'd thanked him for his kindness and asked about the women in the Great Hall. He told them they were standing fast. Good, good, had been the response. They asked about the food supply and said because they were able to come into the city pretty much at will, they could carry in food, if it was wanted. Should they try? Solanj'l felt her heart do another hop, skip, jump. How extraordinary to find such kindness from people who were strangers, actually less strangers than the men of Ramprend, only one of whom was willing to help them in their desire to have whole daughters. She would like to meet these women with whom Doonak was talking. Would he find a wife among them? If he did, he'd have to leave Ramprend, no mountain woman would agree to live in the city. Such thoughts were not relevant.

How could food be delivered? It couldn't be left outside, not with the deputies frequently appearing after the break in attempt. One had seen the basket passing between Doonak and Solanj'l. Doonak told him Hunak wanted a message sent quietly. There was no way to lie about food appearing.

Doonak's visits helped Solanj'l hang on. She, everyone, was so tired. Privileged women were not used to working the way they now did. Keeping girls occupied took a toll. Worrying about the girls' welfare wore them down. Worrying about what would happen to all of them sucked energy out. Too many physical and feeling demands were on them. She thought The Firsts must feel it even more. They were the ones who created this situation; they were the ones responsible for what would happen. Bemla'l, Hopa'l, and others spoke of all women carrying responsibility but Solanj'l wasn't convinced all women agreed. No one spoke directly to The Firsts, but they knew there were mutterings about nothing happening, about how difficult it was living this way. There were also pinings for sex. Petra'l wasn't the only one who liked it. Solanj'l could only snort to herself about this. Maimed for sex but still liking it. There had to be a word to describe that peculiarity but she didn't have it. The grumblers didn't sound as if they were blaming themselves for the various lacks being experienced. Doonak gave her respite, that and, like the Raiders, hope.

47. TIME RUNNING OUT

"YOU ARE ORDERED to leave now." This declaration was made by the Sheriff the day after the women found the flow of water had decreased. He was surrounded by Deputies, but there were no other officials. Hunak, Gung, and Glom must have decided the women were not worth dealing with. Deba'l and Solanj'l had gone to the roof when the Sheriff arrived.

Deba'l said, "We will continue to Stand Fast. Please remind Hunak of our demands." She turned and went inside.

Solanj'l remained at the parapet, one arm around the neck of some forefather, perhaps one of those involved in creating the Ritual. What better place to start it than this Hall? Take girls from the Temple where they were supposed to feel safe to the room of terror and return them to Ploch's Own House, thus offering "proof" the mutilation was of him. Solanj'l felt her arm tightening around the effigy's neck as if trying to strangle it. She'd like to symbolically strangle every one of them up there. Maybe someday she could give herself that pleasure.

The Sheriff was saying something.

"I didn't hear you," she said.

"I said you are ordered to leave now. Patience has ceased."

A cessation of patience. Yes, there had been a cessation of patience—on the part of all.

"As Deba'l said, we are Standing Fast."

The deputies around the Sheriff were shuffling their feet,

looking uneasy. The Sheriff was moving from foot to foot, as if he didn't know what to do. My, how we have confounded them, she thought. What was Hunak up to? He'd ruin his authority and reputation if he kept issuing orders that were ignored by the women. She was glad he was the Minister Second Only to the First. Someone like Metak, or even Glom, undoubtedly would have come crashing in already. Wait, Hunak was a man who tried to be decent, but this weak order made no sense.

"Who issued this order?" she asked.

"Hunak ordered you out days ago. Now it is time to leave."

"Why aren't we hearing this from the Ministry?"

More foot shuffling.

"Did this order come from the High Priest?"

No response.

"Great Ploch, Sheriff, you know the High Priest does nothing without Hunak's consent."

The Sheriff spoke in low tones to his second in command, who raised his shoulders and hands and shook his head.

Had this come from Lumok, pretending he'd gotten an order from the High Priest? Given the Sheriff's silence it was obvious the order was not of the Ministry. How had the Sheriff fallen into such a trap? She'd never thought of him as a stupid man. The deputies weren't equipped with ladders or anything to attack the doors or windows. Was this merely a move to apply more pressure on the women? Was it an attempt to help Hunak, or a threat to him? Get the women out or the men of Ramprend would do it? Or, had Hunak arranged it? A warning? Maybe Lumok had nothing to do with it at all.

She and the Sheriff stared at each other. Had he thought the women would come out when they'd ignored orders from Hunak? Wait, Hunak had never given a direct order to the women. The previous ultimatum had been delivered by Doonak. It was puzzling. Who was responsible for the Sheriff's presence? It didn't matter. Time was running out.

* * *

"Are you certain you're willing to do this?"

Midi'l looked directly into Solanj'l's eyes. "I do what I say I'll do."

There'd been a debate about accepting women like Midi'l into Gatherings. How could you feel at ease with women who may have assisted in the sawing off of your, your sisters', your daughters' legs? Each of The Firsts had argued for admittance, then against it. The debate ended when Morgani'l said, "All women are guilty. Just because we don't actually do it doesn't make us better than those who do."

The Beautifying Sisters were born to their work. They existed between the privileged and servant/worker classes. The men who took them for wives were of Doonak's level, fit to be foremen in mills but not fit to dine with the likes of The Firsts' husbands. These women helped in removing girls legs, had families, had their daughters "beautified" and found them husbands—good Ramprendian citizens. Midi'l, a member of one of Morgani'l's Gatherings, was taken into The Firsts confidence as they planned the Stand Fast. She came to the Gathering of Gatherings equipped to do what she had done before—although it would be somewhat different.

Men now were milling around outside, some shouting at the women on the roof.

"Defilers of Ramprend."

"Haters of Ploch."

"Garbage."

"Filthy Termers."

"You deserve to die."

The women did not reply. A few men threw vegetables and stones but were marched off by the deputies. The Great Hall was not to be soiled or damaged.

Water from pipes had become a trickle; the women assumed it would eventually stop. They conserved what they'd stored as best they could. Clothing wasn't washed, body little, hair not at all. People were scratching and feeling most unclean. They attempted to cook with little water. Dishes were assigned to each woman and girl and were wiped off, not washed unless necessary. Water, not food, had become the major problem, but the food was running out too.

How do you do what you can't abide? If the men would just agree, if they could imagine what it was to be mutilated and left to be less than you had been, if they would look at a daughter as a person rather than a maimed thing to give a man ... if, if, if. They'd known it could come to what they didn't want. They'd prepared for it. The tunnel to the Temple made it easier to accomplish but did not make it easier on their minds and hearts.

In one last attempt to forestall the almost unthinkable, Deba'l agreed to speak with Hunak—on the steps in front of the great doors. Servants came with him to set up a table, chairs, and tea service. When Deba'l sat, Hunak pointed out Glom had sent his famous cream cakes she liked so much. She told Solanj'l she thought her heart might break when she heard that.

Hunak had a plan for gradually phasing out the Ritual. He agreed it was unnecessary—he did not bring himself to say it was barbaric—but to abruptly stop it would be too unsettling for men—and some women. Ramprendians lived on tradition, to cease doing what was so much of their lives would bring an end of Ramprend as they knew it. He had no response for why Ramprend should go on as it was, given it involved mutilation. They, the Ministry and The Firsts, could work to convince people of the wisdom of change. That would not be too difficult because the majority of women already were convinced. The Phylli'ls could be ignored, having no power. Deba'l pointed out no women had power to influence men.

"But the Ministry will be working with you," he said.

"The Ministry can stop it now," she said. "The Ministry has the power. You have the power. Just declare it is to be stopped."

There would be rebellion, something very unRamprendian.

She pointed out he already had a rebellion. Yes, that was true, but one by men would be more dangerous, violence could be done. What did he fear more, violence to the Great Hall or the women? How could she ask such a thing? He asked if the women were willing to be attacked.

"You forget. We all know what it is to be attacked."

He had no response. This husband of hers had become a man trapped. Trapped between the responsibilities of maintaining tradition and his respect for her, for women in general. She believed he did have a degree of appreciation for the lesser Ramprendians. After all, he'd never pressured her to have more children, perhaps producing a daughter who'd have to give up her leg to the saw.

They talked as the sun started its descent. The cream cakes were uneaten, the tea grew cold. They talked until their throats were as dry as unwatered Ramprendian earth. They talked, and parted, two sad people who would never be able to look into each other's eyes again. Years of talking, discussing ideas, agreeing more often than not had ended.

"I always thought myself fortunate in the extreme to have such a husband," Deba'l told The Firsts. "Now I question myself. Did I have influence with him or was I merely a dutiful Ramprendian wife who happened to be married to an agreeable man? One not so agreeable to value kindness and respect over tradition.... We can't wait."

Quiet filled the dining hall during the evening meal. There wasn't much choice but to go ahead with what they wished to avoid. The next morning Doonak delivered a letter to Hunak.

To Hunak, Minister Second Only to the First

It seems you have convinced The Firsts that more talk is necessary. Would you, Gung, Glom, Metak, Doam, and Bantant be so kind as to meet us in the Temple tomorrow evening. We believe it is appropriate to meet in Ploch's

House to find a way to agreement. We request meeting in our original Gathering room. It can be prepared for hospitality. We must have your oath that we will return to the Hall at the conclusion of the discussion. We thank you for your courtesy in this matter.

Deba'l, A First of the Gatherings.

48. MEETING IN PLOCH'S HOUSE

THE SHERIFF AND A DOZEN OF his biggest deputies escorted The Firsts to the Temple, the deputies not pleased with having to carry the refreshments the women insisted on bringing. Not a job for deputies and besides the women should have run out of food by now. Solanj'l thought they'd be pleased if they knew how almost right they were. Cresa'l had created a miracle in making biscuits. There would be no cakes unless Glom brought them.

Word had spread, probably originating from the Ministry, that there was to be a resolution of "the problem." Men standing along the street yelled that it was about time the women came to their senses. A few insults were uttered but stopped when deputies made threatening moves toward the speakers.

"Well, I guess we aren't surprised about this," Morgani'l said as they neared the Temple. Phylli'l was present with cohorts. Lumok was not. "All praises to Ploch," she called out. "All praises for his deliverance. The evil ones have fallen."

Morgani'l called back. "Have you read Ploch's book yet? Have you seen the Ritual isn't in it? Have you found Ploch could be a woman?"

Phylli'l jerked up in her chair. Her face went rigid, as if the sugar water used to secure her hair had encased her entire head.

The Firsts passed into the Temple while Phylli'l yelled about their evilness and the glory of Ploch.

"It's about time you came to your senses," Metak said as

Petra'l step-dragged into the Gathering room. "You will come home with me at the end of this meeting."

Hunak sent the Sheriff and his men away. "We have nothing to fear from each other."

Glom looked at Solanj'l as if he was seeing a face from the past that he couldn't quite place. Bantant walked to where Morgani'l stood and asked. "You are well, wife?" "I am. And you?" He merely nodded. Doam stared at Janka'l and said nothing. She asked him if he was well. After a pause he said he would be better when she returned home.

"The Firsts have recognized the wisdom of my suggestion," Hunak said. It was a declaration, not a question.

"No," Deba'l replied. "We are here to convince you of the rightness of doing away with a barbaric practice."

"What has given you the idea," Metak said loudly, "that women are to be heard."

Solanj'l thought it strange he had not asked about Firsa. If she were a boy would he have done so? Should they have brought the sons into the Hall with them?

"I have to say I agree with Metak," Gung said. "And you, Glom?"

"Of course I agree with him. I think we have been very patient. I think it is time for these women, all women, to be put back in their appropriate place. With due punishment, of course."

"What would be the nature of that punishment, husband?" Solanj'l asked. "Beating us daily. Would that cause great love and respect to fill our hearts? Consider. It could make us hate, have thoughts of killing."

Intakes of breath from the men, and some of her friends. She should not have said that. Discussion must not be cut off. Hunak said attacking each other would have no value. She quickly agreed, she'd spoken out of impatience, as she suspected Glom had done.

"I have a right to be impatient," he said.

Hunak assumed control of the talk, repeating what he'd said

to Deba'l about working to convince the people of Ramprend to give up the Beautification Ritual, assuring them he would do everything he could to make the transition go as smoothly and quickly as possible.

"I don't understand," Petra'l said, "why you just don't order the stopping of it."

"Be quiet," Metak said.

"How are we to have a talk if one side can't talk?"

Solanj'l had never heard Petra'l speak so sharply.

Hunak explained his fears of rebellion if he ordered an abrupt cessation. Change must be gradual. If men had wives with two legs they might not be able to function as a husband should. The stump was considered an essential part of pleasure in marriage. Women could find themselves with no husbands at all.

"How would men have children?" Solanj'l asked.

"There are termers," Metak said.

"I hardly think we would be satisfied with that," Hunak said.

"Are men so limited in their thinking that they couldn't adjust?" Deba'l asked. "Are they so rigid they're incapable of change?"

Janka'l, who'd been busy arranging for the service of teas and biscuits, asked if they would consider beautifying sons as well as daughters, women could then have the pleasure men did. The colour, rather the lack of it, in the faces of the men gave her the response to that idea. "If it is good for our sons to have stumps for pleasure, why not for daughters?" she persisted.

Bantant, in a fatherly tone, said men could not run the country with only one leg. Morgani'l said women could run households if they had two. Stewards would not be necessary, and the money paid them could be put to other uses.

Glom laughed, threw his hands up and said, "Oh, how foolish women can be. I don't know how you have been able to go on with this Stand Fast nonsense for as long as you have."

Deba'l suggested they partake of the teas and biscuits, which would not be as flavourful as the ones from Glom's

kitchen but they could eat in the spirit of cooperation. Three
flavours of tea, each containing large amounts of the drug
that made girls insensible before "beautification," had been
brewed. One pot, with no drug, had been prepared for The
Firsts. It was assumed the men would pay no attention to
the details of what Janka'l was doing. If one of the men
questioned her actions, one or two of the Firsts would drink
from a man's pot.

* * *

Bemla'l opened the door and looked in. "Good, they're asleep."

If it weren't for the agility and tenacity of Nalani, Majana,
and ten other girls they could not have gotten the men to and
through the tunnel to the Great Hall basement. Pairs of girls
dragged a man to the stairs, and even though they'd been doing
the strengthening exercises Furam had taught them, they had
to take a rest. Each pair then lifted and bumped a man down
the stairs to the basement, with a rest at mid-point and another
at the bottom before the final drag to the tunnel where rein-
forcements waited with chairs to roll the men to the assumed
first Beautification Ritual room. The Firsts worried about the
time. How long before the Sheriff became suspicious? They'd
planned for the task to be completed as quickly as possible,
but women's problem with mobility and the girls not being
used to this amount of physical work made quick seem a joke
of an idea.

Nalani and Majana and four other pairs of girls returned
to the stairs in the Temple to help The Firsts descend. Solanj'l
was the last and was so nervous she thought little bits and
pieces of her might start flying off. All the Stand Fasters knew
the husbands of The Firsts would be brought to the Hall and
what would happen when they arrived. As awful as it was,
what choice did they have? Solanj'l's one consolation when
fears of retaliation became too dark and suffocating, causing
the tightening around her head that foretold an axe-cleaving
headache, was the girls would not be killed. Sons needed wives.

When she first thought the girls might lose two legs to the saw, in revenge and example, she'd thrown up until she felt her stomach would come out of her mouth. Deba'l tried to reassure her with the reminder that men liked displaying the legs of their wives. Flesh and wooden. Furthermore, women would never be able to move on two wood legs, making Glom's Glamour Legs useless. He would fight against removing two legs.

The Firsts agreed Midi'l and her assistants, some trained, others in training, would choose the order of removal by lot, with the exception of Hunak. It seemed the only fair way. The men had been transported in that order. Midi'l had learned how to be skillful at the art of beautification. Other beautifiers assisted her.

The first three men came though the operation as well as could be expected—physically. Their mental state was appalling but that had been anticipated. "At least they didn't have to live through the weeks of terror we did," Morgani'l said. The shock to Metak was so great they thought it might make him permanently mindless. His raging screams were terrifying. Midi'l told Petra'l to stay away from the room where he was kept. Doam absorbed the awful knowledge quietly, but it was feared his silence could be as dangerous to him as Metak's rages. Glom looked to where his right leg should have been and cried like a child. He now knew people did mind having their legs sawed off.

49. THE STAND FAST ENDS

"MEN ARE TRYING TO GET ON THE ROOF. Men are trying to get on the roof!" Sasa came running toward the Firsts.

The women on the roof were pushing ladders away before men got up more than a few rungs but Hopa'l told her to tell The Firsts she didn't know if they could keep stopping them and some men were trying to throw roped hooks onto the platform to pull it down. The Sheriff was yelling about Hunak. There were so many men. What should they do?

Solanj'l told Sasa to get more girls on the roof to help push ladders. As she ran off Nalani appeared to report there was banging on the door to the Ministry tunnel. The Stand Fast was going to end—one way or another.

Hunak was groggy but awake. He was tied to a cot, unable to get up. When told what had happened to Doam, Metak, and Glom he closed his eyes and groaned.

"They'll break into the building," he said. "I will not be able to stop them."

"They're already trying to get in," Deba'l said, "By the time that happens Bantant, Gung, and you will also be without a leg. Order the cessation of the ritual, Hunak."

He smiled sadly, then said, "Why would you trust me not to rescind it?"

"Because you're a man of your word, a man of honour," Deba'l said.

Hunak stared at the wall behind her. Solanj'l could see the turmoil within, a man torn between what he'd been selected to preserve and the danger confronting him, a danger that would make him like a woman.

She said, "Hunak, we want you to see and hear something."

The cot on which he lay was pulled and pushed into the dim, dirt hallway that was filled with girls. Several of them sang. "I am great, I am good. I've two legs as I should," over and over, then all the girls, with Majana leading them, recited her composition.

A day will come
Soon too soon
When I will cease to be
You will see me
You will hear me
You will touch me
But I will have left
with the leg
no longer mine
Belonging now
to hungry cats
How can I live
if what held me
straight and firm
is eaten by
creatures
not like me
Creatures with four legs
Don't they have enough?

I want my leg
I want my leg
I want my leg
I WANT MY LEG.

The girls may have had no effect, but Hunak wanted his leg. He was untied, taken upstairs by girls, put on the exterior platform and taken to the roof. He told the Sheriff to stop the men's wall-scaling attempts, and to dispatch a deputy to halt the attempt to get into the basement. Later that day the final banner of the Stand Fast was hung from the necks of the effigies of Ramprend's forefathers.

THE BEAUTIFICATION RITUAL HAS CEASED
ALL GIRLS WILL REMAIN TWO-LEGGED
FURTHER USES OF THE RITUAL WILL RESULT
IN LOSS OF PROPERTY

THIS BY ORDER OF THE FIRST MINISTER
AND HIGH PRIEST OF RAMPREND

EPILOGUE

SOLANJ'L WAS EXILED. All The Firsts were exiled. Punishment had to be meted out. Men had been attacked and maimed, a crime like no other in Ramprend history. This could not be ignored. They were taken out of the city with all the clothing they could wear and what food they could carry or drag. They were not allowed to take their rolling chairs. If they wanted to be two-legged let them survive with one flesh and one wooden. They were left next to a stream flowing out of the mountains.

They were not alone; other Stand Fasters chose to join them, including Cresa'l, Majana and her mother, Nalani, Bemla'l and Hopa'l. And another: Doonak appeared just before they were taken out of the city. He took bags and bundles from women and put them in a wagon he dragged behind him. The deputies who were taking the exiles to their destination asked what he was doing.

"I'm going with the true leaders of Ramprend," he said.

The exiles survived, in part, because of women from the mountains. Solanj'l met the ones who'd offered to bring food during the Stand Fast and thanked them for their kindness every time she saw them. They, and men from the mountains, helped in building shelters and taught the Stand Fasters how to grow vegetables, fruits, beans. They gave them milk and meat animals and taught them how to grow and breed food. Even those who found the wooden legs painful worked beside those who could wear them more easily. And there were girls who could bend, crouch and run up and down rows of crops, and after recalcitrant animals. The cart designed by the mountain women became a tool of the two-legged.

About five years after the exile, babies started to be born. Doonak went into the city from time to time; no one seemed interested in stopping him, even if he'd taken exile status. He told stories to anyone who'd listen about what was happening in The Colony, as he called it. His description of the courage and determination of women who'd once been thought of as having only one use drew men as well as women to The Colony.

Solanj'l and Doonak became partners, lovers, but lived apart. Solanj'l said she would not leave the other Firsts. Petra'l was not with them. Her heart was broken when she could not take Firsa with her and she died a few months after the exile. They all missed her light-heartedness, and sometimes silliness, particularly Morgani'l. Two very different women had become fast friends. Solanj'l thought of her often also. It was possible, after all, to enjoy sex.

The Stand Fast ended but the Beautification Ritual did not—not right away. Most men chose to ignore what had been declared. Some girls continued to have their legs sawed off. No penalties were exacted. Hunak no longer exerted authority; as far as anyone could tell he didn't try. About a year after the Stand Fast his deputy assumed the position of Minister Second Only To The First and Hunak disappeared from public view.

Even if the ritual continued for a time Ramprend had changed; there was no returning to what had been. Women were people not understood by men. So many women committed suicide protesting the ritual that it became alarming. There was on-going confusion over the fact The Great God Ploch had not ordered the Beautification Ritual. Girls ran away from home. Boys attacked girls, apparently in frustration over not being assured of looking forward to fondling and kissing stumps.

Girls had learned something about self-sufficiency and courage during the Stand Fast and fought back, fought the boys, and their own parents.

In time men realized they wanted wives who would not choose to die rather than live with them and watch their daughters be maimed. About ten years after the Stand Fast, death finally came to the ritual. Girls kept their legs. Boys were ordered to not attack girls. The High Priest claimed all this was ordered by The Great God Ploch, two-legged women being a blessing from him. What a state Phylli'l must have been in, deserted by her Great God.

The Colonists were joined by more and more city residents, life outside the city more interesting and vibrant. And girls and women had twos legs. Out of necessity girls and boys, women and men worked together. They also played together. Solanj'l organized races for young people. Girls grew into women with two legs and there were adult races as well.

Solanj'l, with her friends Deba'l, Morgani'l, and Janka'l, all wishing for Petra'l's presence, watched the growth of Ramprendian imagination in sadness and joy.

* * *

Each year we women and girls gather to celebrate. We don't allow males to participate in this ritual, although some may like to. It is not that we are mean-spirited; they have their rituals in which we do not take part.

We dress in our favourite garments and pack our favourite foods. Old women, young women, girls, baby girls in arms. We wend our way out of our homes, workplaces and artist studios. We go to the place The Firsts were taken. We play games, we eat, we laugh.

At the end of the day we form circles within circles. Circles and circles of women and girls. We are turned outward. When we are all in place (which happens only after a lot of shifting around and laughing) the women and girls in the outer circle

JUMP *into the air with a* SHOUT *and start to run. Then the next circle jumps and shouts and runs and the third and on and on and on.*

Soon the field is filled with waves and waves of women and girls who run and jump and shout and laugh.

WE DO THIS TO HONOUR SOLANJ'L
ALL THE FIRSTS
ALL THE WOMEN OF THE GATHERINGS
WHO STOOD FAST FOR
TWO-LEGGED WOMEN.

ACKNOWLEDGEMENTS

Bob Ready, writing mentor, who has kept me going ever since I realized I *have* to write. He said about this work, "I hope someone has the guts to publish it."

Chris McGoey and Judy Gibson, patient friends, who took the time to read and seriously critique *In the Land of Two-Legged Women.*

The Women of Purple Prose—Jane Ebihara, Seema Tepper, and Carol Tremper, who tell me I have something worthwhile to say and should continue to write.

Luciana Ricciutelli, Inanna Publication's Editor-in-Chief, who had the guts to publish this, and who knows how to treat writers very well. She made certain I got a cover I could love, and responded to a *cri de coeur* about editing problems by taking on the task herself. Thank you again and again.

Huey Helene Alcaro has worked on a farm, taught adults in inner city Newark, New Jersey, and taught and directed the Women's Center at Montclair State University, New Jersey. Her fiction has appeared in several North American journals and was a finalist for the 2011 Glass Woman Prize. She lives in Roseland, NJ, and blogs at hueyhelenealcaro.com. *In the Land of Two-Legged Women* is her debut novel.